# NATALIA

Jenni Boyd

Copyright © Jenni Boyd 2010

Revision 1

This edition published by Jenni Boyd Books.
www.jenniboydbooks.com

The moral right of the author has been asserted.

All rights reserved. No part of this book may be reproduced or transmitted without written permission from the author.

ISBN 978-0-9872443-1-4

All characters in this book are fictitious and any resemblance to real persons, living or dead; is purely coincidental.

I dedicate this book to Betty May Rose Hansen, my family and friends. Whose words of encouragement helped me to:

Believe in myself

To keep on writing

And never give up on my dream

## PROLOGUE

It was late at night as she made the long climb up the magnificent staircase. The house was so silent it was eerily still. She did not know why but suddenly felt frightened and stopped midway. The hair on the back of her neck prickled and her mouth was dry as parchment. Her heart pounding so loudly in her chest and her breathing so rapid, she had to grip the richly carved balustrade for support.

Overcome with a feeling of being watched she turned slowly, desperately trying to calm the rising fear. The floor down below was so dark she strained her eyes to scan the area, when suddenly the grandfather clock struck midnight. Crying out in fright she ran the rest of the way up the stairs stopping instantly at the top.

Looking up the long hallway at the many closed doors, fear once again rising as behind any of these doors could lurk danger. After a quick look back down the stairs, she ran to the closest door on the right and within seconds she entered the room closing the door quickly and silently behind her. She leaned heavily against the door waiting for her breathing to settle but also listening for any sounds of movement, warning her of possible danger.

The room was mostly in darkness as the heavy drapes were drawn, but a moonbeam shone through were they didn't quite meet, sending its light to the left of the room like a halo above the baby crib. There was the sound of soft snoring from the occupant in the bed on the other side of the room.

Moving silently towards the crib the moonbeam's soft glow illuminated the young infant, her skin was so fair, her soft downy black hair and long dark lashes were a stark contrast and her ruby-red lips were poised in a cupid's bow, she looked ethereal. Overcome with emotions which only moments before were of fear, she leaned in close and gently gathered her in her arms. The babe made a soft murmur invoking a stirring from the bed close by.

Freezing in sudden panic not game to take a breath or move a muscle, willing them to go back to sleep. After many seconds ticked by she slowly expelled a breath, then carefully placed the child in a piece of cloth underneath her coat and tied securely around her body.

With the precious bundle now close to her heart she retreated quietly and softly from the room, gently closing the door behind her. Pausing, straining her ears for any sound, the old fear was coming back, her heart started to pound harder and her breathing quickened. *Relax and stay calm, you have made it this far.* Moving slowly forward she descended the stairs as carefully and quickly as possible.

The minute she stepped out the front door the cool night air bit at her face, it was a shock after the warmth of the house. Pulling her shabby coat tighter around herself and the infant, she quickly walked towards the estate's front gates and the waiting wagons on the other side.

Without speaking a word, the driver gave a quick flick of the reins and the wagon slowly moved forward, making a gentle sound on the dirt road until finally fading into the night.

By the time the sun had crest the horizon the wagons were long gone and with them the young babe, having travelled all through the night to a destination unknown.

## CHAPTER ONE

ENGLAND, 1870

Her hand trembled as she turned the doorknob, her punishment would be severe if discovered in this room, but it was what she came to see which frightened her most. Despite all this, she proceeded forward.

The door opened smoothly and silently and within seconds she was inside the room; closing the door behind her. As she leaned against the door, her breathing heightened and her palms began to sweat. Her earlier bravado started to slip as she slowly scanned the room *was this a mistake; maybe she should run while she still had the chance?* Then she got a glimpse of something out the corner of her eye; there was no backing out now.

Slowly inching her way across the room ever mindful of keeping her eyes downcast, her mother had said to her many times over the years, *you must never let them see your eyes!*

Suddenly she saw a pair of ugly black boots and without realising it raised her eyes higher, taking in the horrible grey dress. Swallowing deeply – this is the reason she had come here.

Slowly raising her head her eyes widened as she saw the pale white skin of her neck and chin. She had never seen skin so fair, it was as white as freshly fallen snow, Vanessa had said *it was a sign of evil; one who only comes out at night to feast on another's blood!* Despite being frightened, she raised her eyes higher gasping at the sight of the blood-red lips.

As if mesmerised she reached her hand out towards them, but the minute her fingertips felt their coldness she quickly pulled her hand back, breathing so quickly she was beginning to hyperventilate. The fear was so great she was starting to feel faint and without realising it, she looked directly into her eyes gasping in shock. Her eyes were like none she had ever seen, they were so green just like the large emerald Mrs Brampton wore around her neck and were fringed with thick black lashes. Tied tightly around her head was the same ugly grey fabric hiding what was beneath.

"All these years I was too frightened to see for myself, I was expecting to see something so horrible but instead you are beautiful. Why did they keep you hidden, what is it about you they are afraid of?"

Wanting an answer but getting none, she watched as her eyes filled with tears causing them to go an even deeper green. Suddenly angry May paced around the room, how could people be so cruel, what hurt most of all was her mother helped instil that fear! As she paced she opened drawers and cupboards, then she saw the beautiful emerald-green silk dress.

"I think the time has come to take off that ugly dress and uncover your head."

A smile came to the blood-red lips as the ugly grey fabric was removed from around her head, revealing dark glossy long locks that cascaded down past her shoulders. May gasped as she had never seen such beauty and to think all these years she had lived in fear.

Soon the ugly grey dress fell to the floor and May looked at the horrible bleached undergarments and ugly black boots.

"You can't possibly try the dress on with those horrible things; you must take them off, feel the silk against your skin."

The boots and stockings were next, followed by her chemise that covered the fabric that tightly bound her chest, which was designed to disguise her breasts.

Her hands suddenly stilled, hesitating suddenly unsure, finally with shaking hands the fabric was loosened until it also fell to the floor. She quickly removed her pantaloons and could not help a mischievous giggle at what she had done.

May knowing it was wrong looked on, as she had never seen someone naked before.

Her stature was small and petite, she could not be more than five feet tall and her waist was so tiny it had to be smaller than the span of a man's hands.

Amazingly there was not a blemish on her body that she could see; only the red marks her bindings had caused – they had been so tight it gave the appearance of her having no breasts at all.

Suddenly there was an audible gasp causing May to look up and see Mr Brampton, a man who instilled much fear!

"I knew underneath that disguise was a beauty but never in my wildest dreams could I have expected to see what I see now!"

She was so frightened her body began to shake and her eyes darted in every direction looking for a means of escape. Suddenly she felt his hot hands on her naked breasts causing her to let out a scream. Looking directly at the mirror in front of her she realised the vulnerable position she had put herself in.

"Despite your mother and my wife's best efforts to disguise you it only excited me more, just waiting for my chance to see what they so desperately wanted to hide. I often wondered what was hidden under those thick dark lashes, now I see a pair of the most beautiful emeralds I have ever seen. May, it is such a simple name; surely when your mother first saw those eyes she could have thought of a name more befitting."

May desperately wanted to cover her nakedness but he was standing on her discarded clothes, she looked across the room and saw the green dress draped over the chair. With her heart in her throat she ran, quickly snatching it up and clutching it desperately to her body trying to cover herself as best as she could.

"You have chosen wisely, the colour becomes you, try it

on."

Turning her back to him she hastily stepped into the dress, almost ripping it in her haste.

"The dress becomes you and the delicate fabric must be heaven against your naked skin. There is no longer a need for you to wear the clothes of a servant; I will buy you whatever you wish."

May was only half listening, she had to get out of here, Vanessa could come home at any moment which added to her fear, for not only was she in her room; but wearing her dress!

"Come look at yourself in the mirror, it looks far better on you than my daughter, although I must say I preferred the look I saw when I first came in."

He made his way towards her, not wanting him to touch her she ran towards the mirror as he requested.

The first time she saw the dress on Vanessa she had wished she could wear it just once. Now she hated it and never wanted to see it again. Suddenly his hands were on her waist and slowly moved up and around her breasts. She tried to scream but her voice was frozen in fear.

His breathing was now heavy, causing her to look at the mirror in front of her and the sight of his red face and the look in his eyes only heightened her panic. *I have to get out of here!* Franticly turning her head looking for a means of escape, he suddenly spun her around, pushing her hard up against the mirror forcing his sweaty hot lips on hers.

With a combination of fear and revulsion she pushed hard against his chest but he only locked his arms even tighter around her. Suddenly his tongue pushed into her mouth causing her to gag. Instinct taking over she bit down hard on his tongue till she tasted blood, causing him to pull back with a loud roar. She tried to run past him but he managed to grab a handful of the dress pulling her back towards him.

"So you want to play rough my little one? You have no

idea how much that excites me."

He roughly grabbed hold of her hand and pulled it down over the obvious bulge in his pants, letting out a hoarse growl. Repulsed she managed to twist her hand free and once again tried to run to the door, but the dress was too long, causing her to trip and fall painfully up against a chair. Ignoring the pain she quickly got to her feet and grasped the chair firmly with both hands, using it as a protective shield.

He let out an evil chuckle and began to unbutton his shirt, divesting himself of it quickly before unbuttoning his trousers all the while keeping his eyes on her. His fat round face was red and glistening with sweat, so much so that his orange-red hair was now plastered to his head and his ugly potbelly overhung his underwear.

May held the chair closer to her body as her eyes darted towards the door, he was standing directly in line with the door, but maybe with the aid of the chair she could knock him to the floor, giving her a chance to escape.

"Look at me!" He growled.

The sight of his fully naked body caused the bile to rise up in her throat. His skin was covered in freckles and orange-red hair but when she saw his ugly red arousal, she lifted the chair higher and swung it at him, but he still had his belt in his hand and used it as a whip, knocking the chair out of her hands and crashing to the floor. Desperation taking over she tried to run to the door but he was too quick for her, grabbing the front of the dress ripping it open, exposing her naked breasts.

He started to roughly grope them, his excitement growing as he tried to rip the dress from her body. No longer caring who came to her rescue, she took a lung full of air and opened her mouth to scream but before she could, a shrill scream came from behind her. Both May and Mr Brampton turned towards the door to see Vanessa trembling with rage.

Vanessa was outraged. *May was wearing her green*

*dress*! More so, the sight of what she was doing with her father caused her to scream once again, so loud and long it sent chills through the entire household.

Vanessa's mother instantly recognising her child's scream of distress ran as fast as her short fat legs would carry her, all sorts of terrible thoughts running through her mind. Nothing could ever prepare her for the sight of May and her husband, at first she had not recognised May with her long dark hair but the sight of her exposed breasts and her husband's naked body filled her with an incredible rage. *How could they and in her daughter's room!* She ran at her husband scratching, kicking and screaming.

May ran towards the door but Vanessa blocked the way letting May see the hatred in her eyes before lunging towards her.

Realising a new danger had emerged, May ran to the other side of the room in panic but there was no other means of escape. She noticed the large fireplace and the small gap behind, without thinking she ran and tried to squeeze herself in, but in actual fact she'd only endangered herself further.

Mr Brampton finally managed to flee the room and his wife's wrath, but it only increased her anger, she wanted vengeance!

Her eyes scanned the room her mind in turmoil – *how dare they shame her this way? Worse still Vanessa had witnessed their revolting act!* Her eyes rested upon a small pair of pearl-handled scissors on the dresser, quickly grabbing them firmly in her hand, she strode over to a frightened May and pulled her from her hiding place.

Forcing May roughly to the floor and holding her down with her heavy frame, like a mad woman she crazily hacked at May's hair, cutting so close the sharp scissors cut into her scalp, hacking away until there was no hair left at all. Vanessa gleefully picked up handfuls of hair and threw them on the fire that was burning in the grate; as she did an idea came to her mind.

Mrs Brampton stood up panting and wheezing from all the exertion she had expelled, she looked down at May who was sobbing and blood was oozing from her scalp; despite this she still felt the need to inflict more pain.

As if reading her mother's mind Vanessa grabbed the red-hot poker from the fire, an evil growl emitted deep from within her. Mrs Brampton realising what her daughter intended to do once again used her weight to hold May down, ensuring she couldn't escape. Vanessa slowly made her way towards May, making sure she could see the hot poker in her hand, wanting to see her fear.

May struggled desperately to free herself from Mrs Brampton's firm hold, causing the hot poker to touch her exposed breast instead of her face, Vanessa's intended mark. May emitted such a loud heart-rending scream it could be heard down in the kitchen where Mildred was preparing the evening meal. The sound sent a sharp pain to Mildred's chest, instantly alerting her the cry had come from her child, momentarily making her feel faint and weak at the knees. Grabbing a meat cleaver Mildred ran as fast as she could to the top of the stairs, realising the screams were coming from Vanessa's room.

May's screams and the smell of burning flesh only excited Vanessa more and once again she tried to burn May's face, but despite her weakened state she managed to deflect the hot poker, but not without it leaving a nasty red welt on her arm.

"Mother hold her still, I want to mark her face so no man will ever look at her again!"

Mrs Brampton straddled May and pinned her arms firmly to the ground, making it impossible for her to move. Vanessa pressed the poker firmly to May's left check, it left a mark but it didn't blister up like the one on her breast. Disappointment was evident on Vanessa's face as she realised the fire poker was cooling down. Not prepared to give up she placed it back in the hot coals.

Suddenly Mildred burst into the room, hatred and horror welled up at the sight of the scene before her, May's scalp was a mass of blood and she could smell the distinct odour of burning flesh. She lifted the meat cleaver above her head and let out a primal scream, causing Vanessa to drop the poker and flee from the room.

Mrs Brampton took one look at Mildred – she too was a large framed woman, but a few years younger and the way Mildred was holding the meat cleaver left no doubt in her mind, she would use it. She struggled to her feet and made a hasty exit out the door.

All the commotion had caused Walter, the footman to leave his post and venture up the stairs. He had contemplated sending Oliver the stable boy to get the police, but decided to investigate first.

Cautiously making his way not only on alert for an intruder, but also Mrs Brampton, she would not take too kindly to him entering the upstairs domain. Walter knew Mr Brampton was a cruel man, but he also knew he was a coward and would leave the women to defend themselves. He himself was a tall man in his early fifties and kept himself in good physical condition.

As he made his way along the hall he heard sobbing and realised it was Mildred and immediately hastened his pace. He didn't know what to expect, but nothing could have prepared him for the sight of Mildred down on the floor, rocking May in her lap and there was so much blood, it was on Mildred's dress and oozing from May's head. He quickly entered the room and was shocked by the injuries he saw as he neared.

Kneeling down slowly he gently put his hand to May's neck, feeling for a pulse and wondering if she was alive and what horror had happened in this room.

"She is alive but her pulse is weak, we must call for a doctor immediately. Who did this should I call for the police?"

"It was that vile child Vanessa and her mother who did this to her and you know as well as I, there is no point in sending for the police. Please help me take her downstairs to my room, she will be safer there."

After he gently lay May on the bed Mildred asked him to get a clean cloth, a basin of water, and a bottle of antiseptic. When he had left she gently removed the torn dress noting the burn on her breast had become a big ugly blister. She knew they needed to be treated immediately and properly but was unsure what to do. She covered May's naked body with a clean bed sheet and when Walter returned with the basin and antiseptic, bathed and dressed the wounds to her scalp as best as she could.

"Walter she needs proper medical treatment, I have no money what should I do?"

"Take her to the old gypsy woman, she will know what to do."

Both Walter and Mildred turned towards the door and saw Oliver the stable boy, a tall thin boy with a shock of blond hair.

Mildred had heard the stories of the old gypsy woman with her special healing powers, who lived deep in the woods. There was only one problem, there was much hatred between the gypsies and those not of gypsy blood.

"Even if she survived the journey, they would never allow her to set foot on gypsy land," replied Mildred

"I have heard they will not harm one who is sick or injured, as long as they travel there on their own," said Oliver

"How do you suppose she do that, she is barely conscious and what do were really know of the gypsy woman?"

"Mother why? All these years you made me live in fear," whimpered May.

"We would not have been able to stay here if I did not go along with Mrs Brampton's request, besides I thought it would keep you safe."

"All these years I thought I was some kind freak, never allowed to look in the mirror for fear of what I might see, always afraid to be seen for fear of seeing the look of horror on people's faces.

"I knew what Mr Brampton was like. I had every intention of telling you when you were old enough to understand."

"I am almost seventeen; is that not old enough?"

"May darling please forgive me?"

"Mam the mistress is coming and she is looking for May. We can send her on Jasper you know they have a special bond, he will let no harm come to her," said Oliver.

"You have to make a decision now, I will distract her as best as I can, but I don't know how long I can keep her away," said Walter as he left the room.

Mildred started to pace, what was she to do? This was all her fault; she had been stupid to go along with her mistress' devious plan. Deep down she had known it was a ploy so Vanessa, who had the looks of her father, could feel in control. No amount of beautiful clothes could make that girl attractive. Even from a young age Mildred knew May would be a great beauty – one many a man would lust after. She had noticed the way Mr Brampton looked at May; despite everything they had done to make her look unattractive. Suddenly she heard Mrs Brampton's nasally voice and Walter trying to direct her away from Mildred's room. The time had come to tell May everything.

"All right get Jasper ready and bring him to the back door. We will have to tie her to the saddle somehow."

"I will ride with them as far as I can. Don't worry mam Jasper will keep her safe," he said before leaving the room.

Knowing she didn't have much time, Mildred got down on her hands and knees and pulled out a metal box she had hidden under the bed. She rummaged through it till she found the small red velvet bag, then pushed the box back in its hiding place, before struggling back up off the floor and sat on the bed next to May.

"May I now realise what I did was wrong and as this might be the last time I see you; I have another secret to reveal. There is no way of telling you this but to come right out and say it, I am not your true mother and May is not your true name."

"What are you saying, I don't understand?"

"I had just buried my husband and was so stricken with grief I did not think I could go on. I was making my way towards the river when suddenly I heard a baby's weak cry. I openly sobbed at the cruelness of it all, for I had prayed many a night for a babe of my own but when my husband died I realised it wasn't to be. I sat down on the steps of a lavish house, feeling sorry for myself thinking of what others had and I did not. Again I heard a baby's cry and realised it was close by but could see no one about. Standing up I noticed a basket on the top step and realised the crying was coming from within. I ran up the steps and I looked inside the basket and was shocked to see one so small left out alone in the cold. I picked you up and you snuggled into my arms and suddenly my heart was joyous with love – the good Lord had answered my prayers after all. I looked around to see if anyone was about and then I put you inside the warmth of my coat and close to my heart; you were now mine and I was never letting you go."

"My whole life has been nothing but a lie!"

"This was never meant to happen. I couldn't love you more than if you were part of my blood and because of my love for you I must let you go, for if ever you are to have any kind of life, there is only one person who can help you now."

"What do you mean, are you sending me away?"

"It is for your own safety and the old gypsy woman is the only one who can heal you. I won't lie, this journey is fraught with danger as you must enter the deep woods and you must do this alone, your safety depends upon it."

"Please don't make me do this."

"You might die if you don't, besides this woman might lead you to your true parents."

"Why would I want to find them when they left me to die?"

"When I first found you, you had a tiny bracelet around your wrist, it was made of gold and inscribed on it was the name 'Natalia' there was a tiny ruby that formed the letter 'i'. I later discovered a baby by the name of Natalia had been kidnapped and a reward was posted for her safe return to her parents. For whatever reason, whoever the kidnapper was they did not feel they could return you to your true parents, but they wanted your identity to be known. I believe that is why they left the bracelet on you; however by then I could not bear to give you up, I believed you were a gift from God, so I hid your bracelet and christened you May."

May was in shock; she had two parents out there who had been prepared to pay a reward for her return, they must have loved her. She looked up at the one whom she had always called mother, but now all she could see was a stranger, one who had forced her to live a lie.

"Mam we must hurry, Walter will not be able to delay the mistress much longer," said Oliver before May could respond.

"This is the bracelet you had around your tiny wrist, I will pin it inside your dress and hopefully it will help lead you to your true parents; but remember this, I love you as if you are my own and will do so until my dying days. Maybe one day you will find it in your heart to forgive me. Good luck my little poppet and I will pray for you every night," she said as she leant forward for one last kiss to the forehead of her beautiful May.

Not capable of speech, May gritted her teeth as Mildred helped her dress and then outside to Oliver and the waiting horse.

As she climbed into the saddle the pain now so intense, she thought she was going to pass out. Tears were now streaming down her cheeks as she leant forward and linked her arms around Jasper's neck – her one true friend.

"It's just you and me Jasper; please don't desert me too," she whispered before they moved forward.

Mildred said one last teary goodbye and stood on the doorstep watching them disappear into the night, wondering if she would ever see her again.

After riding most of the night they finally reached the outer edge of the deep forest; Oliver knew this was as far as he could go. He knew May was frightened and understandably so, he just hoped it would not be too long before she was found. Her strength was depleting fast as she had lost so much blood, he was not sure how much longer she would last.

He pulled his horse to a halt and let out a whistle to Jasper. There had been no way the horse was going to let Oliver take hold of his reins, as the horse had a mind of his own – something Oliver had learnt a long time ago.

Taking a deep breath before dismounting, he could not let May see his fear; he wanted her to stay strong and not give up. He walked over and pulled off his glove before gently putting his hand over hers, noting how cold it was, realising they hadn't even had time to put on her gloves. He quickly removed his other glove and put them on her hands; they were too large for her small hands, but at least would offer some warmth.

"May this is as far as I can go, I know Jasper will guard you and let no harm come to you. I will pray for you and hope one day we will meet again."

"Jasper it is up to you now, I am counting on you to look after May."

Jasper snorted and shook his head up and down and stomped his front right hoof.

"That a' boy, take her to the old gypsy woman; she is the only one who can help her now, but you must never leave her, you must guard her with your life."

Jasper whinnied and shook his head and May linked her arms tighter around Jasper's neck, trying desperately to hold her tears in check, not wanting Oliver to know how frightened she really was.

"Thank you Oliver."

He climbed back on his horse and watched as Jasper took May into the woods, waited until the thick forest swallowed them up and he could see them no more. He wondered if he would ever see them again, hoping Jasper would lead her to the safety of the old gypsy woman and not fall victim to the evil clutches of anyone else.

With a gentle kick of his heels to the horse's flanks, he headed back to Brampton House wondering what the consequences would be when it was discovered that not only had he helped May escape, a mere servant girl, but with Jasper a very valuable jet-black Warm blood stallion, which in actual fact had been bought for Vanessa!

## CHAPTER TWO

Fonso was small for his age of fourteen years and wasn't always taken seriously by others, so he tended to be bit of a loner, which was unusual for a Romany boy – gypsy. It was not uncommon for him to wander the woods with only his horse for company.

On occasion he would venture on the outskirts of the thick woods; this was something that was forbidden but he did it anyway to prove he was noble, brave and strong, even if it was only to himself. He would definitely be punished if found there by the Gorgio – those not of Romany blood.

His mother had died in childbirth and he had been virtually raised by Luludja. She was the most respected among all the gypsies and was regarded as having special healing powers. Luludja, whose name means 'flower of life', is the oldest of the gypsies, no one knows her true age nor do they care to. Legend has it that when she was born, a bright light burst forth from the clouds and shrouded the newborn and from that day forth she was blessed with special powers.

Luludja named Fonso and his name meant 'noble and ready'.

She believed he would be the one to help free their clan from the terrible curse, one that had banished all gypsies to the dark woods. She had told him this so many times he believed it was his destiny and thus why he ventured further this day, further than he had ever done before.

He suddenly heard a loud whinny, instantly frightening him. *Could he be in danger from a Gorgio, the ones who decreed all gypsies be banished to the deep woods*

Staying close in the shadows of a large elm tree, he scanned the area where he thought the noise had come from, when suddenly the horse whinnied again, causing Fonso to look to his right.

He sat frozen in the saddle, his heart pounding hard in his chest. *What should he do? Should he try to remain hidden or try to make his way back home?*

His eyes darted in every direction ever mindful of a pale-skinned Gorgio, when he suddenly saw movement causing him to let out a gasp.

In a small clearing he saw the most beautiful horse he had ever seen, a jet-black Warm blood stallion, just the type of horse a noble warrior would ride. He could see the horse had on a bridle and saddle, but the rider was nowhere to be seen. Suddenly a trickle of fear came over him. *Was this some kind of a trap?*

Sitting as still as possible, he tried to quieten his pounding heart, hoping both he and his horse blended into the shadow of the tree.

As he strained his ears, the only sound he could hear was the gentle rustle of the leaves as a soft breeze passed through them.

Suddenly the stallion whinnied, causing him to jump in fright and his horse moved nervously.

The black horse turned and looked at Fonso and shook his head, almost as if he was trying to gain his attention.

Despite the dangers, Fonso slowly dismounted and cautiously made his way over ignoring the voice in his head, telling him to get back on his horse and ride as far away from here whilst he still had a chance. As he neared the stallion those thoughts were quickly dashed, as he realised his small brown horse could never outrun him.

Now only feet from the stallion and still no sign of the rider, he was uncertain about venturing any closer.

As he stood there in a quandary of thoughts the horse once again whinnied, but now he was stomping his hoof and shaking his head, almost as though he was trying to get Fonso to come closer.

Cautiously looking over his shoulder before slowly moving forward, his brain screaming at him he was crazy,

*Natalia*

but it was as if the horse had some power over him, as he could not stop moving forward. As he drew nearer the horse suddenly turned and stared at him, causing Fonso to stop in his tracks.

There was something about the look in the horse's eye, almost as if he was trying to tell him something.

"It's all right boy, I am Fonso the noble warrior and I mean you no harm, I am your friend," he said trying to sound braver than he felt.

The closer Fonso got the more agitated the horse became. He put his hand in his pocket and pulled out a lump of sugar he had been saving for his horse.

The black stallion momentarily stopped his snorting and stomping and stretched his head as if to take the treat, then he seemed to think better of it and started shaking his head.

"What's the matter boy, don't you like sugar?"

Fonso slowly inched closer, he was good with horses and usually had one eating out of his hand by now, but something was upsetting him. *Was he trying to warn him? Had he walked into a trap after all?* Suddenly overcome with fear, he quickly turned around and tripped on the thick ground cover, falling painfully to the ground. He lifted his face slightly out of the dirt when he felt a sudden pressure in the middle of his back, *was it the cold barrel of a Gorgio gun?* Trying desperately to be brave he screwed his eyes tightly shut, thinking of Luludja and the rest of his Romany family, wishing he hadn't ventured so far today.

After what seemed like a lifetime, but in reality was mere seconds, he felt a hot breath and then the soft nuzzle of a horse's nose near his ear.

Turning his head slowly, he looked directly into the eyes of the black stallion and thought there was sadness in his eyes, causing Fonso to put out his hand and rub his nose.

"What's the matter boy, what are you trying to tell me?"

The horse grabbed onto Fonso's jacket and tried to pull him to his feet and as he did so Fonso saw a man's thick coat on the ground, it was as if the horse was trying to take him to it.

"You want me to take a look?"

As he knelt down he realised the coat was covering something. Gently lifting it up he was shocked at what he saw. If it hadn't been for the dress he would not have been able to tell the gender.

She was curled into the foetal position and her head was wrapped in a dirty cloth, which was soaked in blood and the side of her face was red and blistered as if it had been burnt and on closer inspection he could make out the shape of an X.

Quickly looking over his shoulder as he realised the injuries were no accident – someone had tortured and possibly killed this poor soul. *What if whoever did this was still about?*

Suddenly he heard a moan causing him to nearly jump out of his skin, then he realised it was from the girl; she was still alive.

"Don't be frightened I mean you no harm, I wish to help you, my name is Fonso."

She opened her eyes causing him to gasp, as he had never seen such beautiful eyes, the most stunning green like a pair of perfect emeralds.

He had heard about the Gorgio being a cruel race but nothing ever prepared him for what they had done to her.

"Please help me, I must see the old gypsy woman," she said in a hoarse whisper.

Fonso was startled. *How does a Gorgio know about Luludja? Perhaps it was a sign; this was how he would lift the curse from the gypsies!* Then he realised his plight, it was forbidden for a Gorgio to enter a Romany camp. He looked back into those beautiful eyes and realised she was fading fast, she would not survive much longer without Luludja's healing powers, something he did not want on his conscience. He whistled his horse over and the big black horse started to get jittery again.

"Calm down big black one, I am going to take her to Luludja; she will help your friend but I need to get her on my horse, I will take good care of her and you can follow."

As Fonso's horse neared the big black stallion started throwing his head and tried to kick his horse.

"What has got into you, do you not want me to help her?"

Fonso tried again but the black horse only got more agitated. What was he to do?

"His name is Jasper and he has been entrusted to protect me. He will only let me ride on his back, if you can help me get back into the saddle he will take me wherever we need to go."

Fonso helped the girl to rise and as she leant on him she spoke softly to Jasper, reassuring him Fonso was here to help and would take them to the old gypsy woman. Jasper immediately stood still, amazing Fonso; *this horse really believed he was her protector.*

It took all her strength to get back into the saddle, so exhausted she leaned forward and linked her arms around Jasper's neck, trying desperately not to pass out.

"What is your name?" asked Fonso.

"Natalia, my name is Natalia," she said, liking the sound as it rolled off her tongue.

Fonso was momentarily taken aback, hearing her name was a shock, one he had heard so many times over his fourteen years: the story of a baby girl called Natalia who was responsible for the terrible curse which befell all Romanies, banishing them to the deep woods forever!

Natalia noticed his reaction to her name. *Did he know who she was?* Taking a good look at his face she realised his skin was much darker than hers, but not from spending many hours in the sun and his hair was a dark mass of unruly curls, it suddenly dawned on her, *he's a gypsy!*

Even though he was only a young boy she felt

frightened; she had been warned about the dangers of the deep woods and the great hatred between the gypsies and those not of gypsy blood. *Was that why he reacted to her name, a name Mildred had kept secret from her all these years, was she now in danger and all hope of finding the old woman lost?*

Fonso saw the fear in those beautiful eyes, causing him to feel ashamed as he realised he must have unwittingly shown a reaction to her name, causing her to think he meant her harm. Wanting to reassure her he held out his hand.

"Pleased to meet you Natalia, my name is Fonso."

Natalia looked at his outstretched hand then up at his face, noting the dimples as he smiled, but it was his dark-brown eyes that made her feel safe, as there was no evil or trickery only kindness.

"I'm ever so glad you came to my rescue Fonso," she said weakly and shook his hand.

Once he climbed onto his horse he came alongside of Jasper and bent down to reach for his reins so he could lead him. Jasper quickly turned around and tried to kick out at him and his horse, letting them both know they were too close.

"You are a stubborn one. Very well, but only I know the way."

With a gentle kick to his horse's flanks he slowly proceeded forward and they made the slow journey back to camp. Occasionally he would look behind making sure Natalia was all right, although he was sure her loyal horse would let him know if she wasn't. His mind wandered to the story of Natalia and what Luludja had told him. She had told him he would be the one to save them from the curse. *Was it written in the stars for him to travel so far today? Was it his destiny to cross paths with Natalia?* He decided to mention it to the others when he enters the camp, for there would be much consternation about him bringing a Gorgio into a Romany camp.

Luludja wrapped her thick shawl around her thin shoulders; her snow-white hair hung limp and lifeless down to her waist. She was tired and old and her thin gnarled hands didn't work the way they used to, making it difficult to tie back her hair. She knew her time was not far off; in fact she welcomed it. She had only hung on this long to see her family free, but she was starting to wonder if that day would ever come.

She was worried about Fonso; she knew he often ventured off on his own in the woods and she also knew it bothered him that he was smaller than the others his own age. Of course she had not let on she knew of his wonderings, for until now, she had felt no need for it. He was a good boy and one day would grow into a trusted and noble man, but he had never been gone this long before. Many thoughts ran through her head. *What if the Gorgio had seen him!* They all knew the punishment if a Romany ventured out of the woods: *Chals* – males – were hung by a rope, and *Chies* – females – were scourged – whipped – or scorched and branded. This was a curse that was put on the entire Romany race and would remain so until that curse could be lifted.

Luludja was shaken from her deep thoughts by a commotion in the centre of the camp – voices were raised. She had never heard such anger. *What was going on, the Romanies were peaceful people; this was so unlike them? She had better investigate.*

Luludja slowly walked out to the porch of her wagon. Pausing on the top step, she looked around and was astounded by the size of the angry mob. They had at least sixty families in their camp and it seemed as though all had congregated in the centre.

Suddenly her eyes focussed on the centre of the mob; there was her Fonso still on his horse and trying to guard a beautiful black steed that could be none other than a Gorgio horse. Luludja put her hand to her mouth. *What had Fonso done, surely he would not bring more trouble to the Romany race?*

Before descending down her wagon steps, she went back inside and grabbed one of her satchels. Moving as fast as her old legs could, she made her way past the angry mob towards the burning campfire, putting her hand inside the satchel then throwing the contents into the fire causing a small explosion.

Immediately the crowd was silenced and all eyes turned to Luludja; she now had the crowd's full attention. She made her way over to Fonso; no one dared speak before she had spoken. Everyone knew of her special powers; some said she even had the power to put a curse on one's head, so if Luludja wished for silence no one would speak until she said they could do so.

As Luludja neared Fonso, she looked at the other horse and realised there was a lifeless form on the horse's back and their head was covered in a cloth, which was soaked with blood. With an impending dread, she made her way towards the black horse, which became jittery the closer she got.

Putting out her hand and speaking quietly, the horse instantly stilled and then she moved to the lifeless form and gently pulled back the heavy coat. Placing her hand to her neck she could feel a faint beat but despite the blood and dirt, she could see skin so fair – *a Gorgio!* Putting her hand to her mouth she looked up at Fonso with questioning eyes. *What was he thinking bringing one of their kind into a Romany camp?* Now she knew why everyone was so angry; this would only antagonise the Gorgio even further.

"Fonso why have you brought a Gorgio here, do you have any idea what you have done?"

"Yes I do. As you can see she has suffered a terrible cruelty, I was meant to bring her here."

The crowd erupted with anger raising their fists, demanding he take her back and be banished from the camp before they suffered further punishment.

Luludja was in a dilemma, she loved Fonso as if he was her own, but she knew the people were right; this would only inflict further hardship on the Romanies. She could see the injuries, but this was none of their business; Romanies did not interfere with Gorgio law. She knew Fonso must have had a good reason for bringing this person here; she had to at least give him a chance to speak.

Luludja turned and held up her hand, demanding silence and glared at anyone who wished to disobey her; once again the crowd became silent.

"Fonso tell us why you believe you were meant to bring her here."

"She asked me to bring her to you."

A murmur went through the crowd and Luludja turned and looked at them before turning back to Fonso.

"She asked for me, how does this young Gorgio know of me?"

"She says her name is Natalia."

An audible gasp went through the crowd and Luludja suddenly felt faint, momentarily leaning on his horse for support before walking back to the unconscious girl.

She gently pulled back the collar of the girl's coat and leant in, suddenly her hand stilled and she felt tears prick at the back of her eyes.

"She must be taken inside my wagon immediately," she said without turning to face the crowd.

Immediately a woman in her late fifties pushed her way through the angry crowd, her face was contorted in anger and her hands clenched at her sides. People quickly moved out of her way as this was Violca, Luludja's pen, meaning sister and she also held certain powers, although not as special as her sister's. Her name meant 'violet flower', although some thought it really meant 'violent flower', as she had a terrible temper. She was much younger than her sister and much larger; her long dark hair that was mildly streaked with grey, was in a braid and coiled around her head. She had pale grey eyes that could turn hard and cold if ever crossed.

"Pen we all know you have a soft spot for Fonso, I like everyone else here would like to know why you believe this Gorgio stays!"

Both sisters stood in front of each other, eyeing each other off as if preparing for battle. Luludja moved in front of the girl; something that surprised her sister as it appeared she was trying to protect the Gorgio girl. Luludja leant forward and spoke softly to her sister, causing Violca to gasp; Luludja grabbed her sister's arm and pulled her closer, once again moving the collar at the back of Natalia's neck.

Violca leant in close and suddenly put her hand over her mouth as she looked at her sister who nodded. Violca turned and looked at all the expectant faces.

"My pen is correct; the Gods have brought this girl here for a reason and it is important we take her to Luludja's wagon before it is too late."

Fonso quickly slid off his horse and walked over to Jasper, taking hold of his reins. He knew the horse could sense the hostility towards Natalia, but also Jasper now trusted him and would listen to his reassuring words as he rubbed Jasper's nose.

A murmur went through the crowd when, suddenly a tall, ruggedly handsome man stepped forward, holding his hand up to silence the others.

They call him Besnik, meaning 'faithful and strong', he was considered head of the gypsies but in actual fact, Luludja's word was final in such matters. He walked over and moved the soiled collar, as he wanted to know what the two women had seen, for whatever it was clearly caused fear in both of them.

He moved closer and noticed the fairness of her skin; it was such a stark contrast against the blackness of the horse. As he moved the collar his fingers came in contact with the girl's skin and a strange sensation ran up his fingertips, causing him to suddenly pull back his hand.

A murmur went through the crowd and they all moved back, as they too had seen Besnik's reaction and wondered if the girl was possessed.

He once again leaned in, this time being careful not to touch her and as he looked closer he could see a mark at the base of her neck: it was a deep purple and was in the shape of a flower.

"What is the significance of this mark and why is it so important to have this Gorgio in our camp?"

"Are you questioning me, I who can foresee things no other can?" asked the old woman with her hands defiantly on her hips.

Besnik could see there was fear in her eyes, but he also knew Luludja would not demand this girl stay if it meant endangering her people. He noted her stance and the way she was holding her body straighter, giving the appearance she wasn't as frail as all thought, but Besnik knew differently. Why was this girl so important to her and why would she not tell them why? It had been many years since he had seen her like this; it was almost as though the Gorgio had given her a new reason for living. He loved Luludja as if she were his own mother and would never do anything to upset her. He trusted her judgement but he would not let it rest there; she would have to eventually give him an answer and he let her know by the look in his eyes.

"I shall carry her to your wagon."

Anger once again welled up through the crowd, causing him to turn giving them one of his dark looks, instantly silencing the crowd; no man wanted to come up against Besnik with his powerful body and rippling muscles – there would only be one winner.

As for the women, he was still single and had yet to choose his lifetime partner; none would dare risk their chance of being chosen. They watched with a mixture of hate and envy as he scooped the unconscious girl up in his arms, before carrying her into Luludja's wagon.

As he laid Natalia on the bed a jolt of pain went through her body, causing her to gasp and she inadvertently clutched at the front of his shirt.

As she opened her eyes, she looked directly into a pair of the bluest eyes she had ever seen, but they were cold, hard, and angry and her pain was momentarily forgotten and replaced with fear. *Where was she and who was this man? What was he going to do to her and where was the young gypsy boy from the woods, the one with the kind brown eyes?*

His face was only inches from hers, frozen in fear she was not able to move or speak, still clutching at his shirt.

He roughly removed her hands from it and they fell limply to the bed. He took a step back, crossing his arms across his broad chest and stared down at her, not saying a word.

Frightened her eyes grew larger as she wondered if he was deciding her fate.

Suddenly a look of disgust came to his face before he turned and left the small room.

Tears welled in her eyes as the previous night's events came flooding back to her; first the shock of discovering she was beautiful and not the ugly ogre she had been led to believe. The anger and sadness that her own mother had deceived her in the cruellest of ways; then the elation and excitement of finally being free, free to see the world and let them see her. She did not know which was worse, discovering her beauty for but a short time, or never having known at all.

Vanessa had finally got her wish, her beauty now outshone Natalia, she had ensured her face was so horribly scarred no one would look at her again, for it they did she would see their horror and disgust, just like she had seen in the ones so blue.

A pain came to Luludja's chest at the sight of the girl's tears; she too had seen the look on Besnik's face and knew the girl was feeling more than pain. She remembered those beautiful eyes; she knew one day she would grow into a beautiful woman. Struggling with her emotions, she quickly ground some leaves before putting them in a cup and adding water from the steaming kettle.

"Drink this child, it will help ease the pain."

Natalia struggled to sit up and do as the old woman instructed. *Was this the old woman Mildred had told her about? Could she really help her or was she in more danger from these strange people who live deep in the woods?*

Suddenly her taste buds came in contact with the contents of the cup and she had to muster all her strength not to spit it back into the old woman's face.

"I know it tastes terrible child, but I assure you I am here to help you not cause further harm."

Natalia relaxed as she looked at the old woman's wrinkled face, realising she must be very old indeed. The young boy had as promised brought her to the old gypsy woman.

The two strangers looked at each other and Natalia could see kindness and gentleness, no sign of horror or disgust.

Suddenly a smile came to the old woman's face and she gently stroked the uninjured side of Natalia's face, the effects of the foul tasting brew were taking effect, the pain had eased, her eyes felt so heavy she relaxed back into the pillows and drifted off to sleep.

Luludja slowly removed what remained of Natalia's head dressing and was shocked by what she saw: it was as if a madman had crazily hacked away her hair.

Some of the cuts to her scalp were so deep they would require a stitch or two; she knew these would heal in time and her hair would grow to cover the scars, but the burns were another matter. Her poultices were known for their special healing powers, but she had never encountered anything like this before. If the gypsy curse was to be lifted, it now rested solely on her shoulders.

After gently bathing and stitching her scalp, Luludja was surprised at how nimble her hands had become – it was definitely a sign. She decided to remove the girl's soiled clothes before tending to the burns. Despite what Gorgio's thought, not all Romanies were grubby. As she cut away the dress Natalia opened her eyes, the effects of the tea was wearing off and when she saw the scissors in the old woman's hand, she struggled to get up.

"What are you doing?"

"I must remove your soiled dress, as it is already ruined I thought it would be less painful this way."

"You were trying to steal my bracelet; it's the only thing I have from my parents!" Natalia sobbed.

"I promise you I am not trying to steal your bracelet, I did not even know it was there."

Natalia relaxed as Luludja carefully unpinned the bracelet from inside her dress, Luludja's hand momentarily closed tightly over it as tears came to her eyes; remembering the last time she had seen it almost seventeen years ago.

*Was she being punished or was this her chance to make things right?* The secret had slowly eaten at her over the years. Violca her sister was the only other living person who knew. She knew Besnik was suspicious and would not let up until she gave him an answer. Looking down at the girl, her tears flowed more freely as she thought of Florica and the injustice of it all.

Luludja gently put the bracelet in the palm of Natalia's hand and closed her fingers over it, then made her drink some more of the brewed leaves, for not only did she need sleep, but if she was going to treat her burns properly the poor girl will feel a great deal more pain.

She sat down on the bed beside her and softly sang a gypsy lullaby until she knew she was in a deep sleep.

"It has come full circle my child, God has given me a

chance to right a wrong. I am so sorry; we thought we were doing what was best for you. I just hope one day you can find it in your heart to forgive, or at least understand."

## CHAPTER THREE

Natalia had been closeted inside the wagon for so many weeks she thought she would go crazy. Despite spending most of her life hiding from others, trying to keep out of the way, she had a great need for the outdoors, away from the house, away from Vanessa's constant tantrums and the strict formalities of Mrs Brampton. She loved to take off her stockings and shoes and feel the grass beneath her feet, but her favourite place was the stables, amongst the horses who she felt were her only friends; she never felt afraid around them, even when they were trying to kick open the stable door.

She still remembered clearly the day a very expensive horse had been brought to Brampton House; it was a gift for Vanessa. She had wanted to join the Foxhunt club where she was sure she would meet a handsome beau and where Vanessa was concerned, only the best would do. However not only was this horse a powerful black stallion, not at all suitable for a mere slip of a girl, but it had a bad temper and no one could control him.

A riding habit had been made especially to Vanessa's requirements and a special luncheon was put on in honour of her receiving her gift. It was not surprising to all the household staff that the horse took and instant dislike to her. He flattened his ears and his eyes had a wild look about them, he kicked and reared up, terrifying Vanessa so much she declared he be shot immediately.

Of course Mr Brampton would hear of no such thing, the horse had cost him a small fortune, so the horse was housed in the stable till he could decide what to do with him.

Natalia decided she had to see for herself; surely no horse could be as evil as Vanessa said. She snuck down to the stables as three men were struggling to lock the horse inside. Not wanting to get in trouble or wishing to be seen, she stood in the corner out of their view. Horse and girl looked at each other and he instantly settled.

Oliver had seen her sneak in, something he had seen her do many times before, but he never let on he knew. He saw the look pass between the horse and May and believed from that day on she had a special power.

As soon as the men left, she ventured over to the gleaming black stallion and let him nuzzle her hand. She decided to call him Jasper and that was his name from that day on.

She would often climb up on the stable door and talk to him, telling him all her secrets and her wildest dreams.

Natalia felt sorry for Jasper, she knew he had been standing sentry at the wagon steps not letting anyone but Luludja enter.

Luludja had said the first six weeks were crucial and she would need to stay out of the sunlight if she wanted to ensure no scars.

Despite Luludja's reassurances, Natalia had her doubts she would ever be beautiful again. Her life would resume to that of her past: a life of forever hiding in shadows keeping her face downcast.

Being confined to such a small space for so long had sent Natalia almost stir-crazy and she knew if she did not go outdoors soon, all Luludja's efforts to heal her would be wasted.

"Please Luludja you can't keep me inside any longer; it has been more than six weeks and you said they were healing better than you expected. I promise to keep to the shade, wear a hat and carry an umbrella at all times if you wish."

"I think you should wait a bit longer."

"I can't wait any longer! Besides my face is still covered in bandages, there is no way the sun can reach my skin. I need to see the sky, feel the grass under my feet! Please?"

The old woman was about to object, but she saw the look on the girl's face. Her mind suddenly went back to a time many years ago and a feeling of guilt and shame washed over her, causing her to look away from those pleading eyes. *Was she Luludja, partially responsible for the plight of this poor girl; had her involvement all those years ago altered her fate?* Closing her eyes tightly, trying desperately to stop the events of the past from flooding back, memories she thought were long dead and buried, a secret she had kept for all these years, a secret that only three people knew of and one of them was now dead. Realising this child had been sent to her for a reason, she now had a chance to make things right!

"You can be a stubborn one. Very well but stick to the shade and as you suggested; wear a hat and keep an umbrella over your head. If I once see you doing otherwise, trust me you do not want to feel the wrath of Luludja."

Natalia hugged Luludja and promised she would do as she was told. Grabbing the rather sorry looking umbrella, which looked as if it hadn't been used in years, she made her way outdoors, pausing at the top of the steps taking in a deep breath – *outside at last!*

Jasper whinnied, shaking his head and stomping the ground, letting her know he was pleased to see her.

She ran down the steps, reaching in her pocket for the lump of sugar that she had pocketed earlier, eagerly handing it to him before rubbing him on his forelock.

"Natalia!" warned Luludja

She quickly opened her umbrella as she ran to the protection of the trees, frightening Jasper in the process and causing him to move away with an angry snort. She turned around and laughed; something she hadn't done in a long time.

"Sorry fella, it's something you'll just have to get used to, as I don't fancy the wrath of Luludja."

Once under the protective cover of the umbrella and the

trees, she stood and took in her surroundings. Standing in awe, as it was a sight she had never seen before, there were many glorious ornate wagons with intricately carved detail, which was highlighted with bold colours of red, gold, blue and yellow. Each had a tiny porch and the colours even extended as far as the steps. As she looked around she could see they were a race who loved colour, as no wagon was the same. She also noticed some appeared as though they hadn't moved in years, as there was grass growing through the spokes of the wagon wheels; some were positioned in amongst the trees, whilst others were more out in the open.

There were many lines strung between the wagons and a sturdy tree, serving as a clothesline with many colourful garments flapping in the breeze. There was the laughter of children and she was amazed at how many there were, all of various ages, most with grubby faces, but all happy at play. She suddenly felt envious, as she herself had many times wished she'd had someone to play with through her childhood years.

It brought a sad smile to her face, thinking of her years as a child and having no one to talk to or play with – a life of terrible loneliness. They all looked so happy and she desperately wanted to go over and say hello, but as she put her hand to her face, *what must I look like?* She could not bear to see the look of fear and horror on their little faces.

As if sensing her sadness, she got a nudge from Jasper as if letting her know he was there and was her friend.

"You have been such of good boy standing guard for me, making sure no harm came to me. Just you wait; when I get the chance I will give you a whole basket of the best apples."

"So you want to repay him by giving him a belly ache!"

Natalia jumped at the sound of the deep voice and nervously turned around to see a tall, powerfully built man with thick raven-black hair. He seemed to tower above her and she noted his hostile stance as he stood with his arms folded across his broad chest.

He was handsome in a rugged sort of way, but despite his size and his bulging biceps, it was his eyes that were the most notable thing about him. They were the most amazing blue eyes she had ever seen and as they stared at one another, she had a sudden feeling of déjà vu. As much as she wanted to she could not look away, making her suddenly feel vulnerable. It was as if he could see right through to her very soul, giving her a funny sensation in the pit of her stomach.

Suddenly his eyes narrowed and she could see he did not like her and wondered why.

Not wanting him to know he intimidated her, she straightened her back and held her head high.

"Of course I don't want to give him a belly ache! I just want to show him my appreciation."

"Well if that is the way you thank someone, by inflicting pain, I will make it a point not to do anything that requires a thanks from you!"

Natalia just stared at him, all her bravado now gone. *Why was he being so hostile towards her, was it the way she looked, had Luludja told him what these bandages hid?*

Before she could voice her questions he suddenly turned on his heel and strode off, leaving her feeling hurt and alone.

Natalia had been wandering around for about an hour and couldn't help notice these people were definitely not happy about her being here. Despite her friendly wave and saying hello, they all kept their distance and if any happened to look her way, she could see the hostility in their eyes. *Was it because of her looks, was she now regarded as some kind of freak one saw at the circus, or was it something else?*

Feeling tired and despondent she sat in the shade on a fallen log by the stream, watching the cool, clear water as it rippled over the smooth moss-covered rocks.

## Natalia

Jasper happily ate the lush green grass and occasionally drank from the stream, there were many flowers in bloom and one could hear the sound of insects and birds. It was a glorious day and such a beautiful spot, but Natalia felt sad, trying to understand why everyone seemed to hate her so much.

Her mind wandered back to the day her kind friend found her in the woods, despite her being in a great deal of pain and going in and out of consciousness, she still remembered the look she saw in the young boy's eyes when she told him her name. *Was that the reason for all the hostility, had they mistaken her for someone else called Natalia? Surely it could not be her personally; she had never been anywhere apart from Brampton House.*

As she sat there pondering these questions, she also wondered why she had not seen the young boy. *Why hadn't he come to see how she was?* Suddenly feeling very tired and realising there was only one who could possibly answer her questions; she slowly made her way back to Luludja's wagon.

As soon as Luludja saw her she noticed not only her fatigue, but the sad forlorn look in her eyes.

"You must take things slowly; let your body have time to heal. Come lie down and rest."

"I can't believe how tired I feel. Luludja, why does everyone hate me?"

"Nonsense they don't hate you! They're just not used to strangers; we don't usually get visitors to our camp."

"Why is that, why do you all hide in the deep woods?"

"There is much you don't know my child, but I will tell you this: we most definitely do not 'hide in the deep woods'."

"Well then explain it to me. It is obvious none of these wagons have moved in years!"

"Child it is time you rest up; give your body time to heal."

Luludja walked over and put some leaves in the mortar, turning her back on Natalia and started grounding the leaves with the pestle.

"Luludja I know you are avoiding my question; what's going on?"

Luludja started grounding leaves in the mortar more fiercely, causing Natalia to get up from the bed and stand beside her; watching the leaves turn into a paste.

"Luludja!"

The old woman suddenly stopped what she was doing and looked sadly at Natalia. She put out her hand and gently touched her bandaged face, then put her thin arms around Natalia and held her in a surprisingly strong embrace.

"Please don't question me on this further. There is much you do not understand, but I promise you this, when the time is right I will tell you all there is to know. Now please lay down and rest; that is what is important now."

Natalia owed so much to this kind and thoughtful woman, she felt it best not to press her in matters that seemed to upset her.

As she lay down to rest, her mind wandered over the last weeks. *What had come of Mildred and Oliver and were they safe, had they been punished for helping her disappear with Jasper?* Her eyes were so heavy; she could no longer keep them open.

As she drifted off to sleep, her thoughts changed to Jasper. The wind was in her hair and the sun on her face, riding carefree through an open field with not a care or worry in the world.

\*\*\*

The next morning Natalia awoke bright and early, hopefully today would be a day of answers. She lit the small stove and put the kettle on to boil. Maybe if she had breakfast ready when Luludja woke, she would be allowed outside again.

The old woman awoke to the whistle of the kettle and Natalia had just finished laying the table.

"Good morning Luludja, breakfast is almost ready."

Luludja looked at her suspiciously thinking she was up to something; usually it was she who made breakfast and woke the girl up.

"I was thinking that as you have been so kind and generous; I would like to take the clothes down to the stream and give them a wash. I am sure you have many more potions to mix up and don't really have time for washing."

"What makes you think I have potions to mix? Besides they are not potions; I am not some sort of witch, I make medicine. You will get me burnt at the stake with talk like that."

"I am sorry please don't get angry with me, I just want to help and I thought it's the least I can do."

"You've done washing?"

"I have washed clothes before and I've cooked, you'd be surprised what I can do."

Luludja looked at Natalia with a look of surprise on her face and Natalia wondered why. *What is so surprising about her doing menial chores?*

"Natalia, would someone be looking for you?"

"Why, has someone been here asking for me?"

"No, but surely you would be missed; surely someone must wonder where you are."

"No! No one would miss me or would anyone waste their time to look for me."

Natalia avoided her eyes, her thoughts going to Jasper, she knew she would not be missed but Jasper would; he was a very valuable horse. *Oh my god, the police were probably looking for me! What if they came here?*

She walked over to the little window and lifted the curtain. *Should she tell Luludja, warn her, or would she be banished from here also?*

Luludja noticed the look of distress on the girl's face; it was obvious the girl was hiding something.

Besnik had been demanding answers; he wanted to know why someone had harmed the girl and why they should take her in – questions she had left unanswered.

Suddenly Luludja thought of Florica, her little flower, tears pricked the back of her eyes. She still remembered that night; it was all still so vivid, even after all these years. Natalia looked up and was surprised to see a look of such sadness on Luludja's face. *What had she said to invoke such pain?* She felt terrible; Luludja had been so kind to her defying Romany law and allowing a Gorgio in their camp. She got up and wrapped her arms around the old woman's thin shoulders.

"I have made something special for you this morning: flapjacks, one of my specialties. So drink your cup of tea whilst I dish up."

The smell of the flapjacks certainly smelt good; much better than the gruel she served for breakfast.

They ate in silence and Luludja looked up at the girl, there were so many things about her she did not understand. She seemed such a gentle creature, so kind of heart; *what on earth could she have done to evoke such a violent attack?*

"Well am I allowed to go down to the stream and wash the clothes?"

The old woman sat and thought for a moment. She had to admit it was a chore she did not like: it was hard on her knees and back, kneeling on the stream's edge and then carrying the heavy basket back. She supposed it would be all right – the stream was well shaded.

"On the condition you use the umbrella on the walk there and back and stick to the shadows."

"Oh thank you Luludja."

Natalia jumped up and hugged the old woman, puzzling her all the more – *this girl was a strange one indeed. Whoever thought doing such a menial chore could evoke such happiness.*

After the dishes had been cleared away, Natalia headed off towards the stream with a basket of washing.

As Luludja watched her retreating back, she realised she had to stay focussed and devote all her attention on healing the girl and give her back the beauty she once had; she owed her that much, besides many lives depended upon it.

On her walk down to the stream, Natalia passed many of the gypsies obviously carrying out the same chore as she, making a point of saying hello to everyone but still met with hostile stares.

"I hope it is just these bandages and not me," she said to herself.

"It's not the bandages, but you do look a sight."

Natalia jumped with fright almost dropping the basket of washing; she didn't realise she had spoken out loud.

There was no mistaking that deep voice.

Nervously turning around her heart did a flip flop as he was standing so close, so close she realised his eyes where the colour of the vibrant forget-me-nots which grew by the stream and as she looked into his eyes, she suddenly felt a mixture of fear and excitement.

"It's not polite to sneak up on people and scare them half to death."

"I didn't sneak up on you."

She stared at him, not wanting to get into a conversation, but for some reason could not will her body to move, nor could she look away from those incredible eyes. *Did he have some sort of special powers?*

He didn't move a muscle or flicker an eyelid.

She could feel herself getting hot and her heart had quickened its pace.

Suddenly the weight of the basket started digging into her hip, snapping her out of the trance.

Adjusting the basket she quickly turned and made her way to the stream, knowing he was still standing there watching her – she could feel his eyes boring into her back.

As hard as it was she refused to turn and see if he was still there, she was not going to give him the satisfaction, as she felt sure he was waiting for her to do so.

After about an hour, the clothes were washed and wrung out as best she could. She lifted the heavy basket and wondered how on earth Luludja managed the chore.

She rubbed her lower back trying to ease out the pain. She had assisted with the washing many times at the house, but had the use of a trolley to assist with the load.

She struggled to hold the umbrella and the basket at the same time nearly dropping the latter, when suddenly a pair of strong, tanned hands took the basket from her.

"I am sure Luludja would not appreciate you dropping her wet clothes in the dirt."

Natalia looked into his handsome face, feeling that strange sensation again in the pit of her stomach and the fact he was standing so close, she could smell his manly scent, a mixture of soap and musk, making her feel light headed.

Her eyes suddenly moved down to his lips, *what would it feel like to be kissed by them?*

His lips suddenly formed a hard line before he spun on his heel and walk away.

*My god, had he read her thoughts?*

Feeling suddenly embarrassed, she didn't want him to think she was that type of girl and quickly ran after him.

"Why do you not like me, what have I done to offend you?"

Her answer was his quickening pace and she had to run to keep up with his long strides.

"Excuse me, I am talking to you."

He stopped so suddenly she ran into his big broad back; which was like coming up against a stonewall; standing still she tried to regain her breath.

He turned around suddenly, his eyes hard as ice.

"I know you have cleverly fooled Luludja, but I know

*Natalia*

your type, so you may as well drop the innocent act."

Hurt as she realised what his assumption of her was, the state she had been in when the young boy had brought her to this place and how she, for no apparent reason, reacted whenever he came close.

"You know nothing about me, but I promise you this: as soon as my skin is healed and I no longer need Luludja's care, I will be out of this place so fast you won't see me for dust."

"I don't really care whether your skin heals or not, I will just be glad to see the end of you; then the rest of us can get on with our lives."

All Natalia's bravado vanished; she could see the anger and hate in his eyes, but she was determine not to let him see the tears that pricked the back of her eyes. He stared at her for a moment and she tried to swallow the lump in her throat, then he suddenly turned and strode off, still carrying the basket and headed in the direction of Luludja's wagon.

By the time Natalia reached the wagon she saw the basket had been placed below the clothesline, but there was no sign of the person who put it there. Natalia decided once she had hung out the wet clothes she would seek out the one who had found her; surely he would speak to her.

Once Natalia had finished hanging out the clothes she felt too exhausted to do anything else. She slowly climbed the stairs to the wagon, feeling as old as Luludja looked. *What was wrong with her, she normally had lots of energy.*

Luludja on seeing how tired she looked scolded her for overdoing it and made her climb into bed.

"Luludja there is a man that seems to follow my every move and it is obvious he does not like me. Have I done something wrong?"

"What does this man look like?"

"He is very tall, ruggedly handsome, strongly built but it is his blue eyes that stand out the most."

"Ah, you speak of Besnik. The others look up to him for

guidance, you are a stranger here; he is just ensuring the safety of his people. Do not concern yourself with him he is a good man. Now get some sleep."

Natalia knew by her tone she did not want to speak further on the matter and she did not have the energy to argue the point; deciding that maybe after she had some sleep she could continue the conversation and hopefully get some answers.

\*\*\*

She woke much later as the afternoon shadows were starting to fall. Surely she hadn't been asleep that long? She sat up looking around for Luludja, the wagon wasn't that big that she wouldn't be able to see her but she was nowhere to be seen. In fact the whole camp seemed quiet; not a sound was to be heard, not even the laughter or cry of a child and there were so many in the camp – that was most unusual.

Quickly getting up from the bed, she walked over to the wagon's door and stood on the top step, scanning the camp area; there was not a soul to be seen or heard. She thought for a horrible moment that they had all moved on, then realised all the wagons were still about.

As she slowly walked down the wagon steps something niggled at the back of her brain and then she realised, *Jasper!* He was never far from the wagon and always there to greet her when she came to the door.

"Jasper where are you boy?"

She looked around the camp and was met with silence, suddenly starting to feel rather frightened. *What was going on, where was everyone?* She wandered further around the camp still not finding a soul. She was near the track that led to the stream when she heard something. Straining her ears, it sounded like muffled voices, she slowly made her way down the path she had taken earlier in the day. Pausing once again, straining her ears trying to follow the direction the voices were coming from, as they were now getting louder and she realised it was down by the stream where she washed the clothes earlier that day.

Ever so mindful of moving as quietly as possible, her senses alert and her instincts telling her to stay as quiet as a mouse and keep to the shadows, something she had learnt from her years at Brampton House. Like a mouse she moved from tree to tree and bush to bush, her senses now on high alert as the further she moved forward, the louder the voices became.

Then suddenly there was a voice louder than the rest; it was deep and angry, one she recognised instantly. Quickly hiding behind a tree, but still near enough to hear what was said.

"We have waited long enough the time has come for answers! Luludja you know as well as all present, having the Gorgio girl here will only bring more trouble; why do you insist she stay?"

There was a great roar of voices all in agreement; Natalia peeked from around the tree to see a large crowd – even the children were present.

Natalia put her hand to her mouth to stop a rising sob. *Why do they hate her so much?*

"I need more time. You must trust me on this; believe me when I say it is for the good of the Romanies. Do you not wish the freedom all Romanies once had?"

Natalia recognised Luludja's angry voice and wondered what she was talking about. *What did she mean, are they not free?* She saw no guards, no fences; *how can they not be free?*

"Of course we want our freedom back but how can this Gorgio give us that? It was because of her we were banished to the woods in the first place," said a voice she did not know.

"That is why you must let her stay, she can lift the curse from us," said Luludja.

Natalia was confused. *What was this curse and how*

*does it involve her; surely they don't think she possesses some sort of power?*

Suddenly that deep voice penetrated her thoughts.

"How do you know we can trust her, what of her injuries, has she told you what happened to her yet? I think she is running away from something or someone and she is using you till she is fully healed; she said as much to me," said Besnik.

"She will only bring the Gorgio's back here, history is repeating itself. What about that horse, only a nobleman would have such a horse; surely no slip of a girl; what if she has stolen it? The police could be out looking for it as we speak; it will only be a matter of time before they come looking here, just as they did before!" exclaimed another voice.

Natalia's blood ran cold. *He was right; the police would be looking for her and Jasper.*

A terrible fear came over her, for she had heard the punishment for stealing a horse was hanging. Her heart was now pounding so hard she could hear the blood rushing in her ears. *What of Jasper, what had they done with him?*

"Enough! You wish to question the wisdom of Luludja, one who has directed you wisely so far?" asked Luludja.

"Then explain to us why this girl is so important, what makes you so sure she will give us our freedom?" asked Besnik.

The crowd erupted over this; it was as if Besnik had incited them into a riot.

Tears sprang to Natalia's eyes. From as far back as she could remember it did not matter what she did or how hard she tried to please, it was always met with anger and hatred. The one whom she'd believed to be her mother, had been the only one to show her love or kindness, but even that had been a lie. *Was there another reason why she had been lied to, the real reason she had to hide all these years?*

Suddenly filled with a terrible fear, she knew she had to

get away whilst she could, as far away as possible before the angry mob came looking for her. Despite the fact Luludja was defending her, she was a Romany and an old woman; she could not hold them off for long.

Running blindly as the tears were streaming down her face, she tried to contain her sobs so not to alert them of her presence. She moved as quickly and quietly as possible, ever fearful of stepping on a twig or kicking a stone.

Her heart pounded hard in her chest and the adrenalin gave her the strength she needed to flee.

Not even stopping for a warm shawl, the need to find a safe haven now overtaking her thoughts, her eyes darting in every direction, frightened someone would see her.

As she finally ran past the last wagon she forced herself to run even harder, ignoring the pain in her chest, her body still weak, only one thought in her head: *must keep running don't ever stop.*

She ran and ran, no idea where she was headed, her legs cramping in pain and a part of her brain telling her to rest, but survival mode had taken over and she couldn't stop.

The sun was setting low and a heavy mist was beginning to fall. She could feel a dampness setting over her clothes and the cold was biting her skin.

The leaves on the ground were now wet causing her feet to slip and slide and the pain in her chest was so intense she could hardly breathe.

Her foot caught a loose stone and she tripped and fell into a pile of leaves. She lay there panting, willing herself to move but her body was spent – she had nothing left.

She lifted her head and looked around, noticing a fallen tree nearby. It was broken in the middle and she could see it was hollow inside.

Realising she could go no further and with darkness descending fast, she knew she would need to seek shelter and find some way of warming her body if she was going to survive the night.

Not capable of standing she crawled towards the hollow of the tree, pausing momentarily, frightened some creature might already be residing inside, then pushing aside her fear and proceeding forward.

Pulling as much of her body inside as was possible, she then scooped handfuls of leaves over herself, hoping they would give her some form of protection against the cold night air.

She lay there totally exhausted, staring at the interior of the log, the smell of moss permeating her senses. Suddenly the sobs she had held in check erupted from deep within and she cried like she had never cried before.

*Whatever had she done to deserve this? Would she ever have a sense of belonging or be truly loved?*

As darkness enshrouded her cold air seeped into her bones, never before had she felt so cold.

Desperately covering herself with more leaves, her body shivered uncontrollably, sapping the remnants of her energy - no longer having the will to fight, her body finally stilled.

## CHAPTER FOUR

It was early morning and there was a heavy fog. They had ridden throughout the night and it had been very cold.

Luludja believed as did Fonso, their only hope of finding Natalia was Jasper; Besnik thought they were both crazy. Luludja had told him the girl had taken no coat or shawl and despite Fonso and himself having on their thick coats, the cold air still managed to seep through, making him believe if they managed to find her there was no way she could have survived the night.

Suddenly Jasper's ears pricked forward and he let out a loud whinny before running off.

Both Fonso and Besnik took off in pursuit, but did not have to go far before Jasper came to a halt by a large fallen tree.

He was stomping his right hoof and nuzzling with his nose at the leaves in a hollowed out section of the fallen tree.

Besnik was the first off his horse, walking over to see if Jasper had found something, but as he neared, Jasper threw up his head showing the whites of his eyes and flattening his ears. Besnik quickly took a step back, trying to avoid being bitten or trampled by the crazed horse.

"What is wrong with the stupid beast? There is nothing here but leaves."

"He knows you don't like her, there must be something here; something that will lead us to her."

Fonso walked past Besnik, holding out his hand to Jasper, letting him know he meant no harm.

"It's alright boy we want to find her as much as you. What have you found?"

Jasper's ears slightly pricked forward but his eyes were still wild. Fonso moved no closer, then after a moment, Jasper once again nudged at the leaves and stomped his right hoof.

"What is it boy; will you let me come closer for a look?"

Jasper shook his head and took a couple of steps back and Fonso moved cautiously forward.

As he bent down he noticed a piece of dirty fabric amongst the leaves, then he slowly moved the leaves with his hand and as he did so he saw more of the fabric and suddenly realised it was a dress. A cold fear came over him, as he realised who it was. Using both hands he frantically swept away the rest of the leaves.

"It's Natalia!"

Besnik quickly moved forward and knelt down beside Fonso, who was now sobbing quietly. Besnik looked down at her and could see some of her bandages had come free and Luludja's special paste had worked miracles, as the scar was now barely visible. She looked like one of the china dolls the children had: the contrast of her long black lashes against her pale frozen cheeks and her perfectly shaped lips which now had a blue hue. Before he realised what he was doing, he put out a hand and gently touched them. He felt that same tingling sensation he had felt the first time he touched her skin. *Is it possible?* He leaned in close to her lips and felt her faint breath. Quickly he began to unbutton his coat, the cold air biting harshly into his skin.

"We must get her back to Luludja as soon as possible!"

"Is she alive?"

"Only just; I'm amazed she survived the night."

By the time Besnik got over to his horse, he was shivering as the cold air took hold. He realised his coat was large enough for both of them and also his body heat would put some warmth back into her body. Once on his horse he pulled her onto his lap, enveloping her in his coat and doing his best to button them both inside it. It was rather tight but he realised it would make it easier to hold her as they would need to ride fast.

Jasper was snorting and shaking his head trying to bite

Besnik's horse, all the while Besnik was trying to control his horse and avoid both Natalia and himself from falling from their precarious position.

"Jasper doesn't like you putting her on your horse!" Exclaimed Fonso.

"Well he has no choice; you need to calm him down, we could be wasting precious minutes by his ridiculous behaviour."

Fonso quickly grabbed Jasper's lead pleading with the horse to behave and the moment Besnik had a chance he gave his horse a quick kick and rode off. He had no time to wait for Fonso, he knew it would not be long before both followed.

On the ride back he was amazed the girl had made it this far and was still alive but what disturbed him more was being in such close proximity of her.

\*\*\*

Luludja heard the sound of pounding horses hooves and realised they had found Natalia alive. She had been keeping her small stove burning through the night, for she realised if the girl managed to survive she would be in urgent need of some warmth.

Besnik hurriedly pulled his horse up close to Luludja's steps and unbuttoned his coat before dismounting.

"She is barely alive; I have managed to warm her slightly with my coat and body heat."

He carried her up the steps and lay her down on the bed.

Luludja immediately began to fuss. She started removing Natalia's shoes and stockings whilst Besnik stood by. Luludja realising he was still inside, quickly turned around.

"You should go outside; I need to remove her damp clothes, go get Violca she is larger than me and will be able to warm her better than I."

On his way he heard the sound of approaching horses

and knew it would be Fonso.

\*\*\*

The next morning Besnik made his way over to Luludja's wagon to see how Natalia had faired through the night. He got as far as the base of the stairs but suddenly could go no further. *What was he doing, why did he care?* Before he realised, he had mounted the stairs and gave a gentle knock on the door, but received no response. Suddenly angry with himself, *he had better things to do than worry about a silly Gorgio girl.* He turned and started back down the steps when he heard someone call out. He paused momentarily before turning, then going back up the steps and entered the wagon.

The sight of Natalia stopped him in his tracks; she was no longer wearing her bandages and he could see her hair had started to grow. The scars on her head were no longer visible. She obviously had a fever as her hair was wet and her face was glistening in sweat. She was tossing and turning which had caused the covers to move, exposing her nudity underneath.

He took in her flawless white skin, the swell of her firm, full breasts and her pale pink nipples erect from the cold air. Then he noticed the small scar near the swell of her left breast and remembered the injuries she had when Fonso had brought her here.

"Besnik! What are you doing?" asked Luludja as she quickly covered the girl.

"I knocked and someone called out, she has a fever," he said before leaving the wagon.

Luludja quickly woke up her sister and then applied a cool cloth to Natalia's face and arms, trying to bring her temperature down.

"She has a fever; keep applying the cool cloth and I will mix some herbs that will help bring down her fever," said Luludja.

"I had to see for myself... I had to know," mumbled a delirious Natalia.

"Do you know what she is talking about?" Violca asked her sister.

"I have no idea it must be the fever."

"All these years..."

"Shhh," soothed Violca.

"Mother why... Why did you have to lie to me?" asked Natalia as she sat up, her eyes glazed.

Luludja rushed over as Violca tried to make Natalia lay back against the pillows, trying to encourage Natalia to drink some healing medicine. She managed to get her to drink a little and within minutes she began to settle and Violca reapplied the cool cloth.

"All these years of hiding... it was all just a lie," she mumbled.

"Shhh, you are safe now; you have nothing to fear," said Luludja.

"Jasper... they have taken him from me... he was my only friend," she cried.

"Hush child, no one has taken him away; he is safe and well. When you get better you can see him."

Her soothing voice calmed Natalia and she finally relaxed in sleep.

Luludja noticed that her temperature was starting to come down as the medicine was taking effect. Once she was satisfied the girl was resting, she walked outside to talk with her sister.

"I know she has a fever, but things don't make sense. We must find out what happened to her and what brought her back here," said Violca.

"I keep thinking of that night all those years ago. We should have waited; we shouldn't have been so hasty to leave," said Luludja sadly.

"I don't understand, what does she mean about having to hide? Are you sure she is Natalia?"

"She is definitely Natalia. You saw the birthmark on the back of her neck and she still has the bracelet; it was pinned inside her dress."

"Then who did this and why? What also bothers me is she came looking for you, do you think she knows?" asked Violca with a look of concern on her face.

"I don't see how, but the thought did cross my mind."

"I am worried this has all been a big mistake, what if Besnik and the others are right and we have put everyone in further danger? What if whoever she is running from comes here? I think it is time we tell Besnik; he will know what to do."

"I understand your concerns Violca but we must keep them to ourselves; we must wait until I have spoken to Natalia. There is a lot we don't yet understand; only she can provide the missing pieces to the puzzle. She is the key to us being free; I firmly believe Fonso was meant to cross paths with her that day."

\*\*\*

It was almost a week since Natalia had been found near death in the forest.

She was currently propped up in bed with a warm lavender shawl wrapped around her shoulders, drinking a warm mug of Luludja's special tea, when suddenly Besnik walked through the wagon door causing her to almost spill the hot liquid in her lap.

The sight of him caused her heart to flutter, avoiding his eyes she focussed on a button on his shirt. Without realising what she was doing, her eyes scanned the expanse of his broad chest; the sleeves of his shirt were rolled up exposing his tanned muscled arms. Her eyes travelled further down, noting his firm, flat stomach, which tapered to a slim waist and the way his trousers moulded to his long muscular legs. Suddenly she heard a cough and her eyes flew back to his, causing her cheeks to grow hot with embarrassment as she realised, he had noticed her thorough inspection of him.

"Are you quite finished, would you like to inspect my teeth also?"

Natalia was wishing the roof of the wagon would fall in and tried to cover her embarrassment by snapping back at him.

"What have you done with Jasper? I demand to see him!"

Suddenly Luludja appeared from behind the curtain.

"I hope you are not upsetting my patient?"

"I came to see how your patient is fairing, but I can see that her near-death experience has only sharpened her tongue."

"Stop trying to avoid my question, where is Jasper?"

"Fonso is looking after him," said Besnik.

"I don't believe you, you have sold him; Jasper would never leave me - Why didn't you leave me in the woods to die? I know you don't want me here, I heard you talking to the others," she exclaimed, tears welling in her eyes.

Besnik was about to make an angry retort but thought better of it and stormed out of the wagon.

Luludja seeing the girl's tears sat down next to her on the bed and patted Natalia's hand.

"Besnik may be many things, but he's not a liar. If he said Fonso is looking after Jasper for you then that is where your horse is."

Natalia looked in the old woman's face and knew she was telling the truth. She also felt guilty for accusing him; after all he did saved her life.

"I'm sorry I just miss Jasper, he's my only friend; the only one who really cared about me," said Natalia, tears rolling down her cheeks.

"Surely it cannot be as bad as that? You know I know very little about you; about what brought you here and about your family."

"I can't tell you much about my real family; I didn't

even know my real name until the night before I came here."

"What do you mean your real name, weren't you always Natalia?"

"I was always called May. It wasn't until my last night at that awful place I found out my real name and my mother was not my mother after all."

"Now you have me confused."

"My mother... sorry, Mildred realised it was no longer safe for me to stay in the house. I was in a great deal of pain and was in and out of consciousness, so things are a bit hazy. I remember her crying and she was trying desperately to make me understand. She told me how she had just lost her husband and wanted to end her life. She was heading towards the river when she heard a baby's cry and saw a basket on a doorstep and was shocked and surprised to see a baby inside. She believed I had been sent from God, but days later found out my parents were searching for me, but couldn't bring herself to give me up; so she christened me May."

"Why was it no longer safe for you in the house, was it the same person who inflicted your injuries?"

"I don't want to talk about it; it is something I would rather forget, all I will say is Oliver, the stable boy helped me get away."

"Natalia it is not good to keep things like this bottled up; please I want to help you. Why did someone hurt you?"

"I did something I shouldn't have."

"What could you have possibly done to warrant such a harsh punishment?"

Natalia's eyes filled with tears and she looked away from Luludja and her hands started plucking at the shawl, so much so Luludja was sure the shawl would start to unravel.

She gently took hold of the girl's shaking hands and held them in her own.

"Child you are safe now; no harm will come to you,

please tell me what happened. Who took a hot iron to your skin and hacked at your hair so violently?"

"You will think badly of me. It was my fault but I had to look; I couldn't stand it any longer I needed to know."

"What child, what did you seek?"

"I was tired of hiding, living my life in fear."

"Why were you afraid, what were you hiding from?"

"Me."

"I don't understand."

"All my life I was led to believe I was some kind of freak; always forced to cover my hair, wear ugly dresses and most importantly of all, never let anyone see my eyes."

"Why could you not let them see your eyes?"

"I would be in mortal danger if I did."

"That's absurd! Who on earth would say such a thing?"

"My mother, least I thought she was my mother and the mistress of the house. I had never seen myself in the mirror; firstly I was never allowed, then I was too frightened at what I would see. One day I could stand it no more I had to know, no matter how bad it would be."

"You say your mother and the mistress, was your mother not the mistress of the house?"

"No she was the house cook."

"I see, so what did you do?"

"I went to Vanessa's room; I knew she had a large mirror."

"Did you see yourself?"

Natalia started to cry and nodded.

"Why are you crying child; what did you see?"

"I discovered they had lied to me, I was not some hideous creature; I was beautiful!" She sobbed.

"This is why you were so brutally attacked; because you looked at yourself in the mirror?" Luludja asked incredulously.

"I was angry and hurt that I had been forced to live this way, forced to make myself look ugly. I wondered what it would be like to wear something beautiful for a change; so I tried on Vanessa's silk dress."

Natalia looked away from Luludja as she remembered Mr Brampton finding her naked, *would she think it was her fault he did what he did?*

"Go on child."

"I was going to I had taken off all my clothes, I know it is wrong but I wanted to see everything; I wanted to see all of me."

"And that's why you were punished?"

"He saw me. I was frightened he had a strange look in his eyes, he came over and started touching me....."

"Who was he?"

"Vanessa's father; master of the house!"

"Go on, child, what happened?"

"I tried to cover myself with Vanessa's dress...then he started to undress....I tried to escape but he was too strong for me...then he ripped the front of the dress... That's when Vanessa walked in and started screaming and then her mother came in. She started attacking him; she was so angry, I tried to run but Vanessa blocked my way – there was nowhere to hide. Her mother grabbed me and held me to the floor, taking to my hair with the scissors; cutting so close it hurt. Then Vanessa got the hot poker out of the fire, she wanted to make sure no one would look at me ever again; the pain was so bad I was sure I would die!"

She was sobbing deeply now, reliving the nightmare all over again. Luludja wrapped her thin arms around the girl trying to give her some comfort, assuring her it was not her fault.

Just then Besnik stormed into the wagon, his face dark with anger as he strode over to the bed.

"You wish to see your horse?"

The anger in his voice stopped her tears immediately and a wave of fear came over her. *Why was he angry, what had she done?*

Luludja stood in front of her as if trying to protect her.

He gently moved the old woman aside, then without warning he bent down and scooped Natalia up from the bed and proceeded to carry her outside the wagon.

She could feel her heart pounding and was sure he could feel it too. She turned her head in panic, hoping Luludja could help her, but he was striding so fast the old woman could not keep up. Suddenly there was a high pitch whistle, causing Besnik to stop in his tracks and he turned around and faced Luludja.

"I am doing as she requested; I am taking her to see her horse," he said gruffly.

Natalia could feel his anger, the way he held her against his broad chest. His hands gripped her so tightly she could imagine the bruises already.

"Besnik please, you are hurting me, I can walk please put me down."

He stopped so suddenly Natalia was afraid she had only angered him further, but instead he loosened his grip and adjusted her position in his arms and looked directly into her eyes.

"Am I hurting you now?"

"No," she whispered, feeling her cheeks go hot.

He then proceeded to carry her towards the stream and surprisingly she felt safe.

Wondering where he was taking her, she twisted in his arms and saw a wooden fence, one she hadn't noticed the day she came down to do the washing.

As they neared she saw her friend, the one with the kind brown eyes, the one who had brought her to Luludja; then she saw Jasper.

"Please put me down; I can walk."

"I promised Luludja I would aid in your recovery, so for now I will carry you."

She realised it was pointless to argue with him, although she did feel a bit silly as they were getting stares from passers-by, who had been either getting water or doing washing by the stream.

As they came up towards the fence Jasper started snorting, stomping and shaking his head. When they came level with the fence, Besnik perched her on the top.

"Hello boy, did you miss me like I missed you?" she asked whilst rubbing his forelock.

Jasper snorted and shook his head in response.

"I have taken good care of him for you, although he will not let me ride him."

"Thank you, I can see that. As for Jasper not letting you ride him, for some reason I am the only one who has had that privilege, so don't take it to heart. I am sorry and I must admit I am embarrassed to say this, as you were the one who brought me to Luludja, but I do not remember your name."

"No need to apologise, my name is Fonso," he said as he held out his hand.

"I am forever in your debt and you will forever hold a special place in my heart," she said as she shook his hand.

"I have never heard of a horse so loyal to one before; you must hold a special power over him," said Fonso incredulously.

"I don't have any special powers Fonso; it is just the way things are."

"Some might disagree with you there," said Besnik.

Natalia turned around and looked at him, those incredible blue eyes bored into hers, causing her heart to flutter. *What was wrong with her and why was he looking at her that way?*

"Could I please ride him, just a gentle ride?" she asked with pleading eyes.

He continued to stare at her and she noticed him clenching his jaw; he stared at her for so long she started to feel uncomfortable.

Finally he shifted his eyes and looked over the top of her head before looking back at her.

"If you give me your word it will be a gentle ride."

A big smile spread across Natalia's face and before she realised what she was doing she reached up and hugged him.

"Thank you!"

His body stiffened and she quickly pulled away, turning to hide her embarrassment.

When Fonso had saddled the horse Natalia started to climb the fence, when a pair of strong arms lifted her up and placed her into the saddle.

"Well boy I made my promise, let's go for a gentle ride," she said as she gathered his reins in her hands and made a clicking noise with her tongue.

Jasper pricked his ears forward and did as she said, moving away into a slow trot.

Besnik noticed she had a calming effect on the horse, noting she also rode astride and not side-saddle like most Gorgio women seemed to do.

He had been standing outside the door of Luludja's wagon when he had heard with anger and horror the story she conveyed.

Her naked body, so young and innocent still a vivid image in his mind. *Her first touch from a man should be gentle and tender, not from one so vile and rough.* He suddenly felt an incredible rage; he could feel his blood boil and without realising it, he clenched his fists.

Natalia was heading back towards the fence when she noticed the look of anger on Besnik's face. *Had she done something to anger him further?* As she drew closer to the fence Besnik's anger seemed to intensify and she started to feel scared.

"Natalia do you think you could weave your magic on Jasper so he will let me ride him?"

Fonso's words penetrated Natalia's thoughts; breaking the hold Besnik's eyes seemed to have over her.

She looked down at Fonso and into his kind brown eyes

and smiled back.

"I don't have any magical powers, but if you like you can ride behind me. I know Jasper will cause you no harm whilst I am on his back, although I am not sure Besnik will allow it as I seem to have angered him further."

Fonso looked at Besnik; he had seen that look before and he knew he hadn't heard a word Natalia had said to him; his mind was somewhere else. To snap him out of it he grabbed him by the arm and gave him a shake.

"Besnik, can Natalia double me on Jasper?"

Snapping back to the present, he looked down at Fonso's pleading eyes then up at Natalia and was shocked to see fear in her eyes. *What was she afraid of?*

As he looked down at his clenched fists he realised she was fearful of him. He looked back up into those beautiful green eyes, realising they grew larger with fear.

"That depends on Natalia and Jasper," he said, not taking his eyes from hers.

Without another word Fonso climbed the fence and was about to get on Jasper's back when the horse moved away, the movement of the horse broke the trance between Besnik and Natalia.

She leant forward rubbing Jasper's neck and whispered something into his ear.

The horse snorted and gently shook his head.

Once again she rubbed his neck and softly talked to the horse.

Neither Fonso nor Besnik could hear what she was saying but the horse settled and made his way back to the fence.

"Now take it easy Fonso, climb on carefully then put your arms around my waist."

Fonso did as she said and once he was on the horse's back he sat very still and his arms tightly wrapped around her waist.

Jasper shook his head as if in protest but Natalia rubbed

his neck and uttered more calming words.

Besnik was amazed; he wondered if she was some sort of a witch and could cast spells, as he had never seen such a thing before.

With Jasper's reins firmly in her grasp and when she was sure Fonso was ready, she gave a click of her tongue, coaxing the horse into a gentle trot.

After they had circled the full extent of the enclosure, Natalia brought them back to the fence.

Fonso's eyes were like saucers and he had a grin from ear to ear.

Besnik knew the girl had won a true and loyal friend with Fonso.

When they drew near the fence, she once again leant forward and whispered in the horse's ear before sitting up and looking at Besnik.

"Maybe next time we will be allowed to go a bit further and faster?" she asked hopefully.

Fonso climbed off the horse and onto the fence and Natalia was about to follow suit, when Besnik lifted her off and back into his arms.

"You don't need to carry me, honestly I am fine."

His only response was to tighten his hold and then he looked across at Fonso.

"Natalia has allowed you to ride her horse, so make sure he is fed and watered."

The walk back to the wagon was done in silence, Natalia having trouble keeping her head from resting on his shoulder, she was surprised at how such little exercise had made her feel so tired.

By the time they reached the wagon, she had given up trying to keep her head off Besnik's shoulder and her eyelids felt heavy.

Luludja noticing how tired she had become, scolded him for tiring her out.

"Please don't be angry with him, for I have had such a

wonderful day. Thank you Besnik and please give my thanks to Fonso also," she said as Luludja tucked her back into bed.

Besnik looked down at her as Luludja fussed over her and saw her finally give in to sleep. He noticed the scar was no longer visible and she had some colour in her cheeks.

"Walk with me; we must talk," said Luludja.

He held out his arm to help her down the steps and they strolled for a while before she spoke.

"Despite your tough demeanour towards her, I can see she is softening your heart."

"What nonsense you talk, she is a Gorgio and I will never forget that."

"Just be careful not to get too close."

"It was I who objected her presence here, do you not remember that? First you berate me for being harsh to the girl and then you berate me for showing some compassion; make up your mind!"

Luludja decided it wise to drop the subject, but she would keep a closer eye on him in the future.

"I think the time has come for you to tell me why she is here; why you went against Romany law and allowed her to stay in our camp."

"All will be revealed, but first I must speak with Natalia."

"I can be patient for only so long Luludja."

He walked her back to her wagon and back up the steps, but did not go inside; instead made his way to the horse enclosure.

As Besnik neared the fence he could see Fonso lovingly brushing Jasper's coat until it shone.

The horse was standing perfectly still, listening to Fonso's excited chatter.

"I knew we would be good friends the moment I saw you; it was just a matter of you getting to know me. You know you can trust me now, as I brought Natalia to Luludja as she asked. You can also see she is getting much better, soon she will be able to ride you like the wind and maybe now that you know me, I can ride you also. You will love it here; there are so many places for us to explore."

"Fonso don't start planning a future with Jasper and Natalia, you know they are only here for a short time," said Besnik.

"Why do they have to leave? Look how much better she looks, Jasper is happy also."

"I have told you this before: she is a Gorgio and does not belong here with the Romanies but with her own kind."

"Why can't the Romanies and Gorgio's live together, why can't she be part of our family?"

"You are young; you don't understand these things, just accept things as they are. One day you will understand."

Fonso was going to argue the matter but realised it would be useless. He would speak to Natalia himself when they had a chance alone, surely if she wished to stay here they could not force her to leave.

Besnik could almost hear Fonso's brain ticking over; he knew he wouldn't let the matter rest. He had grown a deep attachment to the horse and Besnik doubted that Natalia would depart without him, which he was sure Fonso also knew.

# CHAPTER FIVE

Natalia awoke happy and refreshed, she had slept with dreams of riding Jasper through lush green fields that were lined with meadow buttercups with golden petals and knapweed with flowers like tiny purple pineapples and they covered the whole meadow in colour.

She bunched up her pillows and closed her eyes, trying to recapture the wonderful dream. She was sure she could hear the warbling song of a skylark as they rested beside a crystal-clear stream, watching little grebes as they pop up from underwater foraging, whilst grey herons silently stalk at the water's edge.

Laying there with a serene smile on her face, this was how Luludja saw her when she walked in to give her a cup of tea. She sat down quietly so as not to disturb her, as this was the first time she had seen the girl look really happy and at peace, wishing she could see what dreams were in her head, it had been a long time since she herself had a truly restful sleep.

"I'm not asleep; I just wanted to stay in my dream," said Natalia as she sat up.

"I'm glad you slept well, where were you in your dream?" asked Luludja as she handed the girl her cup of tea.

"I was riding Jasper and there was colour everywhere, buttercups and knapweed. We rested by a crystal-clear stream with masses of fluffy, fragrant flowers, I was laughing at the little grebes popping up from the water, I was so happy."

"It does sound wonderful, is it a place you visited often with Jasper?"

"No, that's the funny thing; I have never been to such a place or seen such things, so I don't know if such things exist."

"Well I have seen such flowers and your description and names of them are correct, I have never before heard of a Gorgio to have such visions," said Luludja, truly amazed.

"Do you think it was a vision and not a dream?"

"I do not know child, but it would appear so when you have never seen or heard of such things, but drink up your tea whilst it is still hot."

Luludja had realised it had come time to talk to Natalia about her parents and why fate had brought her here; she could keep her secret no longer and the thought of it brought a pain to her heart. She sat there for a moment, wondering how best to broach the subject, then she thought the girl was so happy at the moment, maybe she should wait and let the poor girl enjoy her happiness for a little longer.

Natalia noticed the look on the old woman's face; it was a mixture of fear and sadness. Quickly putting down her cup and getting up out of bed, she put her arms around Luludja trying to offer some form of comfort.

"I can see sadness on your face and it saddens me too, for you have been so kind to me; I will be forever in your debt. Tell me how I can make you happy?"

"Child, do not worry oneself over me; I am old and suffer many aches and pains, making it difficult to always have a happy face."

Natalia looked at the old woman and realised she was avoiding her question, she would leave it be for now, but would take a closer interest of her from now on.

"I thought after breakfast I would take a walk, maybe pick some flowers. Is there anything you wish for me to do?"

"No my child you go ahead and enjoy your day."

Natalia had been picking flowers when she heard the laughter of children. She paused and looked around to see where it was coming from. They were over near the horses' enclosure and where playing some sort of game. Deciding to walk over and see if they would let her join in, she knew she was too old to be playing children's games, but as she had never done so before wanted to know what it was like.

As she neared a young child of about four tripped and fell and began to cry. Instinctively Natalia ran forward to administer aid and as she crouched down beside the child she was shocked to see fear in her eyes and realised all the other children had gone very quiet.

"It's all right little one; I am not going to hurt you. I see you have grazed your knee."

As she leant forward to take a closer look, Natalia suddenly felt a pain to the side of her head and then saw a rock land beside her. She started to rise and tried to keep the tears and hurt from showing on her face when Besnik suddenly grabbed one of the older boys.

"Nicu! What on earth do you think you are doing? Apologise to Natalia this instant!"

Natalia saw the fear and the tears glistening in the young boy's eyes and her heart went out to him.

"Besnik please don't scold the boy, It was my fault I should have been looking," she said with a smile.

"He threw a rock at you, it would not matter if you were looking he should not have done it."

Natalia could see the look of confusion on the young boy's face, but also the hope she would save him from Besnik's wrath.

"I know it's a rock but we were playing a game, it was my turn to catch but I turned my head because this little one grazed her knee."

"What sort of a game requires one to throw a rock? Someone could get hurt, I can see a bruise forming on the side of your face," he said as he gently touched her skin.

The feel of his hand on the side of her face made her feel suddenly hot and her heart quickened its pace. As he stared at her she realised he was waiting for an answer, but did not know if she was capable of speech.

"Well?"

"I was explaining to them about a game called hot potato and as we did not have one, I was using a rock. I now realise it was a silly thing to do, I am sorry I didn't think."

Besnik stared at her then looked at Nicu, who nervously shook his head, before Besnik looked at her suspiciously.

She was determined not to look away and noticed his eyes suddenly narrowed and she was sure he knew she was lying.

After what seemed like an age, Besnik turned on his heel and without another word walked away.

Natalia expelled her breath, which she hadn't realised she had been holding and then looked at the children and realised they were all staring at her.

"Why did you tell Besnik we were playing a game?" asked Nicu.

"If I had told him the truth, would you have got in trouble?"

"Yes, he would have given me a hiding."

"Really, how would your parents feel about that?"

"They would say I probably deserved it."

"Well let's say I did tell Besnik the truth and you did get a hiding, would that have made you feel any differently towards me, than when you threw the rock?"

"I would have hated you more."

"How do you feel about me now?"

"I don't know, maybe you're not as evil as they say."

"So you all think I'm evil?"

She looked at all the little faces and could see the fear in their eyes. *What had she done to instil such fear in them; did they too believe she had powers to put on a curse?*

"The reason I didn't tell Besnik the truth is because I had learnt a long time ago, if someone is mean to you and you are mean back, the hatred only builds, but if you are nice or just walk away, then they will either become your friend or leave you alone. So I am hoping you will want to be my friend."

Unbeknownst to Natalia and Nicu, Besnik was obscured by a tree and he had been listening to what the two were saying. He knew Natalia had been protecting the boy and was surprised to find out why.

"I will be your friend on the condition you teach me this game you were talking about."

Natalia threw back her head and laughed and soon all the children were laughing with her. With a smile on her face she showed them how the game was played, when she suddenly noticed Besnik standing over by the tree. *How long had he been standing there? Had he heard the conversation between her and Nicu?*

"Natalia, it's your turn to throw the ball."

Turning, she saw Nicu waiting impatiently and all the other children looking at her expectantly. She quickly looked back over towards the tree but Besnik was no longer there and wondered if he would have words to her later about her lie to protect Nicu.

Suddenly she felt a tug on her dress and looked down to see the little one whom she had tried to help earlier. Bending down, she asked her if she would like to play also and was rewarded with a smile and a nod.

The children got themselves into fits of laughter as they played this new game Natalia had taught them. The idea of the game was as soon as one caught the ball, they must immediately pass it on to another without it touching the ground. It was getting on in the afternoon and the children were slowly making their way back to their various wagons, as dirty faces needed to be washed and they had to get ready for dinner.

Natalia was handing the ball to Nicu, when she decided to ask him about something he had said earlier in the day.

"Nicu, why do the Romanies think I am evil, what am I supposed to have done?"

"Because of you, a curse was put on us and we were all banished to the deep woods. If ever we are caught venturing outside, we will be thrown in prison and put to death."

"Oh my God I can't believe this; why me?"

"I don't know; it was before I was born. All Romany fears the name of Natalia; for it was she who put a curse on those of Romany blood."

Natalia just stood there shocked at what Nicu had said and she could see from the look on his face, he was telling her the truth. She realised there was only one person who could give her an answer: the one person who had allowed her to stay in their camp.

"Luludja we have to talk, I need to know why all Romanies believe I am evil and don't try to deny it; I have heard it from the mouth of a young child and I have to admit it makes sense as to why there is so much animosity towards me."

"Very well child, I will answer your questions, but first there is a story I must tell you. It all started with my daughter, but first we will have some warming soup, for what I have to tell you will take us late into the night, possibly the early morning."

They had their soup in silence, Natalia wondering about what Luludja had to say as she could see the fear and sadness; something she no longer tried to hide. Once the dishes were cleared and the pot was put on the stove for more tea, they both settled once again at the table.

"As I said, I shall start at the beginning. It all started with my daughter. I was only blessed with one child as I had her late in life. Both my husband and I thought we would remain childless, but the angels smiled down upon us and my Florica was born, her name meaning 'flower', she was a beautiful child not only in looks but also in spirit. Because of Florica's beauty she attracted much attention from the Gorgio as well as the Romanies, but what you don't realise is a Romanies future partner is agreed upon at birth.

So you see, no matter who vied for Florica's attention, an agreement had been made at her birth and when she came of age she would marry Gunari, whose name meant 'soldier' or 'warrior'. He grew to be a proud, strong man who demanded things done his way. I started to have my doubts about the union between Florica and Gunari, as he also had a cruel streak and my Florica was so gentle.

It was the year of her eighteenth birthday and she would be married on the day of her birth. As the day grew near we were all getting excited; it was going to be a big celebration. When I look back on things now, I should have seen the signs. The day of the wedding had arrived and instead of her feeling as most brides, excited and full of joy, she was sullen and sad.

I was putting flowers in her hair; she would be the most beautiful bride, but I caught a glimpse of her in the mirror and was shocked to see such sadness, it tore at my heart. I turned her in the chair and held her face in my hands. I told her that this should be a day of joy and asked why she was so sad.

She looked at me with her big, beautiful brown eyes and asked me if I had married her father with love. I had told her that love is something that grows with time and she would one day feel that way with Gunari. She then told me she could never love Gunari, as her heart was given to another and that is where it would always remain.

I asked her how could this be and she told me she was in love with a Gorgio and he was the one she wished to marry. I was angry with her and told her she talked nonsense and it could never be. We had an argument and I stormed out of the wagon. When I later returned she had gone. My anger grew more, but as the day wore on and everyone was waiting for the wedding to proceed, my anger soon turned to concern.

As the night descended and there was still no sign of Florica, Gunari became extremely angry, as she had brought great embarrassment upon him. A search party had gone out to bring back the wayward bride. Days turned into weeks and eventually turned into months before my Florica was found. By then she had wed her true love. When word of this reached Gunari he went into a fit of rage, as not only had his betrothed left him at the altar but she had married a Gorgio."

Natalia had been sitting so still and enthralled by the story, but when Luludja had said Florica had married a Gorgio, she could not contain her surprise.

"I thought it was taboo for Romany to marry a Gorgio, how could this be?"

"Romanies and Gorgio didn't always despise each other so, but you are right; if Romany was to marry a Gorgio they would forever be cursed. Before the Romanies were banished to the deep woods we were free to mingle with the Gorgio; that was how Florica fell in love. She was working as a maid in a big estate home as many Romanies did. She met a young footman and they fell in love. He was the one she wished to spend the rest of her life with, even if it meant banishment from her own kind.

When word of this got back to Gunari, he immediately got on his horse and rode many days and nights. His honour was at stake and he would bring his wayward bride home. Florica had been working at the markets, telling fortunes for a silver coin and when she arrived home, she discovered Gunari he had been waiting for her. He grabbed her and tried to drag her to his horse when her husband arrived home, a great fight ensued and her husband was killed. My poor Florica was so beside herself with grief, all the fight had gone out of her. Gunari took advantage of this and put her upon his horse. He rode day and night until his horse almost collapsed with exhaustion. By the time they reached our camp I thought he had killed her.

She was limp and lifeless in his arms. He carried her into my wagon and demand I cleanse her of the Gorgio stench, it wasn't until I undressed her I realised she was with child. If Gunari found out I knew he would surely kill her, I knew I had to keep it from him for the sake of her and the child. I was not sure how I would do this, but I would think of a way.

For three days and nights my Florica cried for her love, she would not eat or drink, even for the sake of her child. On the third night she started to scream in pain, Gunari tried to come into the wagon but I knew I could not let him see her. Hanzi, Gunari's brother came and pulled him away after hearing my protests. In the early hours of the fourth day her baby was born: a tiny girl with black downy hair and the fair skin of a Gorgio. She was born too soon and died a few hours later in Florica's arms. She called her Lala, meaning 'little tulip'. I gave her something to make her sleep, then bundled up the babe and buried her down by the riverbank. Her grave is unmarked as it would not be allowed to have a Gorgio buried beside a Romany – her death was a sign of the curse. Violca, myself and now you, are the only ones who know about the child.

After that night my Florica was never the same. I think something snapped inside her, as the pain was too great for her to bear. In a matter of days she had not only lost her true love, but her child; my Florica was no more."

Tears were pouring down Luludja's cheeks, reliving the nightmare had opened an old wound. She felt she'd failed as a mother; she hadn't protected her child, she should have seen the signs; she should have listened to her. Maybe she'd be here today if she had.

"Luludja this is obviously painful for you but I don't understand what it has to do with me and my parents and Gunari; was he punished for killing Florica's husband?"

"Yes the Gorgio came and took him away and his punishment was at the end of a rope. Even though what Gunari had done was wrong, his brother wanted revenge for his death and told Florica it was her fault. He questioned her about the big house where her husband had worked; it was through her that Hanzi found out about the riches it contained. No one knew of his plan, but his small band of thieves and of course Florica."

"What happened?"

"They made Florica seek employment in the house; they needed her to let them in the estate front gates and also through the heavily bolted front door. When she had previously worked at the house she had become friends with the mistress as she was due to have her baby about the same time as her. It was the day of the planned robbery; it was planned for late that night when all were asleep in their beds. Florica was dusting when the mistress asked her about her baby, causing Florica to break down in tears and she told her about the loss of her child. Feeling touched by her sadness the woman let her hold her own daughter, mistakenly thinking it would help, but as soon as Florica held the babe in her arms she thought the angels had brought back her Lala, as she had black downy hair and creamy white skin just like her Lala.

Many nights later I was awoken by a baby's cry. I remember I lay there thinking why a child's cry awoke me from slumber, as there were many babies in our camp. I heard it again and felt suddenly compelled to go and investigate, so I got up and went outside. I remember the shock of the cold air as it hit me and I walked outside telling myself I must be crazy when I could be in the warmth of my bed. As I stood there I heard it again and realised it was coming from the direction of the stream. I thought this was odd as why would one take their babe out on such a cold night, so I decided to see who would do such a foolish thing.

As I neared the stream the crying seemed to become more insistent and the further I walked, I realised I was heading towards the spot I laid little Lala to rest. I suddenly stopped; was I to be punished forever and haunted by my granddaughter's cries? I slowly moved on and was shocked to see my dear Florica with a babe at her breast. For a moment I thought it was Lala, but realised it could not be. I have seen many things, but I know one cannot rise from the dead. As I got closer my heart pounded with fear; the child's skin was very pale and as she lifted the child to her shoulder, I saw a small purple mark on the back of her neck; it was in the shape of a flower. I had been the one who wrapped and buried Lala and she had no such mark. I realised this child was a Gorgio and wondered what Florica had done.

The child was getting distressed as she was hungry and Florica had no milk. I asked her where did the child come from and she said the angels had given Lala back to her, as they had felt her great sorrow. My heart was pounding, as I knew I had to act quickly, the child must be removed before the others find out. I realised I would have to find some way of feeding her before she woke up the whole camp, so I warmed some milk and dipped a cloth into it so the child could drink and hopefully go back to sleep, which she finally did. I left her in Florica's arms then woke my sister, she was not happy to be woken in the middle of the night, but when I explained the situation she knew what had to be done.

She had a small cart that could travel much faster than my wagon and would draw less attention by us leaving camp. I gave Florica something to help her sleep and we made her comfortable in the back with the sleeping child in her arms, then quietly snuck out of camp to a place Violca knew. It was a grand house, surely the people who lived there would be able to locate the child's true parents.

It was just before dawn and I was concerned about leaving a child out in the cold, so I wrapped her in a thick shawl and put her in a basket and left her on a doorstep. I made sure her identity would be known. You see, she had a tiny gold bracelet around her wrist and the name inscribed upon it was 'Natalia'."

Natalia gasped and tears came to her eyes.

"Yes my child, the babe my Florica took was you."

"Then why is it me who is being punished, why am I being blamed for some curse? I was just a baby who was taken from my home!"

"On our return to the Romany camp we were stopped by some riders who searched our wagon. They said a baby girl had been kidnapped and those found responsible would be punished by death. They followed us back to our camp and all wagons were searched. Once they were satisfied the child was not there they informed us that from that day forth; The Marques of Mansfield decreed all gypsies to be banished to the deep woods until his daughter Natalia was returned. If this was disobeyed our punishment would be death, so you were blamed for the banishment of all gypsies."

"Why did you not tell them where I was all these years? I could have been with my real family; instead I had to suffer in that horrible house."

"We were afraid, we thought it would only be a matter of time before you were returned back to your family; after all there was a reward for your return. Mildred was not supposed to take you; it wasn't meant to be that way."

"But it was."

"I now know that. At first Violca and I could not understand why the banishment had not been lifted and we were too frightened to reveal our involvement to the others, as despite Romany being a quiet race by nature, we were afraid what they would do if they knew."

"Where is Florica, what about her?" she asked accusingly.

"When Florica awoke and realised the babe was gone, she believed her Lala had been taken for a second time. She was so distraught she refused to eat. It must have taken all her strength to walk down to the river. She was found the next day; I laid her to rest beside her darling Lala. I can only hope one day you'll find it in your heart to forgive her. Despite her belief you were her daughter she loved you and by my interference, I destroyed not only her life but yours; but worse still because of my silence, the Romanies have a great hatred towards you for something they believed was you're doing."

Natalia sat there quietly, shocked at what she had heard. *How different her life could have been if her mother had not let Florica see her that day.* She was overwhelmed by a mixture of anger and sadness and could not stand to be in the wagon a moment longer. She got up and picked up the warm lavender shawl, quickly wrapping it around herself.

"I am going outside and I wish to be alone; please don't try to stop me."

Luludja nodded and watched her leave, wringing her hands worried as to what she might do. She gave her a few minutes before walking outside, realising she had spoken all through the night as it was almost dawn. As she stood on her small porch she could see Natalia's faint outline as she headed towards the stream. Suddenly her heart jumped into her throat; *Florica,* then realised Natalia would not do such a thing.

*\*\*\**

Besnik had picked up the bucket and was about to head towards the stream for some water, when he happened to look across at Luludja's wagon and was surprised to see her out at such an early hour and made his way over.

"It's unusual to see you up so early and on such a cold morning."

"I am worried about Natalia; she left over an hour ago and has not yet returned."

"Maybe she wanted to visit Jasper."

"It's possible but she was very upset."

With his bucket still in hand he strode off, wondering what had upset her and his thoughts went back to the previous day of Nicu throwing a rock at her. He knew she was met with much hostility from everyone in the camp; but surely Luludja was overreacting and she was down at Jasper's enclosure.

As he neared the horse's compound he heard Jasper's whinny, but soon discovered he was on his own. He scanned the river and suddenly his memory went back to a cold morning a long time ago; when he found Florica floating face down in the water. He could still see her red dress and her long hair splayed out around her and her lifeless face. He sprinted along the riverbank, hoping desperately history would not repeat itself.

Suddenly hearing a sound he stopped and strained his ears, wondering where it was coming from. He looked around, suddenly realising he was near Florica's resting place and then he heard a voice – it was Natalia. He slowly made his way forward until she came into sight.

She was standing in front of Florica's headstone and wondered what had brought her here.

There was only one person who could have told her about Florica's resting place, but why did she feel the need to visit at such an early hour? He saw she was about to leave and quickly made his way behind a tree but stepped on a twig, announcing his presence, causing her to turn around.

"Is this why you hate me, because of Florica and what my father had done?"

"I don't hate you and what does it have to do with Florica?"

As he walked towards her he could see the tears in her eyes. What had Luludja told her about Florica to cause her to be so upset? As he drew nearer she put her hands to her face and her body began to shake. Instinctively he stepped forward and put his arms around her.

"Natalia, why are you so upset, what did Luludja say to you?"

The feel of his arms around her and the tenderness with which he spoke brought her totally undone; deep sobs erupted from within her. He pulled her closer, bringing her up against his firm, hard chest, enveloping her completely in his strong arms. He didn't utter a word, letting her release her pent-up emotions until she could cry no more. Her body now spent she realised she had soaked his shirt with tears.

Feeling rather foolish and pulling back slightly she looked up into those amazing blue eyes. He slowly lowered his head and gently touched his lips to hers. It was barely a kiss but it sent shockwaves through her. She felt light headed and giddy but wanted more. Being inexperienced she tentatively returned his kiss, evoking from him a deep groan. He pulled her hard up against his chest and deepened the kiss, sending her into a spiral of emotions. Her cheeks grew hot and her heart pounded loudly but she didn't want him to stop.

He smelt of soap and his own intoxicating masculine scent.

She ran her fingers through his hair, then down his broad back and around to his chest.

His hands were moving in erotic circles all over her back and somehow she had managed to unbutton his shirt. The feel of his skin beneath her hands; he felt of muscle and steel, she revelled in the feel of him and wanted to feel more. Her wandering hands evoked a deep moan from him. His hands were exploring her also and they seemed to leave a trail of fire wherever they touched. Her breathing quickened as the kiss deepened further still.

He kissed her eyes and nibbled her ears. She heard a primal sound then realised it had come from her and it seemed to encouraged him more. His lips trailed down her neck and as he did so, he caressed her breast with one hand whilst the other unlaced the front of her blouse. Suddenly she felt his hand on her naked breast, evoking a deep moan from her. He then gently licked her nipple till it became erect, before taking it fully into his mouth; evoking such sheer pleasure it went to her very core, making her hot and damp in her most intimate part. She was now panting loudly not wanting him to stop, when he grabbed one of her hands and guided it to his groin.

"I want you," he said hoarsely.

Suddenly she was thrown back to another place and another time, a place that only brought pain and disgust. The shock of it made her body go as cold as ice and she quickly pulled away, taking in his glazed look, his heavy breathing and the fine film of sweat on his face, despite the cold morning air. She looked down at herself and saw her blouse undone and her breasts fully exposed. *What was she doing, was it her fault Mr Brampton acted the way he had?*

Tears sprung to her eyes as it fully dawned on her the shameful way she had behaved and before Besnik had a chance to speak, she clutched at her blouse with one hand and gathered her skirt with the other and ran off as fast as she could.

He stood there in confusion, fully aroused and still breathing heavily as he watched her retreating back.

As the cold air cooled him and his ardour his breathing slowly coming back to normal, he thought about Natalia's behaviour, trying to understand why she acted the way she had. Once he felt back in control he made his way back up the river and as he neared Jasper's enclosure, his confusion was replaced with anger.

Fonso and Natalia were sitting on the fence; both were deep in conversation and unaware of his approach. They were turned slightly towards one another and he realised she was holding his hand. *What was she doing?* He thought about their ardent embrace earlier and how she suddenly pushed him aside and ran off in tears. Now moments later she was holding hands with a mere boy. Never again would a woman make him feel such a fool. It was time he spoke to Luludja, it was time for Natalia to go back to her own kind; time for the Romanies to resume their lives before she came to their camp.

"Fonso I have been looking for you, we have much work

to do!"

Both jumped at hearing Besnik's angry voice.

Fonso wondered what he had done, as it was he who had been looking for Besnik when he saw Natalia at Jasper's yard.

Natalia could not bring herself to look at Besnik, she knew his anger was directed at her and felt sorry for poor Fonso, for he would feel the heat of his wrath.

"Maybe we could talk later this evening when you have a chance to get away?" she whispered.

"How about I meet you back here just before dusk?"

"Very well but let's keep it between ourselves; I feel Besnik's anger is because of me."

"Fonso!"

Confused at her remark but not wanting to anger Besnik any further, he gave Natalia a quick nod and ran after him.

Natalia watched him leave and sadly realised even though Luludja had done her magic to heal her, she felt Fonso was her only true friend here and the only one she could truly trust.

As she sat on the fence rubbing Jasper's forelock, her mind wondered back to what Luludja had told her, trying to picture what her life would have been if she had grown up in her family home.

"It has come time for us to leave here boy, I must find my parents but I cannot do it on my own and I most certainly cannot ask Besnik. Oh Jasper what should I do?"

Natalia spent most of her day with Jasper, as she was not yet ready to face Luludja; things were different between them now.

As the day wore on and her hunger took over, she realised she could not avoid her forever and on her way back to the wagon she wondered how best to broach the subject of leaving, wondering if she should tell her at all.

Slowly making her way up the wagon steps, she suddenly felt uncomfortable and awkward wishing she had somewhere else to go. She stepped inside the door and hesitated when she saw the old woman sitting at the table facing her; it was as if she had been waiting for her very return.

"Come in and sit down child, we must talk."

She walked over and sat down and waited whilst Luludja poured her a cup of tea.

"I know what I have told you is a great shock and you are now at a loss as to what you should do. It has come time for you to find your parents; I have done all I can for you here, but you cannot do this journey alone and I think you should seek the help of Fonso."

Natalia almost choked on her tea, had Luludja read her mind? What shocked her even more was the suggestion she take Fonso.

"I know he is young and small for his size but young Fonso is wise beyond his years and most importantly, he has a special gift. He has the power to see things that others can't; things that even I cannot see. He will be able to guide you on your way and lead you back to your parents."

"But that would require him leaving the woods; once outside his life will be in great danger."

"This I know but this is his destiny; which is what led him to you that day. You know you cannot do such a journey on your own and he is your only hope; however Fonso's help comes at a price."

"And what is that?"

"You must promise me if Fonso guides you safely to your family, you will plea to your father to lift the banishment; let all Romanies once again be free to roam the land as our ancestors did."

"I will do as you ask, but should we not ask Fonso first if he wishes to go on such a dangerous journey?"

"I know what his answer will be, he has known such a day would come. Now we have much to prepare."

"What about Besnik? You know he will not allow Fonso

to accompany me on such a journey."

"Don't you worry about him; I will make sure he does not interfere and you must keep your distance from him."

Natalia was fairly sure Besnik would keep his distance from her and she wondered if Luludja could also read her mind about what happened between them earlier that day.

"Now firstly we must get you some boy's clothes, your journey will be much safer if you travel as a pair of stable hands; you will draw less attention."

"When do you propose we leave?"

"You shall leave at midnight tomorrow night."

"Is that not too soon?"

"It will be the start of a new moon, enough light to guide you, but not enough for you to be easily detected; besides Besnik and most of the strong men will be out hunting and they will be away for at least two days."

That was a relief to Natalia but she hadn't planned to go so soon. She did not know why, but she felt sad about leaving. She should be happy; she would be finally reunited with her family, finally meet her real mother and father and may even have some brothers and sisters.

Later Natalia walked down to Jasper's enclosure, hoping she would get a chance to speak to Fonso before Luludja did. She wanted to be sure this was something he really wanted to do and not something Luludja pressured him into feeling was his duty.

As she neared the enclosure she was pleased to see he was already there.

He was brushing Jasper's coat when the horse whinnied and alerted Fonso of her presence.

"Fonso could you put down the brush, as I have something very important that I need to discuss with you."

He put down the brush and climbed up next to her on the fence.

"Now I need an honest answer from you; I don't want your answer to be what you think I want to hear, I want an honest answer from your heart."

"I promise to answer from the heart."

"It has come time for me to leave here; time for me to find my family and I was wondering if you would help me find my way?"

"Since I was a young boy, Luludja told me I was placed upon this Earth for the purpose of righting good from evil and it is I who would help lift the Romany curse; so yes I will accompany you."

"Luludja says you have a special gift and will be able to guide our way, do you think you can do this?"

He sat there for a moment and closed his eyes.

She noticed he went very still. She was about to ask him if he was all right when he suddenly began to speak.

"I do not know your parents but I do know where you were taken from; it is a place called Holmesby Manor. It is a grand house. At the entrance of this place are two magnificent front gates and there is a long cobbled driveway that is surrounded by beautiful gardens either side. At the end of this drive there stands a house that is pale in colour and it stands out against the greenery and the blue sky. There is an ornamental parapet that hides the pitched roof, it has many rows of long narrow windows and on the ground level is a neatly clipped hedge, which grows up and around the windows and doors. Once you walk up the entrance stairs there is a heavy timber door with decorative iron hinges."

Fonso suddenly stopped speaking and he opened his eyes and turned to Natalia and he noticed she had her eyes closed as if trying to get a picture in her mind, trying to picture what he could see.

"It sounds beautiful, are you sure that is my home?"

"I am sure."

"Will you help me get there? It would mean leaving the woods and those you love as we would have to keep this a secret; only you, myself and Luludja will know and we would be leaving tomorrow night when the moon is new; Besnik and the others will be away for two nights whilst they hunt for the camp."

"As I told you before, I have been destined for this journey since birth."

"Thank you," she said, giving him a hug.

"I will meet you back here at midnight tomorrow," he said with a flushed face as he climbed down from the fence.

Natalia watched him walk away, a smile on her face as she realised she had embarrassed him. She waited till he had gone from sight before turning towards Jasper.

"Well Jasper, are you ready to go meet my family?"

He responded with a shake of his head as though giving her a yes. She rubbed his nose then made her way back to Luludja's wagon.

\*\*\*

It was late afternoon and the excitement was beginning to build inside Natalia, but before making her journey there was something she had to do. She picked various flowers as she made her way towards Florica and Lala's grave.

As she came near, she spoke in hushed tones before kneeling down and gently placed the flowers on her grave. She sat there in silence for a moment then made her way back to camp; she had much to prepare before they left on their journey.

Hours later when the camp was quiet and everyone else was asleep, Natalia said her good-byes to Luludja and prepared to make her way down to Jasper's enclosure where she would meet up with Fonso.

"Before you go my child I have something to give you; something that will ensure a safe journey."

Luludja pulled at the long silver chain that was around her neck and lifted it over her head. On the end was a large pearlescent stone that was in the shape of a teardrop and in the candlelight one could see colours of blues, pinks and purple. She then placed it around Natalia's neck.

"Please I couldn't; it looks old and very valuable," she tried to protest.

"It is my child on both counts, but I would rest much easier if I knew you had this with you. Whilst you have this around your neck I know you will both be safe."

"Thank you and I hope to return it one day; back to its rightful owner."

Both women hugged for the last time, and Natalia made her way to Jasper's enclosure.

Fonso did not recognise her first of all; she was dressed as he was and just looked like one of the other boys but when she came closer so he could see under the brim of her hat, there was no mistaking those eyes.

"Well do you think I will pass for a boy?"

"As long as you keep your head down and don't let them see your eyes."

Luludja had also helped her bind her breasts as Mildred had done a long time ago – she definitely would not pass as a boy with her full breasts.

Both mounted their horses in silence and left the camp in a slow walk.

After a time Natalia turned to Fonso.

"I trust you Fonso, Luludja said you will know the way, do you think we are far enough away so we can let the horses have full length of their reins?"

Fonso's answer was a gentle kick to his horse's flanks and bolted off into the night.

Natalia had to stop herself from letting out a loud laugh, suddenly feeling total freedom and excitement for what laid ahead and also how much more comfortable it was to ride in breeches and not be hampered by a skirt and petticoats. Her heels barely touched Jasper's side, he needed no encouragement; in a matter of seconds they were following close behind Fonso's steed. Natalia had to rein him in slightly as he preferred to be in the lead.

"You're just going to have to get used to it boy, as Fonso is the only one who knows the way."

\*\*\*

Two days later Besnik walked over to Luludja's wagon with a worried look on his face.

She had been expecting a visit from him and waited for him to speak first.

"Luludja have you seen Fonso, no one seems to have seen him for days?"

"Come walk with me to visit Florica; my legs aren't so steady anymore and I will explain about Fonso's whereabouts along the way."

He looked at the old woman and realised she was looking rather worn out of late. It was all because of Natalia; he had to convince Luludja it was time for her to leave. He helped her down the steps then held out his arm for her to lean on, before making their way slowly towards Florica's grave.

They walked in silence for a time, listening to the stream as it ran over smooth rocks and the occasional sound of the iridescent kingfisher as it dove into the clear waters, moving so fast one only caught sight of a flash of bright blue.

Luludja knew he was becoming impatient for an answer but she also knew he would not press her until she was ready.

"Let us rest for a bit and I will answer your question."

Besnik took of his coat and laid it over a smooth rock, making sure she was comfortable. He did not sit as he had a feeling he was not going to like what he was about to hear.

"Now before you feel the need to rush off, Fonso has my blessing and I do not want you to interfere."

"What is this all about?"

"Fonso left two nights ago; he is taking Natalia to her family."

"What! Have you gone mad? You know once he is seen

outside the woods his life is in mortal danger. I can't believe you would allow such a thing."

"He may be small for his age but he is a wise one. Natalia was planning to leave and I could not let her go alone; a pretty young girl on her own would have been in much more danger than Fonso leaving the woods."

"I must prepare my horse immediately; hopefully I can catch up to them before it is too late."

"No! I said before you must not interfere. Fonso has known since birth such a journey was his destiny. You know of his gift to see things others can't. Have faith in him. Besides they both know the risks and will know when it's the safest time to travel. We organised some clothes for Natalia and have disguised her as a young boy; from a distance they will just look like two stable boys looking for work."

Besnik thought back to the time he had seen Natalia's semi-naked body and the feel of her in his arms the other night; he had grave doubts she would ever be mistaken for a boy.

"I am rested enough, I would like to visit Florica," said Luludja, interrupting his thoughts.

He helped her up and she once again leant on his arm.

They continued on in silence, each deep in their own thoughts until they reached Florica's grave.

Besnik noticed some flowers had recently been placed there and wondered who had done so. He helped Luludja sit down and watched as she put out her hand and gently touch each flower and then her body started to shake and he realised she was crying.

"If I didn't know better, I would think she has Romany blood flowing through her veins."

"Who are you referring to?"

"Natalia of course; she is the only one who would have done this, for no one has ever before placed flowers on her grave other than me. She did this for me. See how she has placed these flowers; she has done this for a reason. Firstly the cattail meaning 'peace'; a poppy, meaning 'eternal sleep'; the purple iris is to summon the goddess Iris to guide them in their journey to Heaven and the daffodil symbolising rebirth and new beginnings. She has forgiven Florica, she holds no hate and she wanted me to know," said Luludja, her voice full of emotion.

"You forgot one flower: the red one that seems to have blown away."

"She deliberately placed it that way. It is for Lala; it is an aster a symbol of love between a mother and her child."

"Who is Lala?"

"She was Florica's daughter; she lived for only a few hours. You see it was Florica who took Natalia; it is because of Florica the Romanies were banished to the deep woods."

"How could this be so?"

"Firstly Florica lost her love and then the baby they created. The death of Lala put her over the edge. Hanzi wanted revenge for the death of his brother and convinced Florica to gain employment in the Gorgio house – a place of great wealth. That is where Florica saw Natalia; she believed the angels had returned her Lala to her – the two were not unalike. As you know Florica had married a Gorgio, so Lala's skin was very fair and her soft downy hair was very dark. As for the eyes, Lala never opened hers so we will never know. By Natalia placing these flowers here this way, she has freed Florica from her demons so that mother and child can be reunited in Heaven and sleep in eternal peace. I have waited so long for this day, please leave me here for a while; I would like to talk to Florica."

Besnik reluctantly walked back up the river. He would return not too much later and check on her, but his thoughts were a mass of confusion, as Natalia seemed to have many sides to her. *Was she really the kind, gentle innocent she wanted everyone to believe? Or was she a witch in disguise, one so clever even Luludja could not see?*

## CHAPTER SIX

Dawn was about to break and they had reached the outer edge of the woods.

Fonso reined in his horse and raised his hand to Natalia to follow suit.

"We are about to leave the safe haven of the woods; I think we should rest up before we proceed any further," said Fonso.

"I'm not tired I could ride for ages and Jasper has hardly worked up a sweat."

"Once we leave these woods I could be arrested at any time. I want myself and my horse to be well rested if we are given chase, because I am not planning on getting caught," said Fonso as he dismounted and led his horse over to a nearby stream to drink.

Natalia was going to protest then she realised he was right; they would have to be on constant alert from now on. She followed Fonso over to the stream and took off Jasper's saddle and rug whilst he drank from the cool, clear waters. Despite being able to see the clearing through the trees, they still had plenty of cover near the stream. After a cooling drink she settled back and made herself comfortable, using the saddle as a pillow, closing her eyes, listening to the sounds of the birds and the buzz of insects as the sun rose announcing a new day.

"Natalia wake up, it is time to get moving," said Fonso as he shook her awake.

It took her a moment to remember where she was, then it all came back to her and she jumped up quickly almost knocking over Fonso in the process.

Jasper was happily munching by the stream's edge, not wanting to leave his patch of lush green grass.

"Come on boy don't make me carry the saddle all this way. We are about to embark on a great new adventure," said Natalia as she tried to lead Jasper closer to the saddle and bags.

Once they were both saddled up and ready to go, Natalia noticed Fonso sitting very still with his eyes closed, almost as though in a trance. She remembered what Luludja had said about his ability to see things, so as to lead their way. She silently looked across the vast expanse of land ahead feeling a sudden prick of fear, hoping no travellers would be about at this early hour.

"This next stage will probably be our most dangerous as we don't have the protection of any trees, so I suggest we let our horses have full rein until we reach the old barn, where we will be able to seek shelter."

Natalia nodded her head and both took off at full speed. Pure adrenaline was now coursing through her veins, which only moments before were filled with fear. With such an open space and no idea of where they were headed, just relying on Fonso's guidance. Natalia had never ridden so fast, the cool air making her eyes water and the brim of her hat blown flat against her forehead, tugging at the fastenings under her chin. She couldn't hold back the laughter as she leant forward in the saddle, horse and rider moved in unison as they galloped at full speed.

Unbeknownst to them both, their fast gallop had caught the attention of a weary traveller who was plodding slowly on the road below. He reined in his horse and watched the magnificent black stallion and its skilful rider as they raced across the field, leaving the smaller brown horse far behind. It took a moment for it to register, but he suddenly realised no man in his right mind would ride such a valuable horse in such a manner in an open, uneven field and more to the point, the size of the rider: he was but a mere boy, sparking him to give chase.

After a time he realised how futile it had been for him to give chase, as the two riders were obviously rested and were now a mere speck on the horizon.

Slowing back to a slow trot, his thoughts went back to the black stallion. Why did it seem familiar? The way the both of them were riding as if they were being given chase: *they were horse thieves*! He knew they would have to rest eventually and there was only one place that could be.

\*\*\*

It was early afternoon when the barn came into Natalia and Fonso's sight, he convinced Natalia to stay in the protection of some trees whilst he ensured they were alone.

She tried to argue the matter, but Fonso convinced her he would draw less attention with his small brown horse, than she would with Jasper.

Once the all clear was given, they unsaddled the horses and led them down to the stream for a drink before looping their reins over the fence, so they couldn't wander off.

Later as the evening was fast approaching and the sun had almost disappeared below the horizon, Fonso lit a small fire inside the barn so they could make themselves a pot of hot tea and also give them some warmth; it was already showing signs of being a cold night.

Natalia set off with the small tin pot to collect water to boil for their tea. As she filled the pot she noticed how grimy her hands were, then looked down at herself and realised it wasn't just her hands. After ensuring Fonso was still at the barn, she quickly took off her hat, shirt, and breast bindings. The feeling of being so exposed in the open sent a shiver of fear and excitement up the back of her spine. She quickly splashed cold water over her face and her breasts, the cold water causing her to let out a loud gasp.

\*\*\*

The weary traveller had the barn in sight; sure the two riders where inside he circled around further down the stream to set up his camp. After tying his horse with enough lead to drink and feed, he cautiously made his way on foot towards the barn, keeping close to the bushes, wanting to get as close as possible; he wanted to get a good look at their faces and also that horse.

Suddenly he heard a loud gasp, causing him to stop suddenly and crouch low, keeping his eyes and ears peeled for where the noise came from. Out the corner of his eye he saw someone bending down at the water's edge. He moved slowly closer, keeping himself low, ever careful as the mere snap of a twig could alert them of his approach.

The figure he had seen at the water's edge suddenly stood up, causing him to gasp in surprise. He quickly put his hand over his mouth and ducked behind a small bush.

The young boy was in fact a young woman of about seventeen, possibly eighteen and she was exposed from the waist up, giving him an eyeful of her creamy white breasts. She must have heard him as she quickly held her shirt close to cover her nudity and turned his way.

"Is that you Fonso? You know it is rude to spy on a naked woman," she said as she came closer to the bush.

He tried to hold his breath and stay as still as possible as she walked closer towards his hiding place. He realised if she kept walking in a straight line he would soon be discovered, but thankfully she stopped.

She turned her head and the last strains of the afternoon light shone fully on her face, causing him to bite at his hand as he nearly gave himself away.

As he stared he realised it was mere luck she'd decided to bathe at the river, as the chances of him discovering her true identity were slim. He had to hand it to her though; she was very clever to go under the disguise of a young boy. Who would have ever thought, but then if it hadn't been for the horse, he would not have given chase – that was her one big mistake.

His mind was racing; *where had she been all this time and how had she managed to remain hidden?* Trying to remain focussed, he noticed her scan the area ensuring she was still alone, thankful he still had his hand over his mouth as she suddenly let the shirt drop; giving him a clear view of her firm, creamy white breasts and her pink nipples still erect from the cold wash. He also noticed the small scar near the swell of her left breast and she was wearing a large moonstone pendant – very valuable indeed.

Moving quickly, she tightly wrapped some cloth around her breast before putting the shirt over top, then walked over and picked up the small pot of water and made her way back to the barn.

Slowly letting out a lung full of air, he sat there in wonderment and his mind raced over what he just witnessed. He wanted to get a good look at the horse and quietly made his way up to the barn.

One of the horses whinnied at his approach and the closer he got, the more agitated the horse became. The horse started shaking his proud head and stomping his hoof, causing the girl to rise from her position by the small fire.

"Jasper, what's up boy?"

"Natalia come inside. I think he is trying to warn us, bring Jasper with you he mustn't be seen."

There was no longer any doubt in the travellers mind; he would have a short rest up and then he would make the long journey back. He needed to be on the road long before them.

Under the cover of the horse's hooves as they were quickly led into the barn, he quickly backtracked down the river. He would only have a few hours rest and then he'd leave under the cover of darkness and ride to the nearest town. He would only stop long enough to have a good meal and obtain a fresh horse before continuing his journey. He was tempted to take them both now, but he knew that would be foolish. He was tired and so was his horse; he wouldn't have a hope if he had to give chase. Besides she wouldn't be too hard to find, not whilst riding a horse like Jasper.

Natalia and Fonso sat and ate some bread and cheese and washed it down with a hot cup of sweet tea. Neither said a word, both keeping their eyes and ears open for what might have upset Jasper.

Not wanting to risk alerting any would be intruders, Fonso put out the small fire. They both sat quietly in the darkness; the only sounds to be heard were of the horses, quietly munching on the hay in the barn.

Natalia's was so tired her eyes felt as if they were full of grit, too afraid to sleep for fear of them being watched, keeping her eyes peeled for any shapes moving in the darkness. Eventually she could keep them open no longer and surrendered to her body's yearning for sleep, Fonso soon followed and within a matter of minutes, both were fast asleep.

***

After only about two hours sleep, the traveller further down the stream saddled his horse and led it a safe distance away before climbing into the saddle and making a fast track towards the road. Feeling quite refreshed, as he never seemed to require many hours sleep; he figured he should make the nearest town in time for breakfast. Whilst there, he would acquire a fresh horse before making his way further north.

After eating a sumptuous breakfast of ham and eggs with thick toast, he made a few causal enquiries as to anyone knowing anything about a black Warm blood stallion; but many said they had never seen such a thing, making him ponder how she had managed to remain hidden.

After agreeing on a price for a fresh horse, he didn't waste any more time and set off at a fast pace.

He rode all day and through most of the night, arriving at the estate gates, dusty and weary just as dawn was breaking.

The sound of his horse's hooves on the cobbled drive at such an early hour had alerted the footman of someone's approach. Upon opening the door, he recognised a familiar face and waited at the bottom of the stone steps, ready to take the horse's reins until the stable boy was called.

"You're awfully early sir. You know he won't be awake," said the footman as he took hold of the reins

"It is a matter of urgency, one that I am sure he would wish to be woken for."

He took the few stone steps in one short leap, suddenly feeling exhilarated. He ran through the front door towards the main staircase, taking the steps two at a time, nearly knocking over one of the maids coming down in the process.

As he had been here many times, he knew his way around and there was no need for his arrival to be announced.

The room was at the top of the stairs and down the furthest end of the hall.

He quietly opened the heavy well-oiled door. The room was in total darkness as the heavy drapes were tightly drawn shut, not even a slither of light could shine into the room. Letting out a huff of disgust, he walked over and firmly grasping the drapes, he pulled them wide open, letting the morning sunlight flood in.

A growl erupted as the sunlight shone on the occupant of the big four-poster bed.

"Who dares wake me up in such a fashion?"

"It is I and I have ridden day and night as there is important news to report."

"It better be good; else I'll have your hide."

"I have found her."

"What, are you sure it is her?"

"Positive."

"How did you find her?"

"She is travelling under a very clever disguise, but if it hadn't been for her riding that black stallion, I might have never known."

"Then how can you be sure?"

"I got to see beneath the mask. Trust me it is her. She has a young stable boy as a companion."

The last comment had him fully awake and getting out of bed.

"Then bring her to me this instant, I have waited too long for this day!"

"She is not here; I didn't think it wise to bring her back at the time. I was in need of a fresh horse and thought it best to report to you first. I will gather some men, we won't have trouble finding her now that I know her disguise and besides, she cannot hide whilst riding Jasper, a Warm blood stallion."

"I don't understand how she has remained undetected for so long; I thought surely the lure of a reward would have exposed her whereabouts before now."

Suddenly the bedroom door was thrown open and a woman walked in, still in her sheer nightgown and she hadn't even bothered to put on a robe.

"For goodness' sake, cover yourself woman; we have a guest in the house."

"Why Lawrence, it's always a pleasure to see you," she said as she stroked one of her long red nails down the side of his cheek.

"Put some clothes on woman and I will see you downstairs for breakfast as I have some important news."

Before leaving the room, she fluttered her eyelashes at Lawrence with an inviting look, sending a wave of disgust over him.

"Organise some men as soon as possible; I want her brought here before sunset tomorrow," said the older man.

He knew he was dismissed and had work to do. He was surprised he was even given as much time as the following evening.

\*\*\*

Natalia was woken by Jasper's gentle nudges and the

sound of soft snoring near her ear. As she tried to get up, she realised she was stiff and sore, not just from the previous day's long ride, but from lying on the cold, hard barn floor.

During the night, Fonso had snuggled up against her, trying to get some warmth.

Deciding to let him sleep a bit longer, she carefully got up and grabbed the pot to make some tea. Surely now it was daylight, it would be safe to light a small fire. She held a finger to her lips so Jasper would remain quiet.

Before going outside, she stood at the barn's entrance, looking from left to right, making sure they were the only ones here.

The sun wasn't yet fully up and as she scanned the vast fields, she could see they were all covered in a white dewy blanket, which also worked in their favour, for if anyone had been about their tracks would have been evident.

Assured that they were alone, Natalia headed for the stream with Jasper close behind. She took in all the pretty flowers, which seemed to be turning their faces to greet the morning sun and as she reached the water's edge, she noted the odd silver glimmer of fish darting below and wished they had a fishing pole. The thought of fresh pan-fried fish for breakfast and some of Mildred's freshly baked bread had her salivating at the mouth. She was still conjuring up all the wonderful things Mildred used to prepare as she scooped the small tin pot in the running stream. The shock of the ice-cold water as it ran over her hand caused her to let out a loud gasp and fling back her hand throwing the tin pot behind her, causing Jasper to run off in fright. Natalia quickly jumped up and cursed herself for her foolish daydreaming, when she was supposed to be alert for passers-by.

The last thing they needed was for Jasper to be running off. *Surely he wouldn't go too far; after all, he is supposed to be her loyal guardian.*

The teapot forgotten, she ran back to the barn to wake

up Fonso, hoping they weren't going to have to waste a day looking for a wayward horse.

"Fonso wake up," she said as she gave him a shake.

Fonso rolled over, taking a moment to register where he was before quickly getting up.

"Jasper has run off, I gave him a fright. I don't know what to do; he has never run off before."

"Probably because he has never been out in the open like this before; he is just enjoying some freedom. I am sure he won't stray too far or for too long."

"What if someone sees him running about and tries to catch him?"

"I think we would draw more attention running after him. I suggest we make a pot of tea and eat the last of the bread and cheese. I am sure he will come back by the time we are ready to leave."

"I hope you are right," said Natalia, worriedly chewing the corner of her finger.

"Trust me; I know more about horses than you think. Now you go get that water and I'll start a fire."

Natalia made her way back down to the stream, looking every which way for any sign of Jasper. Wondering if they would be forced to go on without him, as they wouldn't be able to stay here much longer with very little food left, she filled the pot then made her way back to the barn.

As she walked into the entrance, she noticed Fonso had managed to get a small fire going and had divided up the last of the bread and cheese.

"The bread is stale and hard now, but maybe it won't be so bad if we dunk it in our tea."

Natalia just nodded and handed him the pot of water, feeling down and despondent to the point of tears; she never in her wildest dreams thought Jasper would ever leave her.

They both sat in silence and waited for the pot to boil, Fonso wanting to further reassure Natalia, but then he knew Jasper had a wild streak in him and this was his first taste of real freedom.

The morning was getting on and there was still no sign of Jasper.

Fonso had everything packed back into the bags and made sure that the fire was properly extinguished.

"Natalia I think we should go. If he were coming back, he would have done so by now. We can hide your saddle in the corner and cover it with hay and if by chance we see Jasper along the way, you can ride him bareback as I have seen you do before."

"But your poor horse, can he cope with taking the two of us plus our bundles? If only I hadn't been daydreaming," exclaimed Natalia.

"No point in blaming yourself. We had set out to reunite you with your family and I think we should stay focussed on that. I don't want to sound selfish here, but there are others who are depending on us also. As for my horse, he may be small, but he is very strong."

"I'm sorry Fonso; you are right. Maybe we could lighten the load a little. I could leave behind my dress and undergarments; I was keeping them for when I met my family for the first time, but they will just have to accept me as I am."

"That's the spirit and you could look at it this way: we will be able to go into a village and possibly seek some employment in exchange for food; we won't draw attention to ourselves travelling with my plain brown horse."

Natalia nodded in agreement, but still felt sad about Jasper, still ever hopeful that they might find him along the way. She pulled out her dress, petticoats, and undergarments, and put them underneath the saddle in the far corner of the barn and covered them with hay. She wanted to leave no trail that they had been here – not that she expected anyone to be looking for her now.

It had been much slower going today with only one horse, which now had twice the load.

Natalia thought it was just as well both her and Fonso were small; she guessed their combined weight was no more than a full-grown man and was sure this small horse could not have coped with a heavier load.

They knew they were nearing a town, as the traffic of travellers was becoming more frequent and there were wagons and carriages about.

"I will look for a stable yard or the likes and hopefully we can get some work, but let me do the talking and keep your head down. One look at those eyes and they will know you are a girl."

"But what about you, your skin is darker than mine, won't they know you are a gypsy?"

"We are so dirty and dusty; I am hoping that they will pass off my skin colour for dirt."

They entered the town and the two of them on one horse with their few worldly possessions drew some stares.

Natalia took Fonso's advice and tried to keep her head low, trying to view the town and people from under the brim of her hat.

Suddenly she could hear a sound; something she remembered from her past, but couldn't remember what.

Fonso pulled the horse to a halt and from under the brim of her hat, she could see a man hammering something, she remember seeing the same thing when she was at Brampton House – he was a blacksmith and he was making a horseshoe.

"Wait here and don't speak to anyone," said Fonso as he slid off his horse.

Natalia watched as he walked over to the blacksmith, crossing her fingers, hoping he was right and his true heritage wouldn't be discovered.

The man stopped his hammering and looked at Fonso. She suddenly felt scared as the man turned in her direction.

She lowered her head further and could feel herself starting to sweat, even though the day was quite cool.

*Why was he taking so long?* Expecting to hear any minute, the sound of Fonso's running feet, yelling for her to take the horse's reins for their hasty retreat.

Suddenly there was a hand on her leg, causing her to almost jump out of her skin and only just stopping herself in time from letting out a scream.

"Hey, it's just me. He said he could do with an extra hand, but only for one day and he will only pay for one. I have asked him if he could pay us in food and let us bed in the warmth of the shed for one night; he has agreed to let us do this. He said we could take our horse around the back, where he has a small paddock so our horse can rest and feed. When we have done this, he will show us what needs to be done, but remember don't speak; I told him you are a simple mute and that you're my brother. Most people leave the simple minded alone," said Fonso as he took the reins of his horse.

Once around the back, she could see the small paddock that housed two other horses. They whinnied at Fonso's horse, before continuing grazing on the lush green grass.

"He should be happy here and be well rested before our long journey tomorrow," said Fonso as he started to unload the horse.

The horse now safely in the enclosure, Natalia bent down to start gathering up their things to take into the shed, when Fonso stopped her.

"Wait; your skin still looks too pale to pass for a stable boy; rub some dirt on your face and remember, don't let him see your eyes."

Natalia did as he suggested then lifted her face for inspection.

He rubbed some more dirt on her face and hands, until satisfied she could pass for a stable boy. They gathered all their things and Natalia silently followed Fonso to the front of the shed, making sure she kept her eyes averted at all times.

The blacksmith showed them where they could put their things and then put them straight to work. He had initially told Fonso he was in need of a striker, whose job is to swing a large sledgehammer in heavy forging operations as directed by the blacksmith. He admitted he didn't think Fonso was strong enough for such a job, but Fonso had convinced him to give him a chance.

Natalia's job was much more simple; she was required to keep plenty of coals in the fire to keep it very hot and smooth off any sharp pieces from the new shoe with a metal rasp, once it had been cooled in a bucket of cold water; which she was required to refill from time to time when the water got too hot. Natalia watched in amazement as the blacksmith held the hot iron at the anvil with tongs in one hand and indicated where the iron was to be struck by tapping it with a small hammer he held in the other hand. Fonso's job as a striker was to deliver a heavy blow with the sledgehammer where indicated. Even though she had seen a blacksmith at work before, she had never taken much notice of how the shoe actually got its shape.

They had been working hard for a couple of hours and poor Fonso was starting to feel it in his arms and shoulders, but there was no way he was going to complain. *He was a man now and he had told the blacksmith he could do the job.* He looked across at Natalia and had to keep himself from laughing; there was no need to worry about her pale skin, because she was almost the colour of the black coal she had been shovelling in the fire.

"Well young lad, I have to admit you have surprised me; you have definitely earned a good meal. If you and your brother go around to the back entrance next door, Adele will give you a plate of hot stew and a chunk of freshly baked bread. When you have finished, we will get back to work," said the blacksmith with a smile.

"Thank you sir; I am rather hungry," said Fonso as he took off his apron.

Natalia, keeping up the pretence of being a simple mute, waited for Fonso to tell her what to do. Her mouth was salivating just at the thought of a wholesome stew and some freshly baked bread as they had barely eaten in the last few days, just some cheese and stale bread.

As they walked around to the back entrance of a building, there were many tables and chairs, there was the din of many voices and the clink of plates and cutlery could be heard.

Natalia so wanted to look up and take everything in, but she realised she would just have to be happy with what she could see from under the brim of her hat and maybe Fonso could give her a better picture later that night.

When they got around the back, Fonso knocked on the door and waited for it to be opened.

After a few minutes, a large red-faced woman, who was wiping her hands on her apron, opened the door.

"Well I'd say by the looks of you, you're the young strikers and are waiting to be fed."

"Yes ma'am, we are and it smells real good," said Fonso as he rubbed his stomach.

"Oh, and he has manners and all. Well you just wait here and I'll bring it right out to you."

A few minutes later, she came back with two plates laden with hot steaming stew and large chunks of freshly baked bread.

They both stepped forward and put out their hands to take their plates.

"Thank you ma'am; from the both of us; as my brother doesn't speak; him being mute and all."

"Just leave the plates on the step when you are done and there will be more for you tonight when you finish," she said before closing the door.

Both sat on the ground and not caring that their hands were grubby or that they had no eating utensils, using the bread and their hands to spoon the delicious meaty stew into their mouths. In no time at all, they had managed to devour everything on their plates and even licked it clean.

"I had forgotten how 'good' food could taste," said Natalia, feeling so full she thought she might burst.

"I agree, but try not to talk; you never know who might be listening."

Natalia quickly sat up, looking around hoping she hadn't been heard. Seeing there was no one around, she laid on the grass, tilting her hat to shade her from the noonday sun.

"Don't lay there too long as you will surely go to sleep and if you are thinking about how tired your arms are, just think of me swinging that heavy sledgehammer."

Natalia's response was a chuckle from under her hat.

Whilst the two lay there resting; a man was making enquiries with the blacksmith if he could purchase a fresh horse, but also if he had seen anyone riding a large black Warm blood stallion. The blacksmith informed him he had not, but suggested he get a hearty meal at the inn next door, as Adele would know if there are any strangers about, worthy of owning such a horse.

He had only stepped inside the inn when Fonso and Natalia walked past, making their way back to the entrance of the blacksmiths shed and back to work.

About an hour later, after he had enjoyed a sumptuous meal and questioning the other dinners, no one had seen a horse like Jasper, let alone one ridden by a young boy. He walked back to the blacksmith to collect his fresh horse, which was saddled and ready to go. He was going to thank the man for his suggestion of a place to eat, but he could see he was hard at work with his young striker, pounding into shape a new horseshoe. He marvelled at the size of the lad swinging the large hammer, it seemed to dwarf him and wondered how he managed to convince the blacksmith to give him employment. Swinging onto his horse, he rode off to check in at the various farms and cottages, which were on the outskirts of the town, hoping someone had sighted

Natalia and Jasper. He wasn't overly concerned, as he knew they couldn't have gone too far without being seen.

*** 

Finally the working day had come to an end for poor Fonso and Natalia. They wearily packed away the day's tools and swept out the shed, looking forward to another hot meal.

The blacksmith had said they could heat some water for a hot bath, as they were certainly in need of it.

Once the blacksmith had left for the day, both Natalia and Fonso agreed it would be wiser to have their wash after their dinner, as the dirt and grime that covered them both was a good disguise.

As they had done earlier, they knocked on the inn door and waited for their evening meal, eating it as greedily as before, but this time, eager to get back to the shed to wash and fall into an exhausted sleep.

Neither were concerned about being interrupted during the night, as the blacksmith had padlocked the front entrance before he left, the back door was locked from the inside.

Fonso rinsed out the large disused trough at the back of the shed and filled it with hot water he had boiled over the fire.

Using one of the overhead beams, Natalia draped a large horse rug around their bath, so each could have privacy whilst they washed and dressed.

Natalia was to have the pleasure of the first bath and once behind the screen, she wasted no time stripping off, before sinking thankfully into the large deep trough. *She must be in Heaven!* She had never been in such a large bath before; she could lay out fully stretched with her toes barely touching the other end. She sent a silent *thank you* to Adele, who had kindly given them a cake of soap that was scented with lavender, known to aid aches and pains and ensures a peaceful sleep.

"Natalia, I know it must be really nice in there, but do you think you could come out soon so I can enjoy the pleasure of a hot bath also?"

She had been lying with her eyes closed enjoying the soothing warmth of the hot water and the lavender soap, if Fonso hadn't spoke, she probably would have fallen asleep. Sitting up quickly, she was amazed at the colour of the water.

"Well, I'm afraid if you want to get as clean as I am, you'll have to bring in some more water, because this lot is pretty dirty," she said with a laugh.

"You must have been asleep. I have already thought of that and it's already boiled."

"All right, I'm getting out. Maybe you had another reason for me going first: you get to stay in till the water goes cold."

"You're not just a pretty face are you?" came his reply.

Natalia smiled to herself as she dried and dressed before pulling back the curtain.

By the time Fonso had finished his long bath and emptied out the water, Natalia was fast asleep.

He hoped they wouldn't be too exhausted to wake up early; they needed to leave before the blacksmith arrived in the morning. Their plan had been to leave just before daybreak so they could hopefully leave unnoticed. Fonso knew once they got onto the other side of town, they would once again have the protection of a wooded forest, which should take them almost to the boundary of the large house. He wasn't sure if they would make it in the space of a day, but they would certainly try.

\*\*\*

Lawrence was also tired after his long day, but sleep would not come to him. He had gone to every house, inn and cottage and no one had seen a large black Warm blood stallion; many didn't even know what such a thing looked like and when he described it, all said they would have surely remembered if they had seen such a horse, let alone being ridden by a young boy. He couldn't understand it; it was as though she had once again disappeared into thin air. *How did she do it, how was she able to so cleverly elude him?*

His thoughts drifted to his image of her, naked from the waist up, exposing her creamy white breasts and that pale pink scar in the shape of an X. *It was as if she had been branded!*

He knew she was different from other women her age, in actual fact, all woman in general as they would never consider being seen wearing the clothes of a boy. He found it surprisingly alluring, the way the breeches moulded to her legs, enabling him to imagine what she would look like fully naked and this only excited him more. Despite her short hair, she was very attractive with those incredible eyes.

His thoughts then drifted to what she would be like as a lover, like an untamed tiger and the way she rode that big black stallion. He had never seen a woman ride astride before. She rode like the wind and in perfect unison with the horse. He could picture her with long, luscious hair, riding so fast it trailed behind her and the wind catching her blouse, tugging at the ribbons, exposing her breasts. Yes, he would get great pleasure in bringing her back, for he had plans of his own for her.

## CHAPTER SEVEN

Luck was on their side. Fonso had woken up early and had prepared his horse whilst Natalia slept. He thought it best to do this on his own in case anyone happened to be about.

By the time the sun was coming over the horizon, the town was far behind them and they were now in the safety of the wooded area, offering them protection from any passer-by.

They had decided even though this was the longer way to travel, there was less chance of them being seen; not so much for Natalia's sake, but for Fonso as he was travelling where no gypsy was allowed.

The day had been reasonably uneventful; they had kept away from the roads wherever possible.

Natalia noticed the shadows were getting longer and realised it was late afternoon as the sun was making its slow descent. She was about to ask Fonso if he had any idea how much further they had to go, when he pulled the horse to a halt and sat very still.

Realising he was having one of his trances, something he had done many times along the way, seeking guidance as only he could, as to which path they should take.

After a few moments, he got off the horse and walked through the trees, disappearing amongst the foliage.

Natalia wondered if she was supposed to follow or wait for him, when he suddenly appeared back through the trees.

"We are here. I can see the large house."

Natalia's stomach suddenly filled with butterflies. She had waited for this moment for so long but now the time had come, she felt very nervous.

Slowly climbing off the horse, she followed Fonso through the trees, still screened by the protection of shrubs and smaller trees. She could see a large pale building off into the distance – just as Fonso had described.

The house was situated on a slight rise and from the angle they were standing, gave them a good view of the size and expanse of the place – it was much bigger than Natalia had expected. She could see neatly trimmed hedges and gardens, which encircled the building and the outline of the ornamental parapet and the decorative chimneys that were releasing faint curls of smoke. It looked magical and romantic; something she imagined out of a fairy tale – it was so beautiful.

"How could this be my home? It looks like a place a princess would live."

"Natalia you are a princess and I know this is your home. We are obviously looking at it from the rear, as we cannot see the cobbled drive. If we go around the front I am sure the name on the gate will say Holmesby Manor, you will then know I have led you to the right place."

"Let's leave it till tomorrow, it's getting late and I would like to prepare myself for this. I must admit I am a little scared," said Natalia.

"As you wish but you can't put it off forever; after all this is the reason we have made this long journey."

Natalia just nodded in response.

Fonso made his way back to his horse to set up camp and make a small fire. He had been hoping they could have gone to the house tonight as they had no food left, only a small amount of tea and he was feeling rather hungry.

Natalia just stood and watched the colours of the house change as the sun began to set. *Was she truly home or was this all just a dream?*

She stood there as darkness descended and could no longer see the house, apart from the odd square of light coming from various windows. She walked back to Fonso who now had a fire going and was throwing round objects into it.

"I managed to find some chestnuts, so I am going to

roast them in the fire. I'm afraid that is all we have, plus a pot of tea."

"I'm sorry Fonso, I promise we will leave early in the morning and you shall have some breakfast."

He just smiled at her and handed her a cup of tea, then scraped the roasted chestnuts out of the fire. Both sat there in silence, deep in their own thoughts.

\*\*\*

It was dark when Lawrence arrived back at his home. He decided it could wait till morning before he reported in; besides he didn't have much to report back. He poured himself a brandy and as he let the warm amber liquid slide slowly down his throat, he thought he noticed a flicker of light off in the distance. He walked out into his garden and he saw it again. It was coming from the woods near the boundary of his property and by the way the light moved he figured it was a small campfire – *poachers*. He knew he should really check it out now, but after a long disappointing day and with the brandy taking effect, he decided it could wait till morning.

\*\*\*

Both Fonso and Natalia were up before daybreak, Fonso because of his growling stomach and Natalia because she hadn't been able to sleep.

There was no point in lighting another fire as they had drunk the last of the tea the previous night.

Natalia wasn't convinced they had the right house; it was hard to imagine her family living in one so grand, it was like a castle.

After much consternation, it was agreed they would skirt around the property at a safe distance till they reached the front gates.

The excitement and butterflies were building in Natalia's stomach; they had now reached the road that would take them towards the estate's front gates. They slowly travelled alongside a tall, neatly clipped hedge, obviously a barrier to keep out unwanted visitors.

Suddenly a pair of massive gates loomed in front of them; they stood at least twelve feet high and consisted of wrought iron and each gate had an intricate design across the top, which ended in an arrowhead-like point. Her eyes travelled down to the big bold letters on the front *Holmesby Manor. She was finally home!*

"Fonso I am so excited and scared at the same time; I don't know what to do. How do you suppose we get in?"

Fonso slid off his horse and walked over and inspected the gate, then turned around to Natalia with a big grin on his face.

"It looks like someone forgot to latch it properly," he said as he swung the gate open.

Natalia quickly got off the horse and gave Fonso a hug, then proceeded through the front gate. She had walked a short distance when she realised she was alone; turning she saw Fonso was still outside and holding the horse's reins.

"Come on, what are you waiting for?"

"I would prefer to wait here. You are the one they will want to see not some gypsy boy. If you call for help, I will come to your aid; otherwise I will wait here till I know your father doesn't want to send me to the gallows."

She was about to argue with him but realised he was right. *What if she couldn't convince her father to change his mind?* If anything happened to Fonso she wouldn't be able to live with herself. She blew him a kiss then made her way up the long drive. The closer she got to the house, the more the butterflies grew in her stomach and the palms of her hands had started to sweat. She decided it was probably safer to make her way to the front door via the gardens, because if someone saw a scruffy looking boy walking up the drive, she might never make it.

As she meandered through the beautiful garden, she

thought she could hear running water. *Maybe it would be a good idea to give her face and hands a wash.*

Following the sound, she came upon a pond that had a large marble statue. Natalia reached out to catch the clear running water in her cupped hands before briskly rubbing the dirt off her face. Once again putting out her hands, she looked up and looked at the face of the statue; amazed and shocked her hands fell to her sides. The statue was of a woman, she had her arms outstretched as if welcoming someone, but it was her face that had her so enthralled. Natalia climbed up onto the stones that surrounded the pond's edge and looked into her eyes. *She had seen these eyes before.* The detail the artist had portrayed was amazing, causing tears to come to her eyes.

\*\*\*

Lawrence had also been up early and as he suspected, someone had been camping in the woods on his boundary line, *who would dare camp on his land*? He alerted his grounds man to be on the lookout for possible poachers and decided to notify the neighbouring properties.

He made his way slowly along the perimeter of the neighbouring property when a movement caught his eye. Pausing, he scanned the area and noticed someone was by the fountain. Quickly jumping off his horse he made his way through a gap in the hedge.

He was now on his neighbour's property and knew he should alert the grounds man of an intruder, but he was sure he knew who it was and did not want to risk her escaping. He made his way stealthily keeping close to the bushes, not taking his eyes from her.

She had removed her hat and there was no mistaking the badly cut hair.

Slowly inching forward he watched as she washed her face and hands in the fountain, suddenly having a feeling of déjà vu. He was so close behind her now she was only an

*Natalia*

arm's length away, but still she did not feel his presence, it was if she was mesmerised by the statue.

"Her name is Esmeralda."

Natalia spun around in fright losing her balance falling backwards into the pond, screaming out a warning to Fonso moments before hitting the water.

The water was so cold it took her breath away and as she came to the surface, she felt herself being dragged from the pond. She struggled to free herself from his firm hold, wildly swing her arms at him and kicking with all her might.

"Natalia stop, I mean you no harm!" He said as he pinned her arms by her sides, pulling her close trying to avoid her kicking legs.

She was stunned that he knew her name and looked up at him questioningly.

"You seem surprised I know your name, but I know a great deal about you."

"Who are you and what makes you so sure my name is Natalia?"

"My name is Lawrence and there is no doubt in my mind you are Natalia. The statue that had you so enthralled, you are the image of her. Her name was Esmeralda and she was your mother."

"You said 'was'?"

Lawrence saw the tears form in those beautiful green eyes *of course, how could she have known?*

"I'm sorry it was cruel of me to tell you this way. Unfortunately your mother died years ago, but your father is still alive and eager to meet you."

Natalia was devastated, for months she had been looking forward to meeting her mother for the first time – now that will never be.

"Your father loves you dearly and not a day has gone by he hasn't had someone searching for you. In fact I myself have been helping in that search, that is how I know so much about you," said Lawrence, noting the sad look on her face.

"Are you by chance my brother?"

Lawrence threw back his head and laughed, making her smile in response. He had a handsome face and she could tell by his facial features and the way he wore his neatly styled light brown hair, he was what was termed 'upper crust', one of good breeding. He was tall and his shoulders were broad, but he didn't have that strength and power of another she wished to forget; no he was of a finer frame, one who probably had never done a hard day's work in his life and she was sure there were no rippling muscles beneath his expensive clothes.

"No my dear girl, I most definitely am not your brother but I do live on the neighbouring property. How about I take you up to the house and get you cleaned up before you meet your father?"

Natalia stepped back and looked down at herself: her wet grimy clothes and the fact she was wearing the clothes of a boy; this was certainly not how she wanted her father to see her for the first time. She looked across at his elegant attire and noticed it was also wet.

"I would like to but I don't have any other clothes."

"I am sure you can borrow something of Miriam's, although they would probably swamp you."

"Who is Miriam?"

"I'll let your father explain that. Now let's get you cleaned up."

Lawrence led Natalia up to the front of the house and suddenly the butler opened the front door.

"You catch one of the scoundrels sir?"

"Frederick, I'd like to introduce you to Natalia," he said with the sweep of his arm.

Natalia noticed the look of horror on the man's face as he took in her bedraggled state and tried desperately to wipe the dirt from her face.

As she did Frederick suddenly noticed her emerald

green eyes, the fine bone structure. *She was the image of Esmeralda!* His mouth gapped in shock.

"Frederick?" asked Lawrence.

Frederick suddenly clicked his heels to attention and tried to cover his bad behaviour.

"At your service miss; might I suggest we get one of the chambermaids to draw you a bath before you meet your father?"

"Yes Frederick, that is exactly what we intend to do and arrange some clean dry clothes."

"Of course sir right away," said the butler as he opened the door.

The moment Natalia stepped into the beautiful hall she was awe struck, taking in the highly polished furniture and the beautiful ornate wall hangings. She slowly walked around the room gently touching things, ensuring it wasn't all a dream. As she turned to look at Lawrence, she noticed the dirty puddles she was leaving on the beautiful marble floor.

"My goodness look at the mess I have made, I hope I don't get in trouble."

"I can assure you that won't happen, the maids will soon clean the floor and your father is not an early riser; you will have plenty of time to clean up before he sees you."

A short time later Frederick came rushing back with two chambermaids in tow. If they were surprised by the state of her dress they did not show it.

"Natalia this is Mary and Martha, they will take care of you," said Frederick.

"Come with us miss," directed Mary as she curtsied.

Natalia blushed; she had never had any one curtsy to her before and what made it more ridiculous is they actually looked more respectable than she did. She gave a quick smile to Lawrence and followed the maids upstairs, looking around in wonderment as she went.

Once at the top of the stairs she noted the long hallway

and the many doors, *this is a very large house!*

One of the girls opened a door on the left of the hall and motioned for Natalia to follow her.

The room was beautiful with a large four-poster bed, a fire had been lit and in front stood a beautiful white hipbath that was trimmed with gold – *nothing like the old tin one she used to wash in.* She realised she was still dripping on the floor and must have left a trail all the way up the stairs.

"I'm so sorry I have left an awful mess on the floor. Once I am clean and dry I promise I'll clean it up."

Both maids gasped and put their hands to their mouths in horror.

"Your father would give us our marching orders if we allowed you to do such a thing. Now quickly get out of those horrible wet clothes and into the bath whilst it is still hot."

Natalia was a bit shy about undressing in front of two strangers, when one started to undress her.

"Don't be shy miss, 'tis our job to wait on you," she said with a smile.

Realising there was no point in arguing she let them divest her of her wet clothes.

As she stepped into the beautiful bath, she noticed that they had also put some rose petals in the water and they gave off a wonderful scent.

"Martha get rid of those horrible clothes and see if you can find something for Miss Natalia to wear whilst I help her wash."

Martha picked up the wet dirty bundle and bobbed before going on her errand.

Natalia was enjoying the feel of having her hair washed; feeling like a princess and having to pinch herself to make sure this was not a dream.

The maid was sponging Natalia's body when she noticed the scar near her breast.

"Oh my goodness what happened there?"

Natalia had completely forgotten about her scar: her only reminder from that terrible night.

Luludja had said because it was the first spot the hot poker had touched, it had gone through too many layers of skin for it to fully repair and she should be thankful for small mercies the hot poker had cooled when it had touched her face.

Natalia quickly drew he legs up and tried to cover herself.

"I can wash myself thank you and if you don't mind I would rather be alone."

Not about to argue with her mistress, Mary got up and walked towards the door.

"I will be just outside the door, call me when you are finished."

Martha came up the stairs carrying a large bundle of clothes, wondering why Mary was standing outside the door.

"Don't tell me she is bossy already and given you your marching orders."

"I was helping her wash when I noticed a terrible scar near her breast. I asked her about it and she got upset and asked me to leave."

"What sort of a scar?"

"I have seen many scars in my time and this one was from a burn, which is in the shape of an X!"

"Good Lord what do you think caused it?" Martha gasped in horror.

"Maybe it was the gypsies. You know the story about how she was kidnapped by them when she was a baby, maybe they branded her."

Martha threw up her hands in horror dropping the bundles of clothes on the floor and at that same moment, they both heard a voice from the other side of the door. Mary opened it slowly and poked her head around the corner. Natalia was standing beside the bath trying her best to cover herself with the towel.

"Would you like us to bring in some clothes miss?"

"Yes thank you."

Mary helped Martha pick up the bundle of dresses, petticoats and undergarments and carried them into the room.

"I didn't think you would fit into any of Miriam's things, so I went through the trunk of your mother's as you are about the same size," said Martha.

"Who is Miriam?"

Both maids looked at one another not knowing how to respond.

Natalia had seen the same look earlier from Lawrence and her curiosity about this Miriam was rising. She walked over and looked at the beautiful dresses: one was a soft shade of lavender and was trimmed with a delicate lace and the other of a pale yellow with little white flowers around the neck line. She tentatively touched the fabric and it was delicate to touch. Then she saw the petticoats and undergarments that were made of the softest silk and trimmed with the finest lace.

"I have never seen anything so beautiful, are you sure it is all right for me to wear them?"

Both Martha and Mary looked at each other totally surprised at her reaction, after all the dresses were older than any of those in the room.

"Of course you are allowed to wear them; they were your mother's."

Mary had to coax the towel from Natalia and when the towel was finally removed, Martha nodded at Mary on seeing the burn scar.

They decided on the pale yellow one as Natalia thought the neckline on the other was too low.

Once she was dressed both girls looked at one another, not knowing what to do about her hair.

"Miss who on earth cut your hair?" asked Mary.

Natalia couldn't stop the tears welling up in her eyes and she nervously stroked her hair.

Martha looked sternly at Mary.

"Maybe I could tie a ribbon in your hair somehow," said Mary, feeling ashamed.

Natalia looked up hopefully at Mary, who then rummaged around through some drawers and found some lovely yellow and white ribbon.

After trying various ways she eventually decided on just tying it like a headband and tying a bow just below her left ear, it actually looked quite effective on her short hair.

"I shall make up some special oil which will stimulate healthy hair growth. I can massage it in your scalp each night and you will have beautiful long locks in no time."

"Thank you so much; I will never forget this," Natalia said with tears in her eyes.

Both Mary and Martha suddenly felt protective of their new mistress.

"I think it is time we take you to meet your father," said Martha.

Natalia smiled at both the girls and made her way nervously to the door.

The butler was standing at the base of the stairs when he heard the rustle of skirts and voices from above.

He looked up and his mouth momentarily dropped in surprise, as he was sure he was seeing the ghost of Mistress Esmeralda descending the stairs. Suddenly he noticed she was wearing no shoes and realised it was Natalia. The chambermaids had worked miracles and transformed the dirty urchin he had seen only hours before, but they had forgotten about her feet. *If only her mother had lived to see this day.*

Once she was at the bottom of the stairs he bowed and then whispered in one of the girl's ears about the absence of shoes.

Both girls looked at each other in horror but could do

nothing, as Natalia had already spotted Lawrence and was walking towards him.

He turned and marvelled at the transformation; he knew once she was cleaned up and put on a dress her true beauty would shine through, but he hadn't been prepared for her to look so breath taking.

As she drew nearer he could see she was nervous and shy, but he also noticed her bare feet as they peeked out beneath her dress as she walked. He had to smile, as he knew of no woman who would present herself without shoes. *He was going to enjoy taming Natalia.*

"You look absolutely stunning my dear," he said as he held out his arm.

"You can't give me all the credit; it was as if the maids had a magic wand," she said as she nervously took his arm.

"Your father has been fussing all morning after I told him you were going to join us for breakfast."

Natalia stopped, suddenly remembering Fonso and promising him a big breakfast. Letting go of Lawrence's arm she ran back to the butler.

"Please sir a friend of mine is at the front gates and I promised him some breakfast. Would you mind fetching him, his name is Fonso?"

The butler looked across at Lawrence who was now standing behind Natalia and he shook his head.

"I believe he has already been taken care of miss; he said he couldn't stay and had to be on his way."

Natalia was disappointed; she had wanted Fonso to meet her father and between the two of them they would convince him to lift the gypsy curse. She couldn't believe he left without saying goodbye.

"My dear girl we are keeping your father waiting," said Lawrence, taking her arm.

She nodded once again taking his arm, feeling suddenly very nervous about meeting her father, wishing Fonso was here to reassure her and share this moment. As Lawrence guided her to the great dining hall, she could feel the butterflies building and her legs started to shake. *I hope I am not a disappointment to him* as she noted the plush surroundings, realising her father was a man of great wealth and possibly importance.

Suddenly they were standing before a long table with many beautiful carved chairs.

As her eyes travelled along the length of the table, her eyes first came upon a woman whose face was far too made up, especially for this time of day. Noting the long red nails, which were wrapped around a crystal wine glass and thinking it strange one would drink at such an early hour, she smiled at the woman but the smile was not returned; instead she took a long drink from her glass.

"Sir I would like to introduce you to Natalia," said Lawrence before she could go any further.

Natalia turned to look at the man at the end of the table and for some reason felt disappointment, for his smile was awkward and stiff as if it was something he didn't often do.

His face was blotchy and his large nose was red from drinking too much, his hair was totally white and as he rose from his chair she noticed he leant his large frame heavily on a cane. *Could he really be my father, he looked so old?*

"Come my child; let me get a better look at you."

Lawrence released her arm and gave her a gentle push towards the old man and she walked nervously towards him.

"You are the image of your mother; there will be no doubt in anyone's mind you are the daughter of Esmeralda, God rest her soul. I have waited a long time for this day."

Reassured by this remark, Natalia ran forward and gave him a daughterly hug, but to her disappointment he responded stiffly and awkwardly and said their breakfast was getting cold.

Fighting back the tears, she nodded disappointedly and sat down at the table. *This wasn't how it was meant to be*; she had expected a warm welcome and much laughter, but instead he seemed cold and distant. *Perhaps he needed time to adjust; after all it had been over seventeen years*! Natalia suddenly looked up and looked directly across at Miriam; she was smiling but the smile did not reach her eyes. *Who was she?*

Breakfast was served and Natalia ate everything and anything that was offered to her. She had been so hungry she didn't realise how much she must have been eating till Lawrence made a comment.

"How does a girl so small manage to put away so much food?"

Natalia had a fork full of bacon halfway to her mouth and paused, noticing all eyes were on her. She daintily put her fork back on her plate then put her hands in her lap.

"I'm sorry, it's just I haven't eaten for nearly two days. I just got a bit carried away," she said, feeling embarrassed.

"Child don't apologise; the food is to be eaten, but why have you not eaten?" asked her father.

"We didn't have any money, but we got a good feed before that. We did some work for a blacksmith for payment of food and it was real good; the best stew and bread I had in a very long time," she said with a smile.

Suddenly Lawrence's mind went back to a certain blacksmith he had bought a horse from, and remembered watching the young striker and a smile came to his face.

"My God child, what sort of a life have you had working for food? I promise you will never have to do that again," said her father, totally appalled.

"Don't worry Father I didn't mind. I now have a full understanding of how a horseshoe is made. Besides I got to have a bath in the biggest tub ever," she exclaimed, looking around at the others with a big smile on her face.

Miriam looked at her as though she had gone completely mad, Lawrence was trying his best not to laugh, but her father just stared at her not knowing what to think.

Lawrence got up and walked over to the sideboard.

"Well I hate to see a woman go hungry, how about some more bacon and eggs?" he asked as he lifted the silver covers.

Lawrence's effort at lightening the situation actually embarrassed Natalia further, causing her cheeks to go bright red.

"What a refreshing change to see a woman blush. Natalia don't be embarrassed; I like to see a woman who enjoys her food, to a point of course. Obviously you are one of the lucky ones who don't have to worry about her waistline. If it bothers you we can go for a ride tomorrow once you are settled in, as I know you enjoy riding like the wind."

Natalia looked up at him in surprise. *How on earth did he know she could ride?*

He walked over and put more food on Natalia's plate and whispered in her ear.

"I told you you'd be surprised at what I know about you."

Natalia looked directly across at Miriam and noticed her cold stare. *Is she jealous of the attention he is giving her?*

The rest of breakfast proceeded in silence and Natalia was conscious of other eyes on her and was wishing it would soon be over. Her thoughts wandered towards Fonso and what he was doing. *Had he gone back to the deep woods, or was he waiting somewhere safe?* Her thoughts then drifted to Jasper *what happened to him, did he go back to the old barn?*

Once the breakfast table was cleared her father said he would like to talk to her in the library. He had many questions to ask her as he was in no doubt, she would have of him.

She helped him from the table and followed him slowly in silence, taking in her surroundings: the curtains, the furniture, delicate figurines; everything was so opulent, she had never seen such wealth in all her life and found it hard to believe this was her family home. *How different her life would have been if she had been raised here.*

They entered yet another room and by all the books that lined the walls, she realised they were in the library.

Suddenly her eyes came upon a painting, causing her to gasp and stand transfixed. It was of a woman sitting on a gilded chair. She had long dark hair, which hung loosely over one shoulder and she wore a beautiful lavender dress, but it was her face that had her so transfixed.

"Her name is Esmeralda, your mother. You are the image of her."

"What happened to my mother, how long ago did she die?"

He rose from his chair and walked in front of the painting, looking up into the face of her mother, but at the same time keeping his back to her. He stood there for a while and she wondered if he was going to answer her question. *Was it too painful for him to talk about her?*

"She cried and pined for you for so long. It was all too much for her; she could not bear the thought of life without her beautiful Natalia. Alas my poor child she took her own life. I know it is not the sort of thing one wishes to hear and I think it best if we do not discuss the subject any further."

He kept his back to her, not once taking his eyes off the painting of her mother and she could not help but notice the stiltedness in his voice.

*Was it classed beneath one of aristocracy to let one see how they really feel?* As her mind wandered over these thoughts, she realised she had nothing at all in common with her father. If it weren't for the fact of the painting on the wall, she would surely have doubts if she were indeed his daughter at all.

After a time he sat back down and asked her about her life, as he wanted to know what she had been doing all these years and why it had been so hard for him to find her. He was very angry when she told him about her life as a servant at Brampton House, although she never mentioned its name, nor what happened that fateful night and how that brought her to the gypsies. She told him she discovered by mere accident the one who raised her was not her true mother and so her journey began to find her parents. She told him about the kindness of the gypsies who took her in as one of their own, but the moment she mentioned the gypsies he became very angry!

"It is because of them I was robbed of my child and your mother took her own life!"

"Father it is in the past, they have also suffered. It is a time to forgive and forget."

"I will never forgive or forget," he said, banging his cane on the floor.

"Father you have told me how my mother was when I was taken. Well it was the same reason Florica took me. In a space of a week she witnessed her husband's murder then the loss of her child. She became unbalanced; she believed I was her child. I have forgiven her so you must find it in your heart to do so as well."

"How can you forgive them when the death of your mother is on their hands?"

"If you don't it will eat at you and you will never be free. I have lived with the gypsies and they are not the barbarian's you believe them to be. Please father I beg of you; release them and let them be free to roam again."

"No!" he said loudly, banging his closed fist on the chair.

"Father, please," she begged.

"No! We must never speak of this again!"

Natalia put her head in her hands and started to softly cry. *How could she persuade her father to change his mind, she owed it to Luludja and Fonso?* Her thoughts wandered again to Fonso. *Where was he? Perhaps she could persuade Lawrence to help her look for him; maybe search the full extent of the estate boundaries.*

She turned back towards her father and realised he had left the room. She had angered him, but surely with time he would change his mind. She turned back to the painting of her mother. The artist's impression was so good it seemed as if she was looking down at her with kindness in her eyes. Natalia walked over and reached out and gently touched it with her hand, hoping she would give her guidance, but it only made her feel more alone.

She started to make her way out of the room when Miriam entered, both women stopped and looked at each other when Miriam held out her hand.

"I believe we have yet to be formally introduced. I am Lady Holmesby, your father's wife. I suppose that makes me your stepmother."

Natalia was shocked; *what would possess her father to marry such a woman?*

"I can see I have shocked you. I thought surely your father would have told you about me in your little discussion just now. Just so you know, I am the mistress of this house and not you," she said with a terse smile.

Before Natalia could respond, Miriam turned with a swish of her skirt and walked back out of the room.

Natalia turned back towards the painting of her mother.

"Oh mother what am I to do?"

There was a sudden cough and Natalia turned around to see Mary standing there.

"Excuse me miss, but Sir Lawrence asked me if I could find something for you to go riding in. As you are the same size as your mother, maybe you would like to try on some more of her things."

"Thank you Mary. How many clothes of my mother's are still here?"

"Why all of them miss and just as well I say. I know the fashion and styles have changed, but they will do until we can have some things made up for you."

"I wonder why he has kept them all this time; he must

have been truly in love with her. As for having new dresses made for me there is no need; surely we can adjust my mother's things?"

Natalia followed Mary upstairs, but instead of going into the room she had bathed and changed in earlier, she was led to another room. It was in the softest shades of blue and all the furniture was white and trimmed with gold. There was no doubt this was a woman's room, with the beautifully embroidered silk duvet, also in a shade of blue and on the dressing table was a gold brush and matching mirror. She closed her eyes and could picture her mother sitting on the gilded chair brushing her long hair.

"This room was your mother's. I thought maybe we could go through her things and see what fits," said Mary as she opened the closet door.

Natalia gasped in wonderment, she had never seen so many clothes; even Vanessa hadn't owned so many dresses. She reached out and gently touched some of the garments.

"I thought maybe first we should start with the riding habit, as that is what the earl has requested."

Mary pulled a forest-green garment from the closet and held it out to Natalia.

"Is it possible to ride in such a thing? I know it goes against convention, but I abhor riding side saddle."

"Of course, but I will let you in on a little secret: your mother was not unlike you; she was not always one to conform to fashion and society's ways. Not giving you the wrong idea might I add; she was always a lady. Although whenever possible your mother rode astride as a man, but she knew she would never get away with wearing a man's riding breeches, so she had a tailor make her a riding habit as per her instructions. Look, the skirt is actually joined in the middle as in a man's pants, but once you have it on no one would know it is anything but a skirt."

Natalia inspected the skirt and as Mary said, it was like two skirts joined together and would be worn with a leg in each skirt as one would with riding breeches, but also maintaining a woman's modesty. Natalia noticed there was also a short cutaway coat with a small peplum at the back.

"My mother sounds like she was a very clever woman. How do you know so much about her, you don't look much older than me?"

"My family for generations have worked for the Holmesby family; my mother was your mother's chambermaid as I am now yours," said Mary with a proud smile.

This excited Natalia as Mary could tell her things about her mother maybe even her father didn't know. She let Mary help her out of her dress and put on the riding habit. Once she had put on the modified skirt, she then put on a soft white muslin blouse; then the matching cut away jacket which hugged at her slim waist perfectly; this was followed by a pair of soft black gloves and a black hat, not unlike a man's top hat. She walked over and looked at herself in the mirror: the deep forest-green suited her.

"I think it is beautiful, I just hope I can ride in it. What about my feet?"

Natalia turned around to see Mary holding out a pair of black calf-length boots, they were made of the softest leather.

She pulled them on and they were a perfect fit.

"Fancy that, not only are you the image of your mother but you're also her exact size."

"So there is no need for new gowns; I shall wear my mother's with my father's permission of course," said Natalia, once again admiring the finished look in the mirror.

A couple of hours had passed and there was an assortment of dresses, petticoats, and shoes everywhere. Some things Natalia required adjustments to be made as she felt they were too low and was concerned about revealing her scar. Mary said there would be no problem with that as they could put in bits of lace, which would only enhance the garment more.

"Do you think it would be possible for me to have my mother's room?"

"Of course miss, your father would wish for you to have whichever room you choose."

"It has been fun trying on all the beautiful clothes, but I am feeling rather tired. I thought I might lie down for a while," said Natalia as she sat on the end of the bed.

"Of course miss, I will help you out of your gown then I will clean up here and leave you alone. Is there anything else that I can get you?"

"Perhaps some paper and something to write with, I would like to pen a letter," said Natalia, thinking of Fonso and Luludja.

"Once I have cleared away these clothes, I will bring as you ask. Would you like me to have a tray sent up, or would you be joining the others for the midday meal?"

"Perhaps a tray would be nice; I would like to have some time alone and absorb everything that has happened today."

"As you wish," said Mary as she left the room, with a large bundle of dresses.

Once Mary was gone Natalia laid back on the big soft bed. She couldn't believe how tired she felt, but she was also worried about her promise to Luludja and Fonso. She would have to think of a way to convince her father to change his mind.

*\*\**

Natalia opened her eyes and realised she must have fallen asleep as there was a covered tray of food beside the bed and some writing material over on the small writing desk. Realising she was quite hungry she uncovered the tray and found various delicate sandwiches and a small jug of freshly squeezed juice. She took the plate of sandwiches over to the window which had a seat built into it, so when seated one got a good view of the gardens and surrounding area below. Quietly eating she scanned the area for any signs of a lone rider on a small brown horse.

"Don't worry Fonso, I have not forgotten you wherever you may be. I will keep my promise and maybe we can meet again soon."

With her meal finished, she walked over to the writing desk and started to pen a letter. She had to be very precise and careful in what she wrote as there were many lives depending upon it.

*** 

Meanwhile, Jasper was pacing around his enclosure like a wild animal. The day he had run from Natalia, a horse breeder had been travelling the other way and when he saw this beautiful black stallion running past he gave chase.

Jasper, realising the man was trying to catch him, only ran faster and changed his direction off to the left, but unfortunately for Jasper, as he still had on a bridle, he slipped and almost tripped in the reins, then got them tangled in a hedge.

The breeder, realising the horse was trapped, got out his rope and tried to secure the horse. Jasper reared up and tried to escape, but the breeder was prepared for this and brought out his whip. The first crack and sting of the whip shocked Jasper because he had never had one used on him before. He tried harder to get away, but the harder he tried, the whip administered the more pain. This went on for a time until Jasper was too tired to fight anymore.

With all the fight gone out of Jasper, the breeder was able to safely inspect the horse and noticed he had no markings, so he could rightfully claim the horse for his own. With a combination of rope and reins, he was able to lead the horse back to his property. On the ride back, the breeder was counting the gold coins which would be lining his pockets when word got out he had such a horse, he would have people begging him to let the horse sire their mares.

***

There was a gentle knock on the door and Natalia looked up from the letter she was penning, when the door slowly opened and Mary poked her head around the corner.

"I see you are awake; you were fast asleep when I came in. How are you feeling?"

"Well rested thank you, I was actually thinking of going for a walk out in the gardens."

"I will help you get dressed and I have a message from your father requesting you be present at dinner; he has some things he would like to discuss with you."

"I hope it is about lifting the ban on the gypsies."

"Why on earth would you want him to do that? They kidnapped you and treated you badly," said Mary as she helped Natalia dress.

"They were nothing but kind to me, if it hadn't been for Fonso and Luludja I would not be here today."

"May I ask what happened to you, I noticed the scar near your breast?"

"I suppose you will find out soon enough. I don't wish to talk about the people who did these things to me, but because of them I had to flee. I ended up inside the woods and a young gypsy boy named Fonso took me back to his people. He could have left me there to die, because he knew I was a Gorgio, that is what they call us, one not of gypsy blood. Despite this he took me back to his people and with the healing powers of Luludja, I survived. As a way of thanks to them I promised Luludja I would convince my father to lift this banishment he declared on them. So can you understand how important it is that I change his mind?"

"Yes I do. Can you tell me about them, I have heard so many stories about the horrible things they do, especially to young children?"

"What nonsense you talk, gypsies are gentle natured

people and would definitely never harm a child."

"Sorry miss, 'tis just what I have been told. I would still like to know what they are really like, you having lived with them an all."

"There is much to tell you. How about you accompany me on my walk in the gardens and maybe you can also answer some of my questions?"

"It is unusual for a chambermaid to do such a task, but if my mistress is to insist then I have no choice but to obey," said Mary with a smile.

"Then I insist," said Natalia with a mischievous smile.

Both girls giggled and they proceeded down the stairs, causing Frederick to look up and give a stern frown to Mary reminding her of her place.

"It is all right Frederick, I have insisted on Mary accompanying me as I have many things to learn and she can guide me on how I should behave," said Natalia, giving him a dazzling smile.

"I understand all of this is new to you, but Mary is not qualified to instruct you on these matters."

"I have asked Mary and it is Mary who I wish to accompany me, none other," said Natalia before Frederick could finish

He knew better than to argue, as he also knew his place. He gave a bow to her before walking over and opening the door for them. Once outside the girls again giggled and Frederick realised he would have to bring this to the attention of his Lordship, but he would have to be careful how he broached the subject.

"Mary what can you tell me about my mother; was she well liked?"

"Oh yes, she never spoke a harsh word to any of the help, unless she caught them stealing or something of that nature, which deserved a scold. She didn't always follow convention, but don't get me wrong, she was a true lady, just different from the rest. She just found some of the way

*Natalia*

things were done silly; for example riding side-saddle and having to wear countless petticoats while riding. She thought it was not only uncomfortable but unsafe."

"I agree with her there; I refuse to ride with such a thing and won't let anyone make me. Do you know if my parents were devoted to each other?"

"As you know I am not much older than you, but my mother said your father lived for her, and when she died everyone thought he would surely die of a broken heart, but it was you who kept him going."

"Why on earth did he marry Miriam? She seems nothing like my mother."

"It was only about five years ago and she came along when he was at a great low and vulnerable point. Word has it she drugged his drink and had a priest marry them; he was supposedly unaware of what had happened until she moved in the next day holding their marriage certificate."

"Good Lord that's horrible, wasn't there anything he could do about it?"

"He was afraid of a scandal, which she and her brother had threatened him with. By the way be very careful of her brother; he is a gambler and a lecherous drunk," warned Mary.

"Does he live nearby?"

"He lives on the other side of town, so he can be close to the brothels and gambling houses."

"What is a brothel?"

"It is a place of ill repute where a woman offers herself for lewd purposes to a man in exchange for money," said Mary, feeling embarrassed talking of such things.

Natalia gasped and put her hands to her hot cheeks, shocked that a woman could do such a thing. She would definitely keep her distance of Miriam's brother.

"Maybe I should let you ask me a question," said Natalia, trying to change the subject.

"Can you tell me about the gypsies, what were they like

and how did they live?"

"Shall we sit by the pond and the statue of my mother, as I have much to tell you? They call themselves Romany and we are Gorgio. They live in the most colourful wagons, which are very ornate on the outside as well as in; there are quaint little windows that have shutters that open out and each has a decorative curtain covering each opening. At the front there is a little porch and stairs lead up inside, the stairs are removed when they travel. There is decorative painting around all the cupboards and trimmings. They are people who love colour as it is everywhere, including their clothes and they love to sing and dance. I found them to be very gentle people and all look out for one another."

"It all sounds so wonderful, what about the men are they handsome?" asked Mary with a giggle.

Natalia's mind wandered to Besnik and his incredible blue eyes, his tall strong body, which could turn her body on fire with just one kiss.

"I think you have just answered my question. Was there someone special?" asked Mary, noting the look on her face.

"It's not what you think, but he did stand out from the others, although I am sure he is glad I am gone," she said wistfully.

Natalia got up and wandered further around the gardens deep in thought. Mary followed closely realising this man meant more to her than she was letting on and thought it best if she let her be with her thoughts.

They meandered through the beautiful gardens, Natalia occasionally asking a question and Mary answering as best as she could when Frederick came seeking them, looking rather dismayed.

"You should not be out at such an hour, Mary you should know as much. Miss Natalia, your father wishes to see you in the drawing room," said Frederick, and then shot a scolding look at Mary.

"Please do not scold Mary it is my fault. You see she did

warn me about the hour, but I was not ready to go in," said Natalia as she grabbed Mary's hand and walked past a shocked Frederick.

Once they were inside the house, Natalia patted Mary's hand then turned and made her way to the drawing room to meet her father.

As she walked into the room she could see he had been looking out the window, *was he watching us?*

"You wish to speak to me father?"

"Yes, there are some things I wish to discuss with you privately. Sit down and let me speak. Firstly, I know we have only met today and I know you are naïve as to the protocols of how a young lady should behave, so I have asked Frederick to have someone instruct you in such matters and also instruct you on the intricacies for your coming out ball."

"I do not wish to have one."

"What girl does not want a coming out ball?"

"Me, I don't want one and I don't need one."

"What nonsense you speak. A dressmaker will be arriving by the week's end to make you the dress of your dreams."

"Did you not hear me? I do not wish to have a coming out ball!"

"Please let me finish. When you were but a mere babe, it was decided that on your eighteenth birthday you would be married to the Earl of Sherwood. I would like to hold a ball and introduce you to society, but also make the announcement of your engagement."

"You can't be serious. I don't even know who this man is and as I said, I do not want to have a coming out ball," exclaimed Natalia with her hands on her hip.

"Now, now, sit down. Of course you know the Earl of Sherwood; he is Lawrence and quite a catch. Why on earth do you not wish to have a ball? Every female across the land would give their eye teeth to have a ball in their honour, announcing the engagement to such a fine upstanding man."

"Father please don't make me do this," she said with tears in her eyes.

Her father looked at her tears and wondered what she was so frightened of. He realised he hadn't given her much time to adjust to life living here, but knew Lawrence would not wait forever; it was important they made the announcement soon. Maybe he should let her get to know Lawrence a little better; after all he could be a very charming man. He walked over and put his arms awkwardly around her and held her in a fatherly hug.

"All right I will not push the issue for now, but I would like you to see Lawrence as much as possible and get to know him. We will discuss the subject of the ball some other time."

"Thank you and if it makes you feel any better, Lawrence is taking me riding tomorrow," she said with a shy smile.

Before her father could comment any further, Frederick announced that dinner was being served and both proceeded towards the dining room. Natalia was relieved to see neither Miriam or Lawrence were there, *perhaps they were together*

\*\*\*

Natalia had risen early and looked out the window, still looking for any signs of Fonso and noticed it was a beautiful clear day – a perfect day for riding. She took one last look at herself in the mirror and made a final adjustment to her ridding hat before making her way downstairs. Lawrence was talking to Frederick at the base of the stairs. As she made her descent both men looked up and Frederick leant across and said something to Lawrence.

"Well do I pass?" asked Natalia, causing Frederick to go bright red.

"Of course you do my dear. Frederick was just saying how if he didn't know better, he would have thought it was

Esmeralda coming down the stairs," said Lawrence.

"Why thank you Frederick, I shall take that as a complement," said Natalia.

Lawrence put out his elbow for her to take and led her to the stables.

On the walk there they passed various garden staff and Natalia noticed the odd looks she got along the way. It wasn't until they had reached the stables and she was attracting more stares she commented to Lawrence.

"Why is everyone staring at me?"

"I'm afraid it is something you are going to have to get used to. The fact most of the staff have been here for years and they worked for your mother, to them it is as though she has risen from the dead."

"I just hope I don't disappoint them. I believe my mother was well-respected and well-liked by all the staff."

"I hear you have already acquainted yourself with some of them."

Just then the groom walked out leading two beautiful horses: one a mare, she was dark brown and had a white blaze and four white socks; the other was a pure black stallion.

"This beautiful mare is a Darley Arabian and if she is to your satisfaction, she will be your horse and you will notice I have instructed the groom on your choice of saddle."

Natalia walked over and rubbed the horse's white blaze near its forelock, letting the horse get to know her and whispering words that the others could not hear. Also she noticed the saddle was not the conventional one a woman used. How did he know, had he spoken to Mary?

"What is her name?"

"Her name is Giselle miss," said the groom.

"A beautiful name for a beautiful horse, I think we will get along just fine," said Natalia as she climbed into the saddle before anyone could offer assistance.

Both men looked at each other before Lawrence climbed

onto the saddle of his proud black stallion, feeling the day had got off to a good start with her approval of his choice of horse.

"How are you coping riding in a woman's attire after normally riding in a man's breeches?"

Natalia looked at him stunned. *What else did he know about her?*

"Things are not as they seem. My mother apparently did not like to conform to society also," she said before she gave a quick kick with her heels and was off.

Lawrence was totally taken by surprise and wondered what she meant. Realising she was disappearing off into the distance, he quickly urged his horse into action. He had to admit she was a fine horsewoman and doubted he would ever see another so at ease and at one with their horse.

His horse was much bigger and of a better stock, it did not take them long to catch up. They rode on for a time when he realised she was heading for the boundary where he had found the remains of their camp. He had an idea as to what she was doing and it was only a matter of time before he would be asked the unavoidable question, where was her gypsy companion?

They had come to the boundary line and she reined her horse in, then got off and walked through the thick set of trees.

He dismounted and held loosely onto the reins of both horses, waiting for her to carry out her search; he knew she would find nothing.

A short time later she came storming back out from the trees, an angry look on her face.

"Where is Fonso? And don't pretend you don't know who I am talking about because I abhor liars," she said with hands on her hips.

Lawrence stepped forward and caressed the side of her face. *She had no idea how enticing she looked*; all he wanted to do was take her into his arms.

Natalia noticed the changed expression and warning bells started to go off in her head. She quickly stepped back and out of his reach.

"Well, are you going to answer me or do I have to ask someone else?"

"I am sorry Natalia, it is what your father wished and until he say's otherwise there is nothing you or I can do," he said, noting her step backward.

Without saying another word she marched over to her horse, climbed on its back and rode hard along the boundary line as if her life depended upon it.

Lawrence followed her in hot pursuit and felt both excited and frustrated at the same time. She was definitely an amazing creature, like none he had come across before. She was a mixture of wild animal and puritan and she had no idea how attractive she was. He was definitely going to enjoy wooing her before she became his bride. He must tread carefully though, as he knew despite her father's wishes, if she did not wish for the union, she would fight it tooth and nail.

Natalia thought she must have ridden close to the full extent of the estate boundary and still no sign of Fonso. She was sure Lawrence knew where he was and also her father had instructed him not to reveal his whereabouts to her. She would have to find some other way of getting her answer.

## CHAPTER EIGHT

Natalia was sitting in the window seat, looking out at the vast land of her father's estate, when she heard a gentle knock at the bedroom door. She turned and waited for Mary to enter as Natalia had requested her presence.

"You wish to see me miss?"

"Yes close the door and come and sit beside me, I have something to ask of you."

Mary did as Natalia requested and nervously sat down next to her, hoping she had done nothing wrong.

"Mary, being here in my father's home with all the house staff, having things done for me is all very new to me, as before I came here my position in life was not unlike yours. Things happened in my past life I would rather forget, but that does not mean I will forget those who helped me." Natalia paused and took Mary's hands in hers and looked directly at her.

"What is it miss, is there something you wish for me to do?"

"You are my only hope. I am worried about Fonso. If it weren't for him I would not be here today, let alone be alive. I know he would not have left without saying goodbye, which can mean only one thing: he is in trouble and it is my turn to save him, but I cannot do it without your help. I know it is a lot to ask of you; but you are my only hope."

"I will help you anyway I can, but I am a mere chambermaid. Would not someone of more importance be a better choice; someone like the earl?"

"I feel both he and my father have conspired together about Fonso and wish to keep it from me; after all Fonso is a gypsy and we both know their feelings towards them."

Mary shook her head in acknowledgement as she realised her mistress was right, *but how could she be of help?*

"I know what you are thinking, but I also know how the household staff gossip and someone would have to know something; hence that is where you come in. Bring the subject up. You know how it works; everyone likes to voice their opinion until eventually you get your answer. I don't have any money as such, but I will find some way of repaying you for this."

"I will do as you wish, but I do not require any payment and if I may be so bold as to say, I am hurt that you think I am such a person," said Mary as she pulled her hands from Natalia and stood up.

"I am sorry I have offended you; it is the last thing I wish to do. I consider you more a friend than my chambermaid. Please forgive me."

"You are forgiven and it is an honour you think that of me. As it is that time of day where they will be preparing the evening meal, I will see if I can make myself useful, as you probably know the kitchen staff love to gossip."

Natalia startled the girl by giving her a hug, as she realised Mary would not let her down.

\*\*\*

Luck was on Mary's side as one of the kitchen hand's had gone home to nurse a sick child and the cook was thankful of any extra help.

After about half an hour, Mary casually brought up the subject of Natalia and the gypsies and her thoughts as to what life had been like there. Before long Mary was bombarded with questions as they realised she would be privy to Natalia's past.

Mary was ever careful not to divulge more than she should; after all it was her seeking information from them, not the other way around. She relayed to them that something terrible had happened to Natalia in the home where the gypsies had left her. She did not know what, except she had received some sort of beating as Mary herself had seen the scars. This of course brought many gasps of horror and one declaring all gypsies should be punished for putting the child of their beautiful Esmeralda in such a place. She realised her mistake in saying what she had, as it had only added fuel to their anger towards the gypsies, something Natalia would not wish. She tried to explain what had happened, but nobody was listening; everyone was airing their opinions as to what should be done to all gypsies, until the cook stated that it was just as well the young gypsy boy had been left to rot in a cell and the only thing stopping him from swinging from the end of a rope was his age, but his day would eventually come.

Mary dropped the bowl she had been holding, causing it to crash to the floor with a loud smash. The kitchen went surprisingly quiet and all eyes were suddenly on her.

"What is wrong with you girl? You realise your wages will be docked to pay for the broken bowl," said the cook in her booming voice and with her hands on her large hips.

"You don't understand; the news of this will upset Miss Natalia greatly," exclaimed Mary.

"In heavens name why? After all, if it had not been for those vermin stealing her as a babe in the first place she would never have had to suffer, nor would her mother who was so grief stricken take her own life," bellowed the cook

"Miss Natalia told me the gypsy woman who took her had herself lost her child and caused her to go a bit soft in the head. When she saw Miss Natalia she thought she was her lost child and when her mother discovered what she had done, she tried to return her. She told me she made a promise to the old gypsy woman to convince her father to let the gypsies go free."

"Well I doubt that day will ever happen. Her father would never agree to it and my advice to you is to remember your place and not to meddle into other people's business," said the cook as she returned to kneading the dough for the pie.

Mary cleaned up the broken mixing bowl and food off the floor, then assisted in the preparations for the evening meal, keeping her thoughts to herself, not looking forward to passing on the news about Fonso to her mistress, as she knew it would upset her and could think of no way of helping her friend.

Mary did not get an opportunity to speak to Natalia until it was time to help her prepare for bed. After she relayed her news, Mary saw tears well in Natalia's eyes before she turned and sat in the darkness of the window seat.

"Thank you Mary, now if you don't mind I would like to be left alone."

The sadness in her mistress voice tore at her heart, but she would respect her wishes and leave her be.

Natalia sat in the window seat and cried till she could cry no more. As she turned to look up at the stars, the moonstone pendant that Luludja had given her, gently tapped against the glass of the window. Taking it in her hand she stared at the stars, willing them to give her an answer. *How can I help Fonso?* Suddenly a shooting star shot across the sky until it descended to the ground and seemed to disappear behind the trees on the boundary of her father's estate.

Suddenly she realised she had her answer. Jumping up from the window seat she began to pace the room. *Would it work, could she convince her father, could she really do it?* Natalia paced the room until she was sure she had worn a track in the thick rug. Realising there was no other way and a promise was a promise, she decided to try to get some sleep with what was left of the night.

***

Fonso had managed to climb up to the small window of his cell, as he had done every night desperately trying to overcome the sensation of being a caged animal. All his life he'd had the freedom of the outdoors and this one small window was the only thing that was keeping him from going crazy, like the man in the cell next to his. As he had his face pressed against the dirty bars of his cell, trying to breath in the crisp night air, looking up at the stars; he too saw the shooting star streak across the sky, bringing tears to his eyes as he knew it was a sign from the gods, he had not been forgotten.

Fonso clung to the window until his arms and legs began to shake, as they could not hold him in his precarious position any longer. He slowly slid to the dirt floor and once again, armed himself with his swatter, which he had fashioned out of the hay off the floor, because once darkness descended the floor became alive with rats and he found if he could kill a few of them with his fashioned weapon, the others would feed on them and leave him alone.

***

Although Natalia had been up half the night, she was up before Mary came in to help her dress for breakfast.

When Mary walked into the room, she was surprised to see her mistress struggling to lace up the back of her dress; she quickly rushed over and helped her finish dressing.

"Is my father downstairs yet?"

"Why no miss, he often has a tray sent to his room; he is not known to be an early riser."

"Then you must take me to his room; it is imperative I see him at once."

"Begging your pardon miss, but that would not be right and proper," said Mary with a bob.

"I don't care what is right and proper, Fonso's life depends upon me speaking with my father and if that means going to his room then go to his room I shall," said Natalia with her hands on her hips.

"How about I speak to Frederick miss and he can relay a message that you wish to speak with your father at the utmost urgency?"

"If you insist, but make sure you also relay that if my father is not downstairs within the next half hour, he will be receiving my presence in his room."

"Very well miss," said Mary as she quickly scooted out of the room. She wondered what she had planned; she had never seen her like this.

Mary found Frederick in the kitchen overseeing things for breakfast. She knew he would be here as the cook always prepared something special for him every morning. The cook was not too happy about Mary bursting in, during the one time in the day she had to be alone with Frederick, but that was something to worry about later.

"Begging my pardon but the mistress is demanding she speak to her father in the drawing room within the next half hour; otherwise, she will make her presence in his room."

Without a word, Frederick quickly rose from the table and headed towards his master's room. Without waiting to feel the wrath of the cook Mary also made a hasty exit and headed back to Natalia's room to inform her she had relayed the message.

Frederick walked into the darkened room to the sound of his master snoring. He quickly walked over and drew back the drapes to allow the morning sunlight to lighten the room. He then headed towards the clothes closet and quickly grabbed a pair of trousers and his Lordship's smoking jacket, as there would be no time for a full dress. As he walked back in the bedroom the old man was growling like a bear.

"What is the meaning of this? You had better have a good reason for waking me so early."

"It is under your daughter's instructions. She has something of the utmost urgency to discuss with you and she said if you are not down in the drawing room within the half hour, she will make her presence in your room, which would be most improper," he said as he pulled back the covers and tried to get the old man out of bed.

"What is all this nonsense about?" he growled as Frederick tried to get him out of bed.

"I do not know, but one thing for sure if you do not wish for your daughter to see you in such a state, I suggest you let me help you dress as quickly as possible."

"I would not normally tolerate such insolence, but as you have been very loyal to me over the years, I will overlook it in this instance!"

Frederick had His Lordship dressed in a fashion in record time and they were making their way down the stairs when Natalia suddenly appeared at the base of them.

Her father paused and both locked eyes with each other across the vast expanse of the stairs, before Natalia turned on her heel and headed back towards the drawing room.

Natalia's father proceeded on down the stairs and muttered to himself something about her being her mother's daughter.

Frederick had trouble containing the smile from his face and wondered if he would be privy to this meeting. He soon got his answer. Once he had the old man settled in his chair, both Mary and himself were quickly ushered out of the room and the door firmly closed behind them.

"Natalia what is so urgent that I had to be literally dragged out of my bed and rushed down stairs with such speed, something that I have not done in a very long time?"

"Firstly I have a question to ask of you and I will accept nothing but an honest answer and trust me, I will know if you are lying; something that I learnt in my time with the gypsies." Natalia hoping he would believe her bluff.

Her father looked at her and the way she held herself, if ever he'd had any doubts about her being his daughter, they were now surely banished; she reminded him of himself when he had matters of importance to discuss.

"What is it you wish to know?"

"I wish to know the whereabouts of my friend Fonso,

the one who brought me to you; the one who brought me home."

"He is being held in the Mansfield prison."

Natalia looked at him shocked, trying hard to control her emotions.

Her father noticed the glistening of her eyes and could see the inner struggle of her trying not to cry.

She suddenly turned and walked towards the large French doors, but not before he saw a tear slide down her cheek.

He leant back in his chair and looked at the back of his daughter, who was really a stranger to him and he knew he would have to tread very carefully. He watched as her shoulders momentarily shook, then she took a deep breath and her back went ramrod straight before she turned back to face him.

"I have a proposition to make to you: I will marry the Earl of Sherwood, but only on the condition you release Fonso and lift the banishment on all gypsies throughout the land."

Natalia watched her father's face go from happiness about her agreeing to the marriage, to anger as she stated what she demanded in return. She watched as he struggled to rise and noticed the rising colour in his face. She walked over and sat down on the chaise lounge beside him and took his hands in hers.

"Father I will not be swayed over this. There is no other way you will get me to marry Lawrence. If you do not agree to this then I can see no other reason why I should remain here. I know you are my father and have searched for many years to find me and I have wondered these past months if you thought of me. I know you don't want to hear about this, but if it had not been for Fonso I would not be here today and I wonder if he wished he had left me to die in the woods, as I am sure he thinks I have left him to do so in some rotten prison cell. I will leave you now, as I am sure you need some time to think this over, but I will require your answer by sunset tonight. In the meantime I demand that you at least instruct Frederick to let me visit my friend today until you decide on his fate; you owe me that much."

She looked at her father and could see he was at a loss for words, then she walked and opened the door quickly as she was sure to find Frederick there eavesdropping, hoping to hear something behind the closed door.

As expected, she surprised him before he had a chance to stand back in his position beside the entrance door.

"I am sure you got the gist of that conversation Frederick. I expect to have a carriage organised within the hour to take me to see my friend. Also have the cook prepare a basket, as I promised Fonso a Holmesby breakfast. Make sure the cook doesn't disappoint me."

Without stopping, Natalia made her way back up the stairs and headed towards her room. Once inside and the door was closed and latched behind her, she began to shake. In all her life she had never demanded or took such control of a situation, but it had to be done as the life of her friend depended upon it.

***

The ride to the prison was done in silence. Natalia stared at the passing scenery though seeing nothing, her thoughts focussed on Fonso's welfare and how she was going to get him released from prison.

Mary balanced the basket of food on her lap, for fear it would bounce right off the seat, as the road was so rough. She looked at Natalia and was amazed the rough ride did not seem to bother her and hoped they didn't have much further to go. Mary had never been to a prison before and had never wished to do so, but was required to as Natalia's companion.

Finally the carriage slowed down and pulled to a halt and both girls waited for Frederick to place the steps and open the door for them to alight from the carriage.

"Miss Natalia, I will go in first and explain the nature of our visit," said Frederick.

"Wait, I will come with you." She quickly made her way out of the carriage.

"I don't think it wise; this is no place for a lady and by the look on Mary's face, I am sure she would agree with me."

Natalia turned and looked at the frightened look on Mary's face and her heart went out to her.

"Mary you stay here and mind the breakfast basket, whilst I go inside with Frederick."

Before either Mary or Frederick could speak, Natalia was already making her way up the prison steps.

Frederick rushed after her leaving a relieved Mary in the carriage; trying to convince her it was not proper for her to go inside.

She totally ignored his pleas and surprised a guard by the door as she made to open it herself.

"Miss this is no place for a lady; perhaps you should do as the gentlemen suggests and wait in the carriage."

"Is there a law that states no women are allowed to set foot inside?" she asked haughtily.

"Why, no ma'am, it's just that–"

"Well then let me enter."

He quickly opened the door and shrugged at Frederick, who realised he was quickly losing control of the situation; something he had strict instructions from His Lordship not to do.

Natalia made her way over to a stunned policeman at the counter and stated why she was here.

He just stared at her blankly, not knowing what to make of the situation.

"Excuse me; did you not hear what I just said? I am here for the release of the young gypsy boy who goes by the name of Fonso."

"I have been told nothing of the release of such a prisoner."

"Maybe I should introduce myself. I am Natalia Holmesby; I am sure you know my father Lord Richard Holmesby, Marques of Mansfield," she said as she held out her hand.

The stunned policeman looked at Frederick, who nodded in acknowledgement. He quickly took the outstretched hand and gave it a respectful shake.

"Pleased to meet you miss, but I still can't release a prisoner without any official papers."

"I have not travelled all this way for nothing. I demand to see Fonso and I will not leave until I do," she said with her arms folded across her chest to let them know she meant it.

"Sir surely you can at least let her see the boy; after all he is only a boy, what could it hurt?" asked Frederick.

The policeman looked from Frederick to Natalia, then shook his head and turned and got a large set of keys from the hook behind him. He then lifted the counter and came around the other side and Natalia made a move to follow him when he turned and stopped.

"Now, there is a law that I cannot let you go any further. If you would kindly wait here I will bring the boy out."

Natalia nodded then resorted to pacing the room until the policeman came back with a very grubby and shackled Fonso. She took in his appearance: he looked tired and drawn and he looked like he hadn't eaten since their meal at the blacksmiths. Her hand went to her mouth and tears sprung to her eyes. She had been living in the lap of luxury, whilst the one person who is responsible for saving her life and helping her find her father had been left to rot in this hellhole. She rushed over to embrace him, but she was grabbed from behind before she could do so. She turned around to see who would dare stop her from hugging her friend and looked straight into the handsome face of

Lawrence.

"Natalia I know you have missed your friend, but just take a look at him; he could be infested with lice."

"He is right; listen to what he says. I would not want to embrace you like this; I would forever suffer the wrath of Luludja," said Fonso.

"Fonso I am so sorry; I had no idea. Will you ever forgive me?"

"There is nothing to forgive; I knew you would not forget me," he said with a smile.

"Lawrence you have to do something; we cannot leave him here like this."

Lawrence looked into those beautiful green eyes. Her father had told him about her proposal and that she had come here to release her gypsy friend. He had to admit it wasn't how he had hoped she would agree to be his bride, but she had invaded his thoughts and dreams, if this was the only way to ensure her by his side, then so be it. Her father also had no intention of agreeing to free the gypsies, but he thought if he had the boy released she would believe he would carry out her request.

"I have here on my person a document, which has been signed by the Marques of Mansfield himself and has been sealed with the family seal, requesting the release of this prisoner into my care; to be taken back to Holmesby Manor where he shall be required to work as a stable boy," said Lawrence as he handed across the documents.

The policeman not only recognising the Earl of Sherwood, he also noted the Holmesby seal.

"Looks like you have just been given your ticket to freedom boy. It's not every day someone gets something like this, so you can consider yourself very lucky."

Tears sprang to Natalia's eyes and she turned and hugged Lawrence and kissed him on the cheek.

He put his arms around her, marvelling at the smell of her and the feel of her body so close to his. Instantly she realised her mistake and pulled away. Lawrence smiled to himself *the old rascal was right*! Her father was at this very moment unbeknownst to his daughter, making preparations for her coming out ball where they would also announce their engagement.

"Fonso do you remember that breakfast I had promised you? Well I haven't forgotten; I have Mary guarding it for you out in the carriage," said Natalia with a smile and tears in her eyes.

"No I have not forgotten and I have been dreaming about it," he said with a laugh.

"Well as Fonso has been entrusted in my care, he will have to ride with my carriage, but I don't think that will bother him as long as he has the promised breakfast basket."

Natalia was escorted back to her carriage and the promised breakfast basket handed to Fonso, who was given a seat at the back of the carriage.

Fonso did not mind this; in fact he preferred it as it would be a long time before he would be able to handle any confined spaces. He devoured the entire contents of the basket in no time and spent the rest of the journey taking in the fresh air and all the scenery that the open country had to offer.

## CHAPTER NINE

There was much excitement amongst the staff of Holmesby Manor as there was going to be a grand ball, it had been many years since the manor had held such an event and the ball was in honour of Natalia, it was to be her coming out ball.

The best Champagne and wines were ordered, the menu was extensively discussed, there was to be an orchestra and much more.

Miriam, to the annoyance of the household staff, insisted on being consulted before any decisions were made, inspecting the silver and crystal, demanding it be polished again and again. She alone would draw up the guest list, as this event was of great importance to her, for despite the fact she was now Lady Holmesby, she had not received a single invitation to any society events, something she expected to change after this. Many invitations were sent out across the land and there was much speculation as to where Natalia had been all these years. Of course, not a single invitation had been turned down and many were waiting, hoping they were also on the guest list.

The finest seamstress had been called in to make a new gown for Natalia, something she protested over; there was a closet full of her mother's beautiful gowns, there was no need to make another.

Her protests fell on deaf ears, her father refused to have his daughter presented to society in second-hand clothes. Many bolts of fabric were brought in to find the perfect colour that would best enhance her beauty and all agreed upon a beautiful emerald-green silk, except of course Natalia.

As the seamstress rolled out the fabric, she commented how the colour would offset her eyes and that it was made of the finest silk.

"Remove it from my room at once!" said Natalia, before locking herself in the dressing room.

The offending fabric was quickly removed and after a lot of coaxing and cajoling from Mary, she eventually came back into the room.

They finally decided upon a gold organza, which shimmered lights of blues and pinks and an underlay of gold satin. The contrast against her pale skin and her raven-black hair was quite stunning.

Both Mary and the seamstress had no doubt in their minds once the dress was made and Mary did her magic with her hair, all eyes would be on Natalia.

As the big event drew near, Natalia became more withdrawn, but as everyone was so wrapped up in the preparations, there was only one person who noticed the change in her and it both saddened and mystified him.

Fonso enjoyed working as a stable boy amongst his beloved horses and Natalia frequented them often, but he was missing his Romany family, Besnik and Luludja were never far from his thoughts.

Natalia assured him it would not be long before the Romanies were free to roam the land as they once had, he noticed a sadness in her eyes as she spoke of this; this puzzled him for it should be a reason for happiness and rejoicing.

He'd heard the rumours about the pending engagement between the Earl of Sherwood and Natalia. He had seen them together often, as the Earl always accompanied Natalia on her rides and it was obvious to Fonso he was smitten by her, but he knew she did not feel the same towards him. Even though Natalia was polite and courteous towards him, she seemed nervous and tense around him, not what one would expect, from one who was in love and about to announce their engagement. It bothered Fonso so much, he decided if he could get a moment alone with her he would try to find out what was bothering her.

The next day as he was brushing down the beautiful mare Giselle; he stopped momentarily and thought of another horse, one who was not only proud and noble, but loyal; such perfect lines, not even the earl's black steed could compete; *Jasper!*

"I wish to go for a ride."

Natalia so startled Fonso he literally jumped.

"You know it's not polite or wise to sneak up on someone whilst they are brushing down a horse."

"I'm sorry. My one thought was going for a ride, but I see you have read my mind."

"Where is the earl?" asked Fonso as he looked around.

"He is not here. I am sick of always having a chaperone; I am my own person and I wish to be alone," she said with her arms across her chest.

"I don't know if that is a good idea; besides your father would not approve."

Natalia was about to give an angry retort when she noticed the look on Fonso's face. She realised she was being selfish, as he would be severely reprimanded if he allowed her to ride un-chaperoned. She was aware the others treated Fonso with contempt; he had not divulged this to her, but she had seen the signs.

"Very well; you shall ride with me and I will take no arguments. If it makes you feel any better I will inform the head groom that I insist on you accompanying me today," she said with a smile and made her way inside the stable.

Fonso saddled up Giselle and a horse for himself; realising this would be a perfect opportunity to have a talk with her without fear of anyone else listening.

They headed off at a sedate trot, but as soon as Natalia was sure they were far enough away from the stables, she let her horse have full rein.

Fonso gave chase and heard her let out a joyous laugh; it reminded him of a time not so long ago, but seemed like a lifetime ago. Back when they first left Besnik and Luludja and their hearts were filled with a mixture of excitement and fear of the adventure ahead of them.

Finally she reined in her horse that was glistening with sweat as like his own.

As they approached a running stream, they both dismounted and led their horses over for a drink.

Natalia sat down and took off her shoes and stockings, before putting her feet in the cool water.

Fonso noticed her face was no longer pinched or drawn, she had colour to her cheeks and a carefree smile on her face; this was the Natalia he knew and loved.

"Natalia is it true, that at this ball you are to announce your engagement to the Earl of Sherwood?" he asked as he also took off his shoes.

Immediately the smile was gone and for a moment he could have sworn he saw sadness.

She looked down at her feet in the water then stared out into the distance.

He wondered if she was going to answer, when she turned to him and attempted a smile.

"It is supposed to be a secret, but I suppose not much gets past the gossiping staff."

"It is rather sudden is it not? I mean you have been here but a few weeks and suddenly you are planning a wedding."

"It had been decided many years ago, back when I was a mere baby," she said sadly.

"Do you love him?"

"I barely know him, but with time a love will grow. Lawrence has been ever so charming and thoughtful and he has already professed his love to me."

"Why the rush, why not get to know him better and fall in love before you marry?"

Natalia pulled her feet out of the water and quickly dried them with the bottom of her skirt, then silently put back on her stockings and shoes. She knew he was waiting for an answer, but needed time to compose herself before she spoke. She stood up and took her time dusting off her skirt, then walked over to her horse.

"You are young Fonso and it is hard for you to understand these things. I think it is time we head back before my father sends out a search party."

She had spoken with her back turned towards him, not sure if she could look into those kind brown eyes. She was about to climb on her horse, but suddenly changed her mind and walked over to him and embraced him in a strong hug.

"Thank you Fonso; I will always hold a special place for you in my heart."

Before he could respond she turned quickly and climbed onto her horse. *Don't let him see you cry!*

By the time they arrived back at the stables, Natalia had her emotions in check and decided to make a more concerted effort to give Lawrence a chance; after all they were to be married and as her father had said, with time their love will grow. She was about to dismount when Lawrence walked out of the stables with a look of concern on his face.

"Natalia why did you not wait for me? I was just about to go look for you," he said as he helped her dismount.

Natalia rested her hands on his shoulders as he lifted her off her horse, but instead of immediately stepping away as she usually did, she stood on tiptoe and kissed him on the cheek.

Surprised, he looked down at her as he hadn't expected such a response and was pleased to see a shy smile on her face. Encouraged, he put his hands around her small waist and slowly pulled her closer, letting her know his intention was to kiss her, but giving her the opportunity to pull away. Ever so slowly, he lowered his head then gently touched his lips to hers. Encouraged she still had not pulled away he deepened the kiss. The feel and smell of her were driving his senses crazy; also realising she had most likely never been kissed before. It took all of his willpower to end the kiss when he did. Reluctantly he loosened his hold and then took both her hands in his and looked into her eyes.

"If this is the reaction I get when you ride off on your own, it is hard for me to feel slighted."

"I am sorry I worried you, but I had Fonso with me and he would not let any harm befall me," she said looking across at Fonso, hoping she had reassured him about her pending engagement.

"Is it a crime that I wish to be with you every chance I get?"

Natalia didn't know how to respond to him as her mind was thinking about the kiss and she couldn't help but compare it to the one she had with Besnik. The kiss with Lawrence had not been unpleasant, but he didn't make her pulse quicken or leave her body tingling when his hands touched her. The sight of him did not give her that funny sensation in the pit of her stomach, a combination of excitement and butterflies. The mere thought of him and that kiss caused her cheeks to go hot. Then she cursed herself for thinking such thoughts, after all he had only kissed her to teach her a lesson; a Romany would never marry a Gorgio!

Lawrence noticed the colour rise in her cheeks and was tempted to kiss her again, but knew he had to take things slowly.

"Well I had best escort you back to the manor as I know there is an anxious seamstress who requires your presence for the fitting of a certain dress."

\*\*\*

Natalia stood in front of the mirror and looked at the stranger who stared back at her. *Could this person really be me?*

Mary, Martha and the seamstress were all smiles and commenting on the excellent choice of fabric and colour. The dress had a plunging neckline, which sat on the edge of her shoulders, the fitted bodice showed off her small waist and was covered all over with many tiny glass beads. The skirt cascaded out with many layers of the sheer gold fabric, with an underskirt of gold satin – it was a dress befitting a princess. She had to admit the dress was beautiful, but something would have to be done about the low neckline.

"You have done a wonderful job, but I cannot wear this dress, the neckline is indecently low."

Mary could see the seamstress was going to object, but she knew Natalia was concerned about her scar, even though she herself could not see it.

"Perhaps we could attach a lovely piece of lace to bring the neckline up and enhance the dress all the more," suggested Mary.

Natalia looked hopefully at the seamstress as she held her hand to her chin deep in thought, then to everyone's relief she nodded in agreement and rummaged through her box of ribbons and assorted treasures before finding something to her liking. Standing in front of Natalia, she fussed at the neckline for a short period before standing aside. Natalia looked at herself in the mirror, the heavily embossed ivory lace had a fine gold thread through it and as Mary had suggested, it enhanced the dress even more. She looked at herself from different angles in the mirror, then turned and gave the expectant onlookers a smile.

"It's beautiful and I feel I have to pinch myself to make sure I'm not in a dream."

Suddenly the room was abuzz with chatter, Natalia had given her seal of approval and all were happy and excited.

Because Natalia's hair was barely shoulder length, Mary decided to section it while wet and tie it with strips of cloth, so it would dry in a mass of curls; she would then pin up sections and interweave it with gold ribbon to give the appearance of being much fuller and longer than it actually was.

It had been an emotionally draining day for Natalia; she

could not stand the thought of going down to dinner, having to force a smile on her face while everyone discussed the big 'event' which now was just a week away. She asked Mary to have a tray sent up to her room as she wished to retire early, trying her best to calm her rising panic.

Her father had organised the release of Fonso, but he still did not have his freedom, nor did the rest of his kind. She decided to draw up a document, she would present it to her father on the night of the ball, if he did not agree to sign it; she would call off any announcement of her engagement to the Earl of Sherwood.

## CHAPTER TEN

Jasper's spirit had almost been broken; he had endured many beatings from the cruel horse breeder until luck was finally on his side: the gate had not been latched properly and he finally had a chance to be free.

Fortunately his captor had been busy inside the house, so by the time he got back to the yard Jasper was long gone. He quickly saddled his horse and went in search of his potential money-maker, but no horse was a match for Jasper the fastest horse in the land.

\*\*\*

Luludja awoke suddenly; her hair was plastered against her face, her body slick with sweat. As she lay there reliving the dream, her heart still pounding, her body shaking; a wave of fear came over her as she realised it had not been a dream, but a vision.

Suddenly she heard a whinny and the sound of horses' hooves, shortly followed by the sound of pounding on her wagon steps. Her body was shaking so much she could barely stand and struggled to get out of bed, her fear increasing as she made her way to the front door.

Besnik had also heard the sound of a horse entering the camp, as did many others – a matter of great concern at such an early hour.

Standing on his small porch pulling on his heavy coat, his eyes scanned the area. He heard a pounding noise and realised it was coming from the area of Luludja's wagon. Quickly pulling on his boots he ran towards her wagon. He didn't know what to expect, but was shocked to see a large horse on the steps of Luludja's wagon, his coat was slick with sweat and blood.

As he neared the horse, he could see some wounds had begun to heal and fresh ones were weeping blood, then he realised *Jasper!*

His concern deepened as he realised something must have happened to Fonso and Natalia, as neither would allow such treatment to the horse.

Suddenly, the horse moved and he saw Luludja in nothing but her nightgown. *Had the woman gone mad, could she not see the wild look in the horse's eyes?*

He was about to call out when he saw Luludja put her hands to the Jasper's head and to his amazement the horse settled as if listening to her words. He paused for a moment, trying to decide his next move, knowing the horse had a dislike for him; he knew if he got too close he could be endangering Luludja further.

"He means me no harm. He has come looking for Natalia. Somehow the two were separated and someone has mistreated him. Stay where you are for now. Wait till I explain things to him."

He didn't dare question her, but he thought the cold air had gone to her head; *what on earth was she talking about?*

Luludja went back inside the wagon, only to come out moments later wearing a warm coat and gave something to the horse as she continued to talk.

To his amazement, he saw the horse's ears prick forward and Jasper shook his head, as if agreeing with her. The horse then moved back down the steps, followed by Luludja who still had her hand on his neck.

"Come over slowly; no sudden movements and remember not to raise your voice. It is time you two became acquainted as we have no time to waste."

Besnik did as she said and made his way slowly towards them, wondering what this was all about.

"I had a vision last night. At first I thought it was a bad dream, but the arrival of Jasper made me realise it had been sent to me for a reason. The two of you must embark on a journey and before you question my reasoning, please hear me out. You must take Jasper, as he is the only one who can guide you. Fonso is safe, but Natalia's life is in grave danger and only you with the guidance of Jasper will be able to save her."

"You're not making sense, how can Fonso be safe in Gorgio territory and Natalia be in danger?"

"I cannot explain; unfortunately my visions are not that clear, but trust me when I say he is safe, but if you do not leave as soon as we have treated Jasper's injuries and he has had time to rest, Natalia will not survive the week's end."

Luludja looked deeply into his eyes. There was too much bad blood between the Romany and Gorgio; she knew she could not demand Besnik take this journey, but she hoped he was the man she believed him to be. There was something about Natalia she could not explain; it had nothing to do with her daughter Florica; there was something else, but she could not foresee what it was. One thing she was sure of: if there was ever to be harmony again amongst the Romanies and Gorgio, the survival of Natalia depended upon it.

"We shall leave in the early hours of the next day, the horse will be rested enough for the journey," said Besnik.

As he walked off, Luludja bowed her head and silently sent up her thanks. She had much work to do. First she must make a healing lotion for the horse, but most importantly, she must call on the gods to protect both horse and rider, as there was a strong chance she would not see either one again.

\*\*\*

It was a very cold morning and there was a heavy fog, every time Besnik or the horse expelled air, it gave the appearance of smoke pouring from their mouths and nostrils.

He had been riding now for a good three hours; Besnik didn't think it wise to try to ride Jasper as he knew the horse only allowed one person to ride his back, but also with the injuries he had suffered, a rider would only cause more pain. However, Luludja insisted upon it; she said it was the only way and assured him, after twenty-four hours his wounds would be healed enough to take a rider.

The poultice, which Luludja had made, went on like paint changing the appearance of the horse: he now looked more like a Zweibrucken, which was also a Warm blood, but their black coat was dappled with white.

Besnik realised it would also work as a good disguise, for whoever did this to the horse would probably be looking for him, so he also painted the horse's face and feet. Although, if someone came too close they would see it was only paint, but Besnik had no intention of getting in close proximity with anyone, as he himself would be at risk if seen outside the woods.

By late afternoon Jasper had led them to the barn where Natalia and Fonso had spent their last night.

As they neared the building Besnik tried to rein Jasper in, as there was no way of knowing if anyone was already residing in the barn, but Jasper had other ideas. Besnik pulled hard on the reins, fearing they were going straight into a trap, but the horse did not slow his pace, causing Besnik to curse himself for listening to Luludja and riding the crazed animal. He considered throwing himself from the horse, but the horse was now going at break-neck speed.

As they entered the barn, he twisted in the saddle trying to take in the full extent of the area, ever on the alert for a possible attack.

Suddenly the horse came to a halt at the corner of the barn, almost throwing Besnik forward in the saddle. Then the horse started dragging at the hay with his hoof, trying to uncover what was hidden.

Besnik quickly dismounted, taking in the old bits of rusty farm equipment scattered about and felt reassured they were alone.

Jasper dragged something from the hay and Besnik went

to see what had the horse's attention.

He realised it was clothing, there was a dress and under garments, then he saw the saddle, it had decorative detail, one he had seen before, it had been on Jasper the day Fonso brought Natalia to their camp.

*Natalia what happened to you and where is Fonso?*

"Jasper is Natalia held prisoner by the same person who took to you with a whip, can you lead me to her?"

He realised it was insanity asking a horse for an answer, but Luludja felt Jasper was their only hope and Natalia was their only chance at freedom. *Had the old woman finally lost her mind or could there be some truth in what she said?*

## CHAPTER ELEVEN

The big day had arrived. The manor was abuzz with activity, extra staff had been hired to help out in the kitchen and the head cook could be heard bellowing out orders. Rugs had been taken outside and beaten to remove any signs of dust or dirt and the banisters were given an extra polish – the house shone like it hadn't in years. Decorations had been hung, including a birthday banner, as today was Natalia's eighteenth birthday.

It had felt a little strange celebrating it on this day, as she had never known her true birth date, because Mildred had made a guess at her age. Natalia had been so tiny, Mildred had assumed she was younger than she actually was; hence she felt she was celebrating her birthday two months early.

Natalia looked across at the beautiful dress and the matching pair of shoes. Mary had laid them out carefully in preparation for the night's ball. She remembered a time not far back, when she wished she could wear such a dress, believing it would make her the happiest girl in the world; now she was not so sure.

She walked over to the window seat, a place she had spent much time of late.

It was a beautiful clear day, the flowers were out in full bloom and there was not a leaf or blade of grass out of place.

Her eyes wandered across to where she would live when she became Lawrence's wife, he had taken her there with Mary as chaperone. Lawrence had wanted her to see the home where she would one day be mistress and her title would be the Countess of Sherwood; it all seemed so surreal.

Despite being surrounded by people, she had never felt more alone. As she leant against the windowpane, Luludja's pendant tapped against the glass. She grasped it firmly in her hand and closed her eyes, remembering the colourful wagons and the sound of the children's laughter as they happily played. Remembering a pair of incredible blue eyes that felt as though they could see to her very soul, eyes that could be cold and hard, but also burn with passion. If only he had never kissed her, never caressed his hands over her naked skin, bringing her body alive, making her feel the most glorious sensations, turning her blood hot like molten lava. She so desperately wanted to feel those things again, but knew she never would.

She opened her eyes and once again looked at the boundary line; realising Lawrence could never make her feel these things and she was only torturing herself by thinking these thoughts, only making life more difficult. Even if she wasn't to become Lawrence's wife, there could never be a life for her with Besnik; she being of Gorgio blood and he Romany; a union of the two could never be.

*Stop being foolish girl and accept life as it is!*

After deciding the only way she could lift herself out of this mood was to go for a ride and called for Mary to help her change.

As she came down the stairs Frederick notice she was dressed for riding and felt it was his duty to inform her, as the Earl was not present to escort her, she had best leave it till another time.

"Please Frederick; consider it a birthday present to me from you. Could you not yourself, escort me down to the stables and then Fonso could escort me on my ride? I feel if I do not go now, I will surely go mad. I am not used to all this fussing over me; I find it so overwhelming."

Frederick took one look at her face, he had learnt to read people 'well' over the years and he could see she was putting on a brave front, but he could also see the sadness in her eyes. He would never admit it, but he had developed a soft spot for the child of Esmeralda; she was so like her mother, so kind and thoughtful, if only she was here today. This was a time a daughter needed her mother and Esmeralda had such a calming quality about her, something he felt Natalia needed now.

"How can I refuse the daughter of the beloved Esmeralda? I shall do as you wish, but just this one time, seeing as it is your birthday wish," he said with a smile and held out his arm to escort her to the stables.

They walked along in silence and Frederick sensed she was not in the mood for small talk. Natalia noticed there was as much activity going on outdoors as there was inside. Lanterns were being strung and tables and chairs were being strategically placed around the garden, for those wishing for a more private place, away from the noise and activity that would be in the main hall and the ballroom tonight.

As they neared the stables, Natalia saw Fonso walk out with Giselle and noticed he had her ready to ride. *Had he been able to read her thoughts as she sat up in her room?* It never ceased to amaze her the things he could see. She was tempted to ask him about her future, but of course she would do no such thing.

"I see your horse is all ready for you. Had you pre-planned this?" asked Frederick.

"No I did not; it is a gift Fonso possesses. He sees things, things which you and I cannot, he is not the ogre you all seem to think he his; he's kind and sensitive to one's feelings," she said defensively.

"Miss Natalia wishes for you to escort her on her ride today and she assures me she will be safe in your hands," said Frederick.

"I will guard her with my life. I can assure you no harm will come to her," said Fonso, stretching to the full extent of his short stature.

Frederick could see he meant every word and it was obvious he held a high regard for Miss Natalia, perhaps she was right; maybe they all had prejudged him.

As he walked back to the house, he realised she had tried her best to seem happy and excited about the evening event. *What did she not want me to see?* He had a sudden feeling of déjà vu and his thoughts drifted to Esmeralda. He remembered as if it was yesterday, when Esmeralda first came to Holmesby Manor. She was like a breath of fresh air; no airs or graces and it wasn't long before everyone loved her. Natalia so reminded him of her mother, so gentle and caring, but she too had that stubborn streak, for when her mind was made up, one was hard pressed to sway her otherwise. Looking back, he now realised the signs where there, Esmeralda had changed, yes her child had been taken from her, but Frederick now wondered, *was it more than that?* He still remembered clearly the day they carried her out, it had taken him a long time to accept she'd given up so soon.

Fonso sensed Natalia did not wish to talk. *Maybe if I focus enough, I will see what is bothering her.* He had noticed lately whenever she was with the earl, she always made a point of showing her affections towards him; something Fonso felt was done to appease his fears.

They rode the horses hard before stopping at the stream, as they had done once before, but this time he would not ask any questions; he would let her do all the talking.

As before, they cooled their feet in the stream and she sat there in silence. He closed his eyes, centring his thoughts, willing his mind to see.

Suddenly he could see red, not the deep red of blood, but the red one saw in a flame of a fire where it becomes almost orange, there was a face and the eyes were hard and cold and the lips were twisted in a cruel smile; it was a woman, he could hear her laugh, but it did not make him smile, as it was pure evil, sending a chill to his bones. He saw her turn and there was another, but he couldn't see a face; that person was wearing a hooded cloak and a grey mist was swirling around, but he could see there was something in their hand; it was a -.

"Fonso, Fonso!"

Suddenly he was back to the present and realised he was wet with sweat. His heart was racing as if he had been running for his life, but he felt no fear for himself, but for the one he loved!

"Fonso are your all right?"

Fonso sat up and noticed the look of concern on Natalia's face, then was overcome with a feeling of dread. *Oh my God Natalia!*

"Please speak to me. Are you all right?" Asked Natalia

"Yes, I am fine, it was just a vision; you have seen me have them before."

"I have never seen you react this way. What was it about, is someone in danger, is it Luludja or Besnik?"

He was surprised she had mentioned their names, as she hadn't done so in such a long time, so long he had wondered if she had forgotten them. He wished Luludja were here; she would be able to help him understand what he had seen, as she was more experienced at these things than he. One thing he was almost certain of: Natalia's life that was in danger.

"Natalia will you promise me you won't go anywhere on your own, don't be so trusting of these people, we know very little about them!"

"I'm relieved Luludja and Besnik are fine, but don't you think you are being a bit melodramatic?"

"I am serious Natalia, promise me, else I will ensure you never ride again, I will tell them you had an accident and whatever is needed to ensure you are safe!"

"Fonso what is this all about, surely you would not do such a thing to me?"

"I mean it, give me your word you will be careful, trust no one; especially tonight!"

"Yes if it makes you happy, I will be extra careful."

He was wishing things hadn't been so difficult for her with his people. He felt she fitted in with his kind more than she did her own. *What was really keeping her here?*

"Natalia do you really want to be here?"

"Of course, what would make you ask such a silly question? I have finally been reunited with my family and am soon to be married. If you wish to go back I will understand and I will do my best to ensure a safe journey back home for you."

Even though she was smiling, the tears were streaming down her face, which Fonso felt she was unaware of. Despite the temptation of going back to the simple life of the deep woods and being with his own kind, he could not desert her, not now.

"I think we should be heading back. Mary will have her work cut out trying to do something with my hair. She is determined to make me look like a princess so that all eyes will be only on me," she said with a hollow laugh.

They rode back to the stables and Fonso noticed the look of relief on her face that neither Frederick nor Lawrence were waiting for her when they arrived. He decided once he was alone, he would summon up all his strength and see if he could revisit the vision, he needed to know who wished Natalia harm, for it could save her life!

Mary was chattering non-stop about how exciting tonight would be, she had never experienced a grand ball and was so glad she had been given the honour of preparing Natalia.

Of course, Natalia hadn't listened to a word she had said; her thoughts were elsewhere.

She was staring at the mirror in front of her, but she was not seeing her reflection or what wonders Mary had done with her hair. She could not forget the incident at the steam and felt sure Fonso was not being totally honest, she could not stop thinking of Luludja and Besnik, for she could not bear it if something was to happen to them!

"Miss Natalia, do you not like it?" asked a worried Mary.

Natalia was shaken from her thoughts and looked at herself in the mirror; *is that me?* She put her hand to her face then gently touched her hair and saw that the reflection moved as she did. The way Mary had pinned her hair and interwoven the gold ribbon was amazing.

"You have truly worked miracles Mary. I had to pinch myself to make sure it was me," said Natalia, looking up into Mary's worried face.

"Twas no miracle, miss, I just enhanced your beauty. Now let us help you get into your gown."

Natalia had been sitting in her petticoats, as Mary had not wanted to crush the beautiful golden gown; she wanted to make sure no one could find fault with the way she prepared her mistress. Mary carefully with the help of Martha got Natalia into her gown then buttoned up the back over the many gold pearl buttons. Her dainty shoes were placed upon her feet then Mary gave her a spray of a delicate scent, one she had been told would send any man crazy; of course she did not tell Miss Natalia that.

"Martha go ahead and let Frederick know Miss Natalia is about to come down. We want everyone ready for her grand entrance," said Mary proudly.

Martha ran out of the door excitedly, pulling herself up just in time before anyone could see her and scold her for such behaviour. She made her way sedately down the stairs as she had been instructed many times.

As she neared, Frederick looked up and Martha gave a nod, alerting Frederick who walked over to His Lordship, informing him he was about to announce Natalia's entrance. Miriam was busy letting the guests know who she was; she was not there to stand by her husband's side, but to score favour with the many guests. With the help of Lawrence, Natalia's father made his way to the base of the stairs, ready to accept his daughter's arrival. Frederick raised his white-gloved hands and tapped the gold bell to gain everyone's attention.

"I would like to present Miss Natalia Holmesby, the daughter of Lord Richard Holmesby and the late Lady Esmeralda."

All eyes were at the top of the stairs when she suddenly appeared. There was an audible gasp from the crowd, as they had never seen such a vision of beauty. She had truly exceeded the beauty of her mother. Tears came to her father's eyes and he leant heavily on Lawrence's arm; he had refused a chair as he wished to be standing to accept his daughter.

Lawrence was lost for words; he could not believe that this vision at the top of the stairs would soon be his bride. His heart swelled with pride just at the thought of it.

Natalia looked down and saw all the people looking up at her, she froze with fear and was about to turn and run, when Mary came up behind her.

"'Tis all right miss, I am right behind you; there's nothing to fear. Just imagine you are a princess, for you surely look like one."

Natalia turned and looked at Mary, who could see the frightened look in her eyes.

"You promise you will walk down with me?" she asked as she reached out to Mary.

"I promise; let's not keep your father waiting," she said, giving her hand a squeeze.

Hesitantly, she made her first step down the stairs, then looked down at her father and saw the pleased look on his face.

"I can do this, I made a promise and I must remember that."

Natalia thought she had said these words to herself, but in fact had spoken aloud, loud enough for Mary to hear. *What did she promise?*

Suddenly Natalia moved down the stairs and Mary had no time to ponder on this further; her job was to ensure her dress did not catch and cause her to trip or fall.

When she was finally at the base of the stairs, her father let go of Lawrence and embraced his daughter.

"You have made me so proud."

"You have no idea how scared I feel," she said as she gripped his hands tightly.

"I know this is all new to you, but don't worry; you are in good hands. Lawrence will help guide you," he said, indicating that it was Lawrence's cue.

"It will be my pleasure, sir," he said as he tucked her hand in the crook of his arm.

"Frederick I hear no music; is this not a celebration?" asked His Lordship.

Frederick nodded and quickly instructed the orchestra to begin playing and people made their way to the dance floor.

Lawrence waited patiently whilst introductions were being made, as everyone wanted to meet the daughter of the Marques of Mansfield; the daughter who had been kidnapped by gypsies and was finally reunited with her father after all these years.

After a time, the crowd began to thin and Lawrence turned towards Natalia.

"I must say you are an absolute vision of loveliness and I won't let you leave my side. Shall we dance?"

Natalia looked around her to see if anyone was watching, she then turned in front of him so no one could hear.

Lawrence tried to look at her, but she was looking down at her hands and nervously twisting her lace handkerchief. He gently stilled her nervous hands and lifted her face up to look at him.

"Natalia what is it, what is bothering you?"

She had no choice but to look him directly in the eyes, thinking how best to say it, when Lawrence noticed the blush rise to her cheeks.

"My darling how ignorant we have all been. Your life before here; you've never been taught to dance have you?"

"Perhaps it would be better to avoid embarrassment and we let her sit with her father and you dance with me."

Both turned to see Miriam standing there in a blood-red gown with a plunging neckline, which Natalia thought was bordering on indecent and was further shocked to see her flutter her eyes at Lawrence.

"Maybe another time; tonight I plan to devote all my time to Natalia," Lawrence said politely.

Miriam's smile suddenly disappeared from her face and she looked at Natalia with cold hard eyes, then turned dramatically and made her way over to a man who Natalia thought was young enough to be her own son and to make things worse, was leaning in so close he could see down the front of her gown. She felt sorry for her father and wondered if he was aware of the way his wife was behaving tonight.

"Don't let her bother you, perhaps I could teach you a few steps."

Natalia saw the smile on his face and thought he was mocking her. He saw the hurt look in her eyes and realised he had not handled this well, he gently pulled her rigid body towards his and bent down and whispered in her ear.

"I am not making fun of you my darling. How about we find a spot out in the garden away from prying eyes, but still close enough to hear the music and I shall teach you a few simple steps?"

Natalia looked up at him and could see the kindness in his eyes, so nodded in agreement.

He bent and gently kissed her on the forehead, then guided her outside to a private spot in the garden.

"Now you place your left hand on my right shoulder and your right hand in my left, I place my right hand on your waist. There are only three simple steps to this waltz, but we will start nice and slow."

Natalia was stiff and awkward in such close proximity to Lawrence, which caused her to constantly step on his toes.

"Lawrence I'm sorry; it's not going to work," said Natalia despondently.

"You need to relax; you're too stiff. Try closing your eyes and focus on the music. We don't have to move; just sway when you feel the rhythm."

She did as he suggested and stood there with her eyes closed, but still standing in the dance pose.

After a few minutes of concentrating on the music, she could feel the rhythm and started to sway with the beat.

"That's it; now keep your eyes closed and move with me. Just let the music flow."

He started out very slowly and was pleased she was keeping her eyes closed. He gradually increased the speed of their steps until they were up to the pace of the dance. He looked down at her, still with her eyes closed and a smile on her face. All he could think of was pulling her close and ravishing her lips. He was so overcome with emotion that he faltered and stepped on her foot. Her eyes instantly shot open and she saw the look in his eyes. She knew he was going to kiss her, but decided not to stop him. *I have agreed to become his wife.* She surprised him by slowly sliding her arms up around his neck – he needed no more encouragement.

Many who had ventured out into the garden and witnessed their private dance. A dance that turned into a passionate embrace; sparking rumours of a possible engagement. The intruders went quickly back inside, informing others of what they had seen.

However there was one observer who was not happy about this turn of events and turned angrily in search of their loyal servant, as a rider must be despatched immediately. They would have to act on their plan tonight, before any announcement could be made.

"My darling as much as I love having you out here all to myself, your father has gone to great lengths in your honour and I am sure would like to show you off to all the guests.

How about we have that dance inside now?"

"Dancing with you out here with no one watching and going into that crowded ballroom are two very different things," said Natalia nervously.

He smiled down at her and pulled her close and kissed the top of her head, feeling like the luckiest man in the world.

"You know you are a natural; you have nothing to fear. If it bothers you, you can always close your eyes and pretend we are back here in the garden."

"Do I really have to go in there?" she asked, looking up at him hopefully.

"I'm afraid so. Don't worry; I won't keep you on the dance floor too long," he said, feeling like he could drown in those green eyes.

Reluctantly she allowed him to take her into the grand ballroom and when she saw the many faces and swirling ball gowns, she clutched tightly to Lawrence's arm as if her life depended upon it. Many heads turned to look at the handsome couple and soon room was made for them on the dance floor.

Natalia was so filled with panic she began to feel faint.

"Natalia it's all right. Just look at me and forget about the others. Focus on the music and pretend we are alone and back in the garden."

She tried to do as he said and when she looked into his eyes, she could see they were filled with love and it was for her. She nervously smiled back at him, wishing she could feel the same way, letting him slowly lead her into the waltz, doing her best not to take her eyes from his. Many noticed and commented about young love. Her father was watching and was pleased to see things going so well, for he had no intention of it being a long engagement; he wanted to hear wedding bells before the year's end.

When the music stopped and everyone applauded the young lovebirds, Lawrence bent down and whispered in

Natalia's ear and suggested they make their way over to her father and maybe ask him for a short dance.

She looked up at him, then across at her father, she could see the look of pride on his face, but the thought of going back out on the dance floor frightened her. However Lawrence was right; she should do this and besides, he was frail and not well and people would think nothing if they faltered.

"As much as I hate the idea of going back on that dance floor, I do have to agree with you," she said with a nervous smile.

With her hand safely tucked in the crook of his arm, they made their way over to her father.

"Father is it improper of me to ask you for the next dance?"

"Are you sure you want to dance with an old fool like me?"

"I have never thought such thoughts of you and I would love to have the next dance with you, but I will warn you I might step on your toes."

Her father threw back his head and let out a loud laugh, causing others to look their way and comment on how good it was to see the old man happy again. He leant heavily on the arm of the chair as he made to get up.

"I would be proud to take my beautiful daughter out on the dance floor," he said as he held out his hand.

As they made their way over to the dance floor, people began to clap, causing the conductor to turn and when he saw the Marques approaching the dance floor, he quickly instructed the orchestra to play a slower waltz.

Natalia turned and faced her father, then tried to remember the steps Lawrence had taught her, but she need not have worried, because even though her father seemed old and frail, he held his own on the dance floor and didn't let her falter a step. When the music ended a great cheer went up and everyone once again clapped.

"It's been a lot of years since I have done that. You certainly made me feel young again, but I think one dance is enough for now."

"That's fine by me, I didn't know how to dance until a short time ago. Lawrence gave me a lesson out in the garden, he said people were expecting to see us on the dance floor and I must say I was so scared I thought I might faint."

"Yes, I heard whispers about two lovebirds dancing in the garden and if you were scared, you covered it well."

Natalia felt she had done enough dancing for one night and walked with her father back to his seat. Once he was seated, he suggested to Lawrence they should mingle and he introduce Natalia to the guests.

Everyone was eager to meet her in the hope they would be included in any future celebrations.

As they slowly made their way around the room Natalia got a glimpse of a face, throwing her back to another time; she was so overcome with fear she could barely breathe and the room started to spin. She clutched so tightly at Lawrence's arm he could feel her nails through the thickness of his jacket. He looked down at her and noticed her pallor and her body had begun to shake. Quickly making their excuses, he guided her outside the glass doors and into the cool air.

"Natalia what's wrong, are you ill?" he asked, his voice full of concern.

She was so frightened she was incapable of speech.

Lawrence was really worried now and helped her over to a seat.

"Darling please speak to me. Tell me what's wrong. Should I call for a doctor?"

The cool air bit into her skin and she began to shiver, prompting Lawrence to take off his jacket and wrap it around her shoulders. He brought his face close to hers, blocking everything from her view, trying to get through to wherever she was. He gently caressed her cheek until her eyes began to focus. Suddenly she was brought back to the present and realised his face was close to her and his eyes were full of concern. The ringing slowly subsided in her ears and the earth no longer tilted.

"Natalia can you hear me?"

Not sure she was capable of speech, she nodded.

"What happened back there?"

Natalia looked past him and scanned the faces inside the glass doors, but could see no sign of what caused her fears.

Lawrence watched her eyes as they looked past him and noticed the colour come back to her cheeks and her breathing had returned to normal. He scolded himself; he should have realised this was all too much too soon. Both he and her father had been selfish and wanted to move things along. He sat on the chair beside her and took her hands in his.

"How are you feeling, would you like me to get you a drink?"

She definitely did not want to go back inside; at least not yet. Maybe a drink would be a good idea and she could stay here till her heart settled.

"I would like that and if you don't mind, maybe my coat as I would like to stay out here for a while and I don't want you to catch cold because I am wearing your jacket."

He placed both hands on either side of her face and gently kissed her lips, her eyes and the tip of her nose, before looking deep into her eyes.

"Darling I would freeze any day for you, but I will get your coat if you wish."

She smiled back at him and nodded.

Before rising he gave her a gentle kiss on the lips, then made his way back inside. She sat and watched him as he disappeared into the crowd. She leant back in the seat and tried to focus on the music and clear all terrible thoughts from her head. Suddenly she felt the need to distance herself from all of this and decided to take a short stroll through the garden.

She made her way past the neatly clipped hedges and the ornamental flowers, distancing herself away from the music and the bright lights, until she finally began to relax.

"I underestimated you May."

Natalia's blood ran cold and the hairs stood up on the back of her neck. She turned slowly in the direction of the voice.

"I got the shock of my life when I saw you. I thought surely my eyes were deceiving me, but I see they have not."

Natalia turned to where the voice came from and as the bushes parted her heart jumped into her throat. The last time she had seen her was still vivid in her mind, the fear she had felt was still as intense when she had walked towards her with the hot poker. Natalia's mouth went dry and was incapable of speech. *Run, run while you can!*

"Obviously I didn't leave that poker in the fire long enough. How does a lowly servant girl get an invite to such a grand affair, or afford such an expensive dress, who did you seduce this time?"

"I am the earl's fiancée. I am Natalia the daughter of the Marques," she said, angered at Vanessa's remark

"You conniving little tramp, I obviously underestimated you; I would have never thought you capable of seducing such an old man, like you seduced my father?"

"How dare you. I never seduced your father he attacked me. As for the Marques, he is my true father; I was kidnapped from him when I was a mere baby."

"My God, you have the audacity to go with that ridiculous story?"

"It's true. Why do you hate me so much? I have never done anything to hurt you."

"Oh and there are tears as well. Very well for old times' sake, I am actually going to give you the chance to bow out gracefully and avoid a scandal, because mark my words, if you don't, I will walk in there right now and announce to them all the fraud you are. I will tell them you are a thief and how you seduced my father and in case you think they won't believe me, my mother is also here."

"I have suffered your intimidations for many years, but you can intimidate me no longer. How do you think my father will react when I tell him it was you who inflicted such cruelty to me and forced me to run for my life?"

"You wouldn't dare."

"Just try me," said Natalia with more bravado then she felt.

"Then you leave me no other choice."

Before Natalia knew what was happening, she was grabbed from behind. She opened her mouth to scream, but a heavy cloth was placed over her face and a terrible taste came to her mouth. She tried to struggle, but her body and limbs became so heavy and everything seemed to move in slow motion. Suddenly she could feel herself falling and the lights began to dim, until everything went black.

When Lawrence returned to the garden he was surprised Natalia was not there. *Perhaps she had gone for a walk,* remembering how upset she was earlier. He quickly searched the garden and soon found his jacket. Full of concern he called out her name and searched further till he found one dainty gold shoe. Suddenly frantic, he ran further down the garden towards the cobbled drive and noticed something glistening in the moonlight. Quickly running over, a cold fear came over him, for the glistening object was Natalia's moonstone pendant, one she was never seen without and the chain had been broken.

## CHAPTER TWELVE

Besnik realised he had no other choice but to listen to Luludja's craziness and let the horse lead the way, he was in a land that was totally foreign to him. However he did maintain enough hold on the reins to make sure they travelled at a sedate pace. They were now on a cobbled road with many more people about; he wanted to avoid at all costs drawing attention to himself. Despite the fact they were now travelling under the cover of darkness, he still kept his collar turned up and his hat pulled low, never forgetting he was a Romany in Gorgio territory.

The toll of such a long journey was starting to bear down on him. As Luludja had been so adamant there was no time to waste, both horse and rider had little rest.

Suddenly the sound of a fast approaching carriage had him sitting straight in the saddle. *Had he been spotted, did someone notice a gypsy had ventured out onto Gorgio land?* As it neared, Besnik had to pull tight on Jasper's reins as he became jittery and appeared to be trying to run towards the oncoming carriage.

"Jasper, settle down! We are not here to draw attention to ourselves but rescue Natalia."

Jasper flattened his ears and began throwing his head. The closer the carriage came, the crazier the horse became and Besnik struggled to keep the horse under control, but also keeping his eye on the fast approaching carriage.

He noticed it was totally black and was pulled by two black horses. He realised if it hadn't been for the break-neck speed at which it was travelling, it would most likely have gone past unnoticed, as there was no marking on either horse or carriage, it could have easily blended into the night.

As the carriage sped past, Jasper reared up and almost unseated Besnik from his saddle, but with his experience and by using all of his strength, he managed to get the horse under control and over to a nearby tree.

He quickly dismounted and held the reins tight, looking around to see if they had drawn any attention. He saw a couple who were taking an evening stroll and they were looking his way, suddenly their attention was drawn to a man riding a horse at a dangerous speed. Besnik realised to his dismay it was a policeman and pulled Jasper deeper into the shadows. Thankfully Jasper had settled, almost as if he understood the importance of the situation.

To Besnik's dismay the officer started to rein in his horse, so he climbed quickly back into the saddle, hoping Jasper was not too tired to outrun the officer.

As he was contemplating these thoughts, the policeman turned his horse in the direction of the couple across the road.

"Have you by chance seen a black carriage drawn by two black horses come by this way recently? He would have been travelling very fast."

"Why yes, he went by only moments ago and looked to be headed in the direction of the Moors. What has he done?" asked the woman.

"We believe he has kidnapped Natalia Holmesby," said the policeman as he rode off.

Suddenly there was another sound of horse's hooves riding at break-neck speed, barely missing the policeman.

\*\*\*

Natalia felt as if she was being violently shaken about. Her mind was fuzzy and she had a terrible taste in her mouth. She opened her eyes, but everything was so dark. *Where am I, what happened?* She tried to sit up, but then it was as if the earth disappeared from beneath her and she could feel herself falling, until coming to a sudden halt with a hard surface. Frightened, not knowing where she was or how she come to be in such a place, not game to make another attempt at getting up in case of falling further, she tried to listen to the sounds around her and tentatively put out her hand to feel the ground beneath her.

She could hear a pounding noise and was not sure if that was from the bump on her head. She slowly moved her hand and realised the surface she was laying was smooth. Very slowly, she pushed herself up into a half-sitting position and suddenly the surface was gone from beneath her. It was so dark she couldn't see a thing and desperately put out her hands, trying to grab hold of something, anything that would stop her from falling to possible danger below. Her hands felt something and she grabbed hold, but to her horror it seemed alive and moved. Letting out a scream, she immediately let go before once again landing on a hard surface, tears came to her eyes, *if only I could see something.*

"So my pretty, you are finally awake," said a deep voice.

Startled, Natalia didn't move, hoping he couldn't see where she was. Suddenly she realised what the pounding noise was, it was horses and she was in a fast moving carriage. She quickly pushed herself across the floor as far away from the voice as possible. She suddenly felt a hard wall against her back and knew she was on the other side of the carriage. Using her hands she managed to find the seat and slowly pulled herself up.

"Who are you and where are you taking me?" she asked, trying not to show her fear.

"I'm taking you to a special place, a place where we can be alone and not worry about being disturbed."

She couldn't see his face, but she could see his silhouette from the faint moon glow and the sight of his large frame caused her heart to pound even harder and her breathing increased.

"Settle down my pretty, save the heavy breathing for later. Just sit back and enjoy the ride; it won't be much longer now." He laughed.

His laugh sent chills down her spine; it sounded evil.

She realised she was sitting near the door and contemplated jumping out, but the pace at which the carriage was travelling, she would surely be killed, *but would that not be preferable to what horrors he had in mind*? She suddenly lunged forward, grabbing the handle, bracing herself for a hard fall. However, to her dismay the handle did not turn. She pulled at it franticly, but it would not budge.

"You don't think I would forget a simple matter of locking the door do you?"

Natalia sunk down to the floor, her hands still clutching the handle, no longer able to contain her tears. *This is all Vanessa's doing!* She felt so angry that her tears stopped. *I have not come this far to let her win again!* Suddenly she could see the face of Luludja and remembered her words of encouragement; Natalia instinctively put up her hand to clasp her moonstone pendant, *it's gone*! Instantly her panic began to rise, Luludja had told her she must always wear it, as it was blessed to keep her safe.

Suddenly the motion of the carriage slowed and the pounding of her heart became louder. Quickly pulling herself back up into the seat she realised her best tactic would be to let him think she had given in and perhaps he would relax his guard. Her nerves jangled as the carriage came to a stop and the driver placed the stairs outside the door, then she heard the key turn slowly in the lock. It was as if there was a spring tightly wound inside her, she wanted to jump as soon as the door was opened; but she willed herself to wait, as she would only get one chance.

The door opened and a voice in her head screamed *Run*, but she managed to stay in control and slowly stepped out of the carriage, hoping he would think she had conceded defeat. Ever so slowly, she inched away as if making her way towards the cabin door. She even turned to look at him as if making sure he was following, but when she saw his face. *Run, run now*! With her heart in her throat she lifted her skirts and ran.

She heard the sound of a cracking whip, followed by an evil laugh. She had no idea where she was going; she just knew she had to run. The surrounding area was thick with shrubs and trees and her dress with its many petticoats kept catching and tearing on the branches, making it difficult to move fast and unbeknown to her, she was leaving him a trail to follow.

Her breathing had become so laboured her chest was hurting and she had to pause to catch her breath. She looked quickly around her, making sure she was far away from the cabin while listening out for her pursuer. She could see the distant glow from the cabin and a smile came to her face, when suddenly the hairs on the back of her neck prickled. Turning quickly she screamed like she had never screamed before, he was only a few feet behind her – all this time, she had been running towards him. She quickly darted to her left, but suddenly felt pain and felt herself being pulled backwards so hard she stumbled and fell to the ground.

"Enough! This game is beginning to bore me, I think it's time for another game."

He suddenly loomed above her and she was pulled unceremoniously to her feet and the realisation that he had ensnared her with his whip, which was tightly wrapped around her waist.

Natalia tried to untangle herself, but he pulled his arm back hard, bringing her up against his large belly. She struggled and screamed, but it only excited him more, then in one swift movement he picked her up and threw her over his shoulder like a sack of flour. Natalia pummelled his back as hard as she could and struggled to free her legs of his firm hold, screaming as loud as she could, hoping someone will come to her rescue.

"Scream all you like my pretty; I love to hear a woman scream, why do you think I brought you to such an isolated place?"

Natalia's screams turned to tears and she struggled all

the more franticly, causing him to let out an evil laugh.

Suddenly she noticed the ground beneath them had changed and they must be nearing the cabin. The realisation of it brought on more screams.

She banged her head as he carried her through the doorway of the cabin, then he threw her from his shoulders and onto the bed. Her head was pounding in unison with her heart and watched in horror as he took off his coat and started to unbutton his shirt.

"I think it is time to make oneself more comfortable and divest of some clothes, but don't worry my pretty; the pleasure of removing yours is mine alone."

He had rid himself of his shirt and was now in the throngs of removing his trousers.

Natalia quickly scrambled off the bed, only to feel the pain of the whip as it wrapped around her arm. She screamed in pain and fear, kicking and swinging her arms as he once again threw her on the bed, then she realised he had a knife in his hand.

"As you can see I have rid myself of my clothes, now it is time to remove yours."

He leaned in so close she could feel his hot, fowl breath on her face, then he slowly started to cut away her dress, taunting her, occasionally dragging the blade against her skin. A wave of despair came over her, as she realised there was no escape, he had now removed her dress and it would not be long before he rid her of her undergarments. *I would rather die than have him touch me!* As he slowly brought the knife towards her, she pressed her hands firmly on the bed, ready to propel herself forward, hoping the knife will plunge deep into heart.

It was as if time had slowed, she kept her eyes focused on the blade of the knife as it moved towards her, then when the moment was right, she pushed herself up with all her might, suddenly feeling the blade as it pierced her skin; she heard a loud scream not knowing if it had come from within, before closing her eyes and sinking thankfully into the darkness.

***

"Natalia, Natalia!"

She opened her eyes and realised she was lying on the ground outside as she could see the stars above. Her heart was pounding hard in her chest and her body was trembling with fear. Suddenly a face loomed above her, causing her to breakdown and cry, for she was looking directly into the face of Besnik.

"You are safe now; there is no need to be frightened," he said as he gathered her in his arms.

Despite his words she couldn't stop the tears, the combination of the night's events and the fact he had risked his life to save her.

Finally her tears were spent and she realised it felt good to be in his arms and wanted to stay this way forever.

"What happened, where are we?"

"You fainted and we are a few hours ride from your family home."

"And him?"

"He is dead. I could see what you were going to do, I called out, but you could not hear me; I thought I was too late when I saw the blade touch your skin."

Natalia looked down and saw the knife had only just pieced her skin.

"How did you know?"

"Luludja, she had a vision, she knew you were in danger."

"I can't believe you risked your life to save mine."

She looked up into those blue eyes and wished she could read what he was thinking. Her eyes travelled to his lips. Before she realised what she was doing, she leaned forward and touched her lips to his, it was as if a fire had been ignited. Besnik pulled her hard up against him and deepened the kiss, but too soon he pulled away and looked deep into her eyes.

"Are you sure this is what you want?" he whispered.

"Yes."

His lips reclaimed hers, before leaving a hot trail down to the valley between her breasts, unlacing her chemise as he did so.

She ran her fingers through his hair and arched back her neck as one of his hands caressed one breast, whilst his tongue licked and teased the other before taking it fully into his mouth. The pleasure so great she let out a moan and he slowly pushed her back against the blanket. She fumbled with buttons, trying to undo his shirt, wanting to feel him, when suddenly Besnik pulled back and he looked down at her, his breathing heightened and she wondered what was wrong.

"Natalia; is this really what you want, or are you going to suddenly push me away and run?"

At first his words hurt, then she remembered when he kissed her down by the river and as she looked deeply into those blue eyes, it suddenly dawned on her she loved him with her heart and soul and had been fooling herself that she felt otherwise.

"Yes Besnik, this is what I really want and no, I will not push you away."

"Even if I do this?"

His hand suddenly went under her petticoat and touched her thigh. She instinctively froze, but she did not try to push him away. His hand slowly moved higher up her thigh until he found her most intimate place, a place no one had ever touched her before; all the while, he kept looking into her eyes. She stared back and even with the shock of where he placed his hand, she did not push him away. Suddenly his hand started to move in a slow circular motion and the pleasure it gave caused her pulse rate to quicken and a moan escaped from her lips.

"Are you sure this is what you want?"

"Yes, yes please don't stop!" she said breathlessly.

Her body was on fire, but with the most incredible pleasure and she could feel a tension building inside her, like a tightly wound spring.

He leant back down and alternately suckled each breast; all the while, his hand kept massaging her most erogenous area, winding the spring even tighter.

She could feel herself getting hotter and she was breathing much faster. She could vaguely hear a primal noise and realised it was coming from her.

Suddenly an explosion of the most intense pleasure came over her body and the blood was ringing in her ears and she arched her back and screamed out.

He gently caressed her face and waited for her breathing to settle, pulling her to her feet before looking down into her eyes.

"I want to see all of you."

He slowly pulled down her petticoat and finished unlacing her chemise, before letting it fall to the ground. He looked at her semi naked body and slowly put out his hand and gently traced her scar with his finger.

She quickly pulled away from his hand and tried to cover the scar with her own hand.

"There's no need to be embarrassed; you are beautiful and I am not bothered by a mere scar."

He gently moved her hand and kissed the spot she had tried to cover, then tugged at the ribbon on her pantaloons and stood back as they fell to the ground.

"You are beautiful; perfect in every way. Now it is your turn to undress me' I want to feel your hands on my skin."

She shyly stepped closer and finished unbuttoning his shirt, then slowly pushed it off his broad shoulders, caressing his skin as she did so.

Once it fell to the ground, she slowly ran her fingers across his broad chest, moving slowly down the ripple of muscles to his flat stomach and noticed him quiver wherever her hands touched. Encouraged by this, she leant forward and licked at one nipple until it became hard, causing Besnik to moan.

He then pulled her up against him, letting her feel his arousal and letting her see the look in his eyes before kissing her deeply.

"Finish undressing me, I want you to see all of me," he said hoarsely against her lips.

She slowly moved her hands to the front of his trousers and shakily started to undo the buttons; all the while fully conscious of his arousal as it strained against the buttons. She could hear his breathing becoming more ragged and finally the last button was undone, then as she tried to push down his trousers, she realised they were caught. She looked up at him, taking in his heaving chest and the look in his eyes; she knew he was waiting to see if she would carry out his request. Not taking her eyes from his face, she moved her hands to the front of his trousers and slowly put her hands around his erection causing him to gasp. Then ever so gently, she eased it out and looked at it in amazement and without thinking, erotically stroked it.

"You have no idea what pleasure you are giving me," he rasped.

He stepped out of his trousers and scooped her up into his arms, before gently laying her back down on the bedroll. He lay down beside her and once again reclaimed her lips; all the while his hand was caressing her body, causing her temperature to rise. She could feel herself becoming wet and moist, then he slowly positioned his body over hers before gently lifting her hips and slowly entering her. She suddenly felt pain, causing her to cry out and he stilled his body and gently kissed her lips until the pain subsided, then very slowly and gently he began to move. She expected to feel more pain, but was surprised by the pleasure she felt.

He moved very slowly, waiting for her to fully relax and

accept him.

The sensations she felt was even more pleasurable than before and instinctively she started to move in unison with him.

Her hands were in his hair, then they moved down to his shoulders and could feel the bulging muscles beneath, then they travelled across to his broad back moving lower to his firm buttocks.

The spring inside her was ever tightening and she wanted more of him, she wanted him to increase his pace. Gripping his buttocks firmly she pulled him closer, letting him know what she wanted.

Her breathing was now heavy and she was moaning in pleasure.

The spring inside her was wound so tight when suddenly, it was as if there were stars at the back of her eyes and she was devoid of all sound around her and her body was engulfed in the most intense pleasure, so great it caused her to cry out and dig her nails into Besnik's skin. Then she felt his body shake and he released a deep primal growl.

They were both slicked in sweat and breathing deeply, he looked deep into her eyes before rolling onto his back taking her with him.

As she lay on his chest, she could hear his pounding heart, neither capable of words.

Natalia had never felt such intense emotion and tears pricked at the back of her eyes. Her heart felt as if it was bursting with love and she had to tell Besnik how she felt. She lifted up her head and looked at him, taking in his thick glossy hair and noticing for the first time, he was in need of a shave. Then as she looked into his incredible blue eyes, she wanted this moment to last forever.

"I love you," she said.

Besnik stared at her and she saw the muscle in the side of his jaw twitch, as she had seen so many times before, then he put his hands to her shoulders and gently lifted her off him and lay her back on the bedroll and then pushed himself up on one elbow and stared down at her.

"I think we should both get some sleep; we have a long day ahead of us tomorrow."

It was like a slap in the face, her throat felt tight and there was a sick feeling in the pit of her stomach. Trying hard not to show her tears, she quickly rolled on her side, putting her back to him and forcing her hand into her mouth, trying hard not to cry. The lump in her throat got so tight it began to hurt and her heart felt as if it had been trampled beneath a stampede of wild horses. How long she lay like that she didn't know, but she could taste blood on her hand.

Suddenly she could hear soft snoring and very slowly turned and saw Besnik was fast asleep. Slowly getting up, she quietly retrieved what was left of her clothes and silently dress, making sure not to wake Besnik.

She didn't know what to do, but she knew she needed to get far away from here, the more she thought about it, the more she realised she could not face Besnik ever again; there was only one thing for her to do, she had to make her own way home. Surely they could not be that far from her home. She no longer cared who or what was in the woods; she couldn't hurt any more than she already did. Her body was now numb and her heart felt as if it had been ripped in two.

Natalia had no idea how long she had been walking, but suddenly heard the sound of horses and realised they were coming towards her. She stopped in the middle of the road, waiting for them to get closer, not caring if they saw her in time to avoid her being trampled.

As they neared she could see there were at least four horses in total. Suddenly the one in front spotted the lone figure dressed in only her undergarments and held up his hand for the others to slow up.

They approached her in a slow trot and she could see the one in front was a policeman and slowly made his way

*Natalia*

towards her.

"Are you alright miss?"

Natalia suddenly burst into tears.

He quickly got off his horse, taking off his jacket as he did and placed it around her shoulders.

"What happened, did someone hurt you?"

"Please, can you take me home?"

The policeman looked at her and wondered if this was the girl they were looking for.

"Is your name Natalia Holmesby?"

Not capable of speech, she nodded her head and burst into another bout of tears.

"Do you know who did this to you?"

"Yes."

## CHAPTER THIRTEEN

Natalia sat numbly in the drawing room. She just wanted to go up to her room and never come out again, but the officer had insisted on her recounting what had happened the previous night. She told them briefly about Vanessa's involvement and about being grabbed from behind and later waking up in the fast moving carriage. Not wanting to tell them about Besnik, she made up a story of how she managed to turn the knife on her attacker and that he was now dead. Barely holding the tears in check, she told them she was tired and wished to retire to her room. Both Mary and Martha were waiting expectantly at the base of the stairs.

"We are so glad you are safe miss. We've all been worried out of our minds and the earl has been searching the countryside. He hasn't slept a wink, not even stopping for something to eat."

The thought of Lawrence sent Natalia into a fresh bout of tears; she hadn't thought of him once, or their impending marriage.

"Oh you poor thing, here's me nattering and you've been through such a terrible ordeal. We have drawn a hot bath for you and a tray has been sent up."

Natalia followed the girls up the stairs with a feeling of impending dread. The image of Besnik and their night together kept flashing in front of her eyes like a form of torture; one minute wishing he hadn't been the one to save her, but then glad he had. She told the girls she wished to be alone and would not need their assistance further and when they left the room, she turned the key in the lock, wishing she could lock out the world forever.

As she undressed herself and looked at her reflection in the mirror, she wondered if this was how one looked after being totally ravaged. Walking over for a closer inspection of herself, she noticed a few wisps of ribbon in her hair, wondering if it was her attacker or Besnik's lovemaking that left it looking such a state. She looked down at her breasts; then closing her eyes, she remembered Besnik's hands and mouth caressing them, which brought on a fresh bout of tears. Their lovemaking had been so passionate; how could he have been so devoid of emotion when she professed her love to him? Did it not mean anything to him? Then she remembered it was her and not him who gave the first kiss and she felt hot with shame as she had practically thrown herself at him and he had asked her many times if they should stop.

Disgusted and ashamed, no longer able to look at herself in the mirror, she walked over and hopped into the bath.

The hot water felt good as it eased the aches on her body. If only it could ease her aching heart and the sick feeling in the pit of her stomach.

She dried herself and practically fell into bed, her body exhausted both physically and mentally, not even bothering to dress as what was the point; she was never going to leave this room nor ever see anyone again.

She must have fallen asleep and was woken by a loud banging on the bedroom door. A sudden fear came over her as she pulled the bedclothes up to her chin.

"Miss Natalia, its Mary, please open the door."

"I told you: I wish to be alone."

"The doctor is here to see you."

"I don't need a doctor."

"Your father called for me; he thinks it best I check you over," said the doctor.

"I told you: I don't need a doctor," she yelled.

"Please miss, unlock the door. The earl is anxious to see you, also," said Mary.

"How many times do I have to tell you, I wish to be left alone?"

Natalia threw a pillow at the door, once again bursting

into tears, there was only one person she wanted to see, but he didn't want to see her. She cried so hard those standing outside the door could hear and the doctor just shook his head before walking downstairs to talk with her father.

Natalia woke up the next morning feeling like a limp rag doll, as she had cried herself to sleep only to wake up in the middle of the night and go through the whole process again.

As she lay in bed, staring at the ceiling, she wondered if this hollow feeling inside her would ever go away, feeling like she was dead inside, when a loud knock on the door made her jump in fright.

"Miss Natalia, are you awake? Your father has instructed for a locksmith to be ordered if you do not unlock your door. Please will you let me come in?"

*How could her father do this to her, did he not understand her need to be alone?* Then she suddenly felt angry. *How dare he? Men, they were all the same!* She thought of poor Mary who was caught in the middle and which would be preferable: the embarrassment of having a locksmith open her door or letting Mary in. Throwing back the covers she quickly pulled on a robe and slowly walked over to the door.

"Mary if I ask you something, will you promise to tell me the truth?"

"Yes miss I promise."

"Are you alone?"

"Yes."

Natalia leant against the door for a moment. *Could she trust Mary, would she trick her into thinking it was for her own good? No Mary was not like that.*

Slowly turning the key in the lock, she opened it a crack, ensuring Mary was in fact alone before letting her in.

Once inside, Natalia quickly closed and re-locked the door.

Mary was shocked at the sight of Natalia; her eyes were red and puffy and it was evident she had been crying most of the night. She saw the untouched tray of food.

"How about I draw you a fresh bath and organise something else for you to eat?"

"Thank you Mary, but I'm not hungry; I just let you in so you can tell my father I am fine and wish to be left alone."

"You must eat, else you will surely become ill, and beggin' my pardon but you certainly don't' look fine. Everyone is worried about you and the earl is anxious to see you."

"I just can't face anyone yet; why can't they understand that?" she asked tearfully.

"Oh miss I wish I knew what to do to make you feel better. Why won't you let the doctor see you? He might be able to help."

"No doctor can help me; there is no medicine in the world that could make me feel better."

"Your father is adamant about the doctor and I know he will not leave until he has seen you."

"Very well; I shall see this doctor, but on the condition you do not leave my side."

"I promise, now we must get you dressed."

Natalia put on the most modest blouse in her closet, one that buttoned all the way to her throat and the sleeves came all the way down to her wrists, matched with a demur grey skirt, giving her more the appearance of an old school mistress.

The doctor noted her appearance and immediately made his own assumptions. After taking her pulse, he put his stethoscope in his ears and asked her to unbutton her blouse so he could check her heart. He was standing so close to her it made her feel uncomfortable and she had to summon all her strength not to scream, when he put his hand near her breast.

"Now I know you have gone through a terrible ordeal, but for me to finish my examination I need to examine a more delicate area. I will step outside to respect your modesty and if you can remove your clothes from the waist down, Mary can drape a sheet over you before calling me back in. I am afraid it won't be pleasant, but it is something that has to be done."

"I can assure you I have no intention of removing my clothes for you or any other man for that matter, so you can leave this room right now."

"It is important you let me finish my examination."

"In God's name why?" she asked angrily.

"We need to make sure you weren't, violated; we have to ensure no chance of–"

"I can assure you that vile man did not touch me. Now get out!"

Natalia was so angry she could have hit him and angrily stormed over and pulled open the door.

He stood there for a moment before realising he had handled the situation badly and in hindsight should have brought a nurse.

He had barely exited the room when Natalia slammed the door and turned the key in the lock. She paced the room. *Was this her father's doing or was it Lawrence, was he worried he was getting soiled goods?* Then her anger turned to realisation; she could not marry Lawrence now, it would not be fair to him and besides, even though Besnik did not love her, she could never be with another man again.

She walked over to the window seat and looked out despondently, a movement caught her eye. Leaning in closer to the glass she could see it was a man on a horse and as she pressed her face against the window, the man and horse stopped before turning his head, almost as if he knew she was watching him.

Even from this distance, there was no mistaking who it was. She would recognise his strong, proud body anywhere.

After a few moments, he turned his head and both horse and rider continued on their way.

Natalia bounded out of the window seat so fast nearly knocking over a startled Mary. She raced over and grabbed the door handle, desperately trying to pull the door open, before realising it was still locked.

Frederick had just closed the door to the drawing room after taking tea into His Lordship and the doctor when he heard the sound of running feet. He was surprised to see Natalia bounding down the stairs, almost tripping in her haste.

"Miss, is everything all right?"

Natalia ran past him; she didn't have time to stop or speak and almost slipped as she opened the heavy door.

Once outside, the bright sunlight temporarily blinded her after being closeted inside for so long, but that didn't stop her as she ran blindly towards the stables.

As she neared the stables she could see Fonso with a tall black and white horse. Her heart pounded even harder and her mouth suddenly went dry. *Was he here?*

By the time she reached Fonso, she was out of puff and had to lean on the rail to catch her breath.

"Look who is here, at first I didn't recognise him with all the white paint. He has been treated badly, but he is on the mend."

Natalia was only half listening as she looked around her, then she realised he wouldn't be standing out in the open for fear of being spotted.

"Where's Besnik?" she asked quietly.

"He's gone. How did you know he was here?"

"Gone, gone where?" she asked, biting back the tears.

"Back home. He just came to bring back Jasper."

"Did he ask you to go back with him?"

"Yes, but I told him I would come back after your wedding as there was much to do and by then I should have the papers."

"You told him I was getting married?"

"I know it is not official yet, but if it hadn't been for the kidnapping, you would be engaged now."

"What did he say?"

"He seemed shocked; then he said you could consider Jasper as a wedding present."

Natalia looked away as she could no longer hold back the tears. She had so desperately hoped he would come back for her. The fact he had risked everything by coming here, was it just to return Jasper, or had there been other reasons as well? Now all hopes and dreams were dashed and what must he think of her now, an engaged woman making love to another man?

"Natalia darling, I have been so worried about you."

Natalia turned around and before she could say a word, Lawrence pulled her to him and kissed her passionately on the lips. She pushed away from him, tears running freely down her face.

"I'm sorry Lawrence; you are a wonderful man and will make a wonderful husband, but I cannot marry you,"

"Darling, you have been through a terrible trauma, please don't make any rash decisions? I will give you all the time you need."

"You don't understand…"

"Natalia please don't say anymore. I am prepared to wait."

She looked into his handsome face and could see the hurt in his eyes. She knew full well how that hurt felt. She decided not to say anymore, not wanting to hurt him further and she knew in reality, he would not wait forever; he was a handsome man and deserved to find someone who would return his love. She made her way back to the house and the privacy of her room, once again locking the door and throwing herself on the bed and crying herself to sleep.

\*\*\*

It had been over two weeks and Natalia still could not be coaxed out of her room. Although, Mary had convinced her if she did not eat she would make herself ill, then she would be in the doctor's care, so she agreed to have light food sent up to her room.

It was late afternoon and Natalia was sitting in the window seat, looking out despondently when she heard a knock at the door, not bothering to answer, as it would most likely be Mary.

"Natalia, do you plan to spend the rest of your days closeted up in this room?"

Natalia spun around, the last person she expected to see here was her father; he was such a stickler for following the rules of etiquette and it was most improper for a father to be seen in the bedroom of a young woman, even if she was his daughter, especially without her maid present.

She noticed he was holding a beautiful, intricately carved silver box as he walked over towards her and sat in the chair beside her.

"Lawrence tells me you are having doubts about getting married."

"I have no doubts father. I told Lawrence I couldn't marry him."

"I know your experience must have been frightening, but you are safe now and Lawrence is a good man; he will be kind and gentle to you."

"I know he is a good man, but father I do not love him and it would be wrong for me to marry him."

"As I told you before: you will grow to love him; you are right for each other."

"How do you know we are right for each other, what would make you say such a thing?"

"I am your father; trust me, I know these things. Listen, the reason I came here is I wanted to give you this; it was your mother's."

He handed the box to Natalia and she reverently opened it and couldn't help but gasp at what was inside. There were necklaces of diamonds, emeralds, and sapphires all with matching earrings. She gently ran her finger over each one, realising her mother had worn these.

"I thought they might cheer you up. Just think of what jewels you will add to this box when you become the Duchess of Sherwood."

"Do you actually think shiny baubles would change my mind about marrying Lawrence? What sort of person do you think I am?" she asked angrily.

"Obviously I have not handled this well. You can keep the jewellery box; after all, they were your mother's, but just think about what I said. I will leave you in peace, but mark my words: I will not tolerate you confining yourself to your room for much longer."

She watched angrily as her father left the room. *Didn't he care about her feelings at all? It was as if he cared more about Lawrence than her and to think he could bribe her with jewellery!* She spun around in the window seat, knocking the box to the floor, not caring as she had no intention of wearing them – they could stay on the floor forever. She pressed her face to the window, scanning the countryside below, still ever hopeful of seeing a lone rider, hoping he would come and whisk her away.

As she turned her head a glint caught her eye, but as she moved it disappeared. She slumped back disappointedly before seeing it again, but once again as she moved, it disappeared. Moving ever so slightly, hoping to see it again, she then realised it was not outside, but in fact a reflection on the window of something inside. Turning around, she saw the jewellery strewn across the floor, which must have caused the reflection on the glass.

She realised it was her mother's after all and should be more careful of her things, as apart from a few of her clothes, she had nothing really special of hers.

As she picked up the scattered pieces and carefully placed them back in the box, she noticed the bottom had come apart from the box. She carefully turned it over, feeling ashamed at damaging such a beautiful thing. As she looked at it closely, she realised it was different to the rest of the box, almost has if it had been added on later and there was something sticking out. It appeared to be a piece of paper. Trying carefully not to tear it, she gently pulled at the corner managing to pull a portion of it out and realised the paper was in fact a photo. She excitedly pulled at it before hearing a slight tear. Feeling frustrated, as she wanted to see what was hidden, but did not want to damage it further.

*Who had put the secret compartment there, had it been her mother, was she hiding something she didn't want her father to know about?* Just then she heard another knock at the door and quickly put everything back in the box, before jumping up and shoving it in her dresser drawer, moments before Mary walked in carrying a tray of food.

"The cook has cooked a hardy stew and baked your favourite bread especially for you."

Natalia walked over and for the first time in these last weeks, actually felt hungry.

"Thank you Mary. it does smell good and give my thanks to the cook also."

Mary was pleased to hear this and once the covers had been removed, she left the room to tell the cook the good news.

As soon as the door was closed, Natalia ran over and locked it then retrieved the silver box from the dresser drawer.

Carefully using the knife, she tried to prize off the bottom of the box and as it loosened, something fell to the floor, it was a silver chain and pendant.

When she picked it up, she thought it looked familiar, then gently pulled out the photo. It was of a child of about eight sitting on a woman's lap. The child was obviously her mother as it was like looking at a younger version of herself and the woman, by her skin colour and the way she was dressed, Natalia knew she was a gypsy.

Natalia knew before she was born, gypsies were allowed to roam free across the land. Obviously this woman meant something to her mother, but why did she feel the need to hide the photo? Taking a closer look at the pendant, she wondered why it was so familiar. It was flat and round, about the size of a silver dollar. The image on it looked like a wheel of a carriage or wagon, and on the right-hand corner was a crescent moon. She turned it over and the name Esmeralda was inscribed on the back. *Why would her mother hide this very simple pendant when she had far more expensive jewellery in the main compartment?*

Suddenly her stomach rumbled as the aroma of the stew and freshly baked bread reached her nostrils. She placed the photo and the pendant on the tray and looked at them whilst she ate; hoping they would give her an answer.

## CHAPTER FOURTEEN

Natalia sat bolt upright in bed. Her room was in darkness and it was late at night. She had remembered why the pendant was so familiar; putting her hand to her neck it gave her comfort to know it was there. She walked over to the window seat and looked at the pendant in the moonlight. *It is the same as Besnik's.* There was only one person who could possibly answer her questions: *Fonso and morning was hours away!*

She had hardly slept a wink and was already dressed before the sun crested the horizon. Cautiously opening the door, making sure no one was about, she made her way slowly down the hall to the top of the long staircase, peeking her head around the corner, making sure Frederick was not down below. Relieved to see he was not, she quickly made her way down the stairs, carefully turning the key in the lock of the front door, pleased to know Frederick kept it well-oiled so it opened and closed silently. She quickly made her way to the stables, keeping to the cover of the garden, darting in and out of the shrubs as she went. As she neared the stables she saw Fonso and he looked as if he had only just got out of bed.

"Natalia you nearly scared me to death. What on earth are you doing up at such an early hour?"

"I need to talk to you and it is important that nobody else knows. I'll help you saddle the horses."

"Are you crazy, you want to go riding now?"

"Please just trust me on this."

Fonso begrudgingly saddled two horses. He hadn't even had breakfast and she wanted to go for a ride; there would probably only be scrapings left by the time he got back.

Neither said a word on the ride, the cold air biting at their faces.

As soon as Fonso thought they were a safe distance from

the house, he demanded to know what this was all about.

"I need you to tell me about this pendant."

"You dragged me out here, missing my breakfast, just to tell you about a pendant," he said angrily.

"Will you just look at it?"

Fonso looked at it, turning it over in his hand before handing it back to her.

"Where did you get it?"

"I found it. Do you recognise it?"

"Yes, all Romanies have one. Where did you find it?"

"It was hidden in my mother's jewellery box along with this photo. What do you mean all Romanies have one?"

Fonso lifted the chain from around his neck and handed it to her as he looked at the photo. Natalia compared the two pendants and noticed Fonso's name inscribed on the back.

"They're different," said Natalia as she held them out to Fonso.

"It just means we are from different clans. See this symbol of a *chakra* or wheel; it represents the sixteen spoke wheels of the *vardo* or wagon. It is on both pendants. That is the Romany symbol and the other is the symbol of the clan you come from. As you can see, on mine is a star and on the other is a crescent moon. I thought you were taken from your mother as a baby; how come she has this photo of you as a child?"

"It's not me; it's my mother, we apparently looked very much alike. Are you positive this pendant my mother had hidden is Romany?"

"Yes, each child receives one at a young age and their name is inscribed on the back. Wait a minute; wasn't your mother's name, Esmeralda?"

"Yes, are you saying my mother was Romany, how can that be; she was fair like me, look at the photo; have you ever seen Romany so fair?"

"No, but then how do you explain the pendant, do you know anything about your grandparents, your mother's family? The woman in the photo; the way she is dressed, her skin, she is definitely Romany."

"I thought so too and strangely I have never asked my father about my mother's family. I think I was so wrapped up in finding my parents it hadn't even occurred to me to ask about grandparents or uncles and aunts. It still doesn't explain why my mother felt the need to hide these things; who was she hiding them from?"

"Perhaps she was hiding them from your father."

"Why would she feel the need to, it doesn't make sense?"

"Everyone knows how your father feels towards the Romanies; he would not have been pleased to know she had such things."

"His dislike for them is only because I was kidnapped and he blames them for her death. This hidden compartment would have been there long before, because she died not long after I was taken."

"Maybe there was someone else she was hiding it from, but one thing I can assure you, that pendant with your mother's name inscribed on the back is definitely Romany."

Natalia looked at Fonso stunned *what does this mean?*

"Natalia, what happened to you that night? I know you were kidnapped, but I feel there is something else, something that caused you to call off your engagement and you do not even seem to care Jasper is back?"

"I would rather not talk about it, as for Jasper, yes I know I have neglected him, but that will soon change. Now I think we should go back before we are missed."

"You're right; we should be getting back."

They made their way back and both Natalia and Fonso were relieved there was no one else about. She quickly helped him unsaddle the horses before making her way back to the house, wondering who could help her solve the mystery of the photo and the pendant.

She was deep in thought when the front door opened and

she nearly jumped out of her skin when Frederick spoke.

"Where have you been and what caused you to go out alone at such an early hour? Mary has been worried sick and has been searching the whole house."

"I'm sorry Frederick, I just had to get outside for a while and I couldn't wait till everyone was awake. Tell me, how long have you worked here?"

"Since I was not much older than you. Why do you ask?"

"So you would have been working here when my father and mother first met?"

"Yes," he said hesitantly.

"Obviously my father was much older than my mother; how did they come to meet?"

"I don't think this is a topic you should be discussing with me; perhaps you should ask your father."

Natalia could see she was making Frederick uncomfortable and wondered why; *it was an innocent enough question, was it not?* She liked Frederick and did not want to make him feel uncomfortable, she decided to ask someone else, *someone who liked to gossip.*

"Oh miss I have been so worried about you; worried you had been kidnapped again."

"Sorry Mary, I didn't think; I just needed to get outside for a while. Tell me, where does your mother work now, where did she go after my mother died?"

"Why do you ask?"

Natalia noticed she seemed nervous and was frantically twisting her apron in her hands.

"I was wondering if I could ask her some questions about my mother."

"What sort of questions, surely someone here could tell you?"

"I thought she would be the best person to speak to; after all she was my mother's chambermaid and as you know, privy to things others are not."

"Um, what sort of things?"

Natalia noticed Mary was getting more nervous and wondered why.

"I was wondering how my parents met as there is such a great age difference. What attracted my mother to such an older man?"

"Maybe you should speak to your father."

"I was hoping to hear it from my mother's point of view and the only one who could tell me that would be your mother."

"Well, you see, my mother is also dead."

"Oh, I am terribly sorry. When did this happen?"

"Ah, not long before you came here. Look, I would rather not talk about it if you don't mind, I must go; they are short staffed in the kitchen."

"Yes of course, I am sorry if I have upset you."

"'Tis alright miss," she said with a quick bob.

Natalia continued up to her room, thinking that was the strangest conversation she had ever had with Mary. *I wonder why she had never mentioned before her mother was dead?* She went back down the stairs and asked Frederick if he would inform her father she would like to speak with him, after he has risen and had breakfast.

Natalia was sitting in the window seat, holding the photo of her mother in one hand and the silver pendant in the other, willing them to speak to her. Suddenly there was a knock at the door, quickly tucking the pendant and photo inside her blouse before Mary walked in.

"Your father is waiting to see you in his library," she said with a bob.

Natalia noticed Mary was avoiding direct eye contact and this puzzled her.

"Thank you Mary, I shall be right down."

Making her way down the stairs, she went over in her mind the questions she would like answers to. After giving a firm knock to the library door, she waited for permission to enter.

He was obviously curious about her requested meeting as he spoke before she even had a chance to take a seat.

"Does this visit mean you have finally come to your senses?"

"After you gave me my mother's jewellery box it got me thinking. There is very little I know about her and I was hoping you could tell me."

"What do you need to know? She looked the image of you; she was well liked by the staff and sadly she took her own life."

"How did you two meet?"

"What a strange question to ask, we met as most couples do: at some gathering or other."

"I don't want to offend you, but you were obviously much older than her; what was the attraction?"

"Well I can't answer for your mother, as she is not here, but as for myself she was a very beautiful woman."

"What did you have in common?"

"Natalia what is this all about?"

"I know little about my mother; I never got to meet her, surely it is not so unusual for a child to want to know everything about their mother? For instance, did she have any brothers or sisters? Do I have aunts and uncles out there whom I am yet to meet?"

"No, she was an only child."

"Then what about my grandparents, her parents, are they still alive?"

"No."

"When did they die?"

"Natalia all these questions; I really don't see the point to them. I am sorry to say I am your only living relative. Does this have something to do with your marriage to Lawrence?"

"No, as I told you before we are not getting married; it wouldn't be fair."

"What nonsense! You know he loves you and as I said before: you will grow to love him with time. I really don't want to get into an argument with you over this. I was going to leave it till the end of the week to tell you, but I have rescheduled announcing your engagement; it will be at the end of the following week. Both Lawrence and I agreed there is no point in a long engagement."

"Are you serious?"

"I have never been more serious in my life. I know what happened to you was rather unpleasant, but it is time to move on; you have spent enough time sulking in your room – life goes on."

Natalia looked at him shocked. *Unpleasant! How could he be so cold?*

"If it makes you feel any better, they managed to catch this Vanessa woman and she is now behind bars."

She was pleased Vanessa was where she belonged, *but how long ago did this happen?*

"It has also been brought to my attention you have been spending time with that gypsy boy. As of now, it must cease and if you disobey me on this matter I will be given no other choice, than to put him back behind bars."

"You can't be serious; surely you would not do such a thing."

"I am and I will. Now if you don't mind, I have some important matters to tend to."

She knew she had been dismissed, but also realised he never had any intention of releasing the gypsies; her marriage to Lawrence would have been for nothing. *I must warn Fonso!*

Natalia stormed angrily up the stairs slamming closed the door to her room and then proceeded to pace back and forth. *What was she to do?* The more she thought about it, the more she realised there was no point in her staying here. *This place was not a home; there was no laughter or love.* Suddenly there was a knock at the door and Mary walked in;

she was holding a small box.

"Pardon me miss, but your moonstone pendant is now repaired."

"Thank you Mary and could you please organise a tray to be sent up to my room; I don't feel up to company at the moment."

Mary bobbed all the time keeping her eyes averted, before leaving the room. *What is going on?* She opened the little box and looked at the moonstone pendant and remembered Luludja's words; *it will keep you safe.* She gently lifted it out of the box and remembered her father's warning; *if anyone needed this pendant now, it was Fonso.* She had to find a way to warn him.

As she paced the room she suddenly noticed a piece of white paper sticking out under the door. She walked over and picked it up, it was an envelope someone had slipped under her door. She quickly opened the door and looked out, but the hallway was empty, she quickly ran down the length of the hall hoping she could catch them, but there was no sign of anyone. Puzzled by who could have left it and how long it had been there, she locked the door behind her, then opened the envelope and pulled out a single sheet of paper. It read:

> *I know what your father is planning to do to your friend the gypsy. If you care for him, like I think you do; ride out at first light to the place only the two of you go, make sure you are alone, or your friend dies!*

A cold fear came over Natalia. *Who would put such a letter under her door, was Fonso really in danger?* She realised she had no other choice but to go; she couldn't risk something happening to him, not knowing who she could trust anymore; she had to do as the letter stated, she could not risk Fonso's life.

***

It was an exceptionally cold morning, her hands were so cold and stiff it took longer than usual for her to saddle up Jasper. Her next big worry was to get Jasper as far away from the stables as possible before he started snorting, which he always did in the cold air.

On her ride there, it suddenly dawned on her about what was written in the letter, telling her to go to the place only she and Fonso knew. *How did they know of this place, had she been followed?* Then, she remembered what her father had said about her spending time with Fonso; *was he behind this letter somehow?*

As she neared the spot they used to visit, she realised it could not have been her father, that would make no sense at all.

The place was eerily quiet and there was a heavy mist about. Twisting in her saddle as she pulled Jasper to a halt, she looked for any sign of anyone else here, but the only sound was the quietly running stream, even the birds didn't appear to be awake yet.

"Hello, anyone here? I have come alone."

There was no response and Jasper started to get jittery. *Maybe this was just someone's idea of a sick joke, but then what if it was not?*

She climbed down off Jasper and cautiously looked around, but as she walked away from Jasper he became agitated, snorting and shaking his head. Natalia looked back and could barely see him, as the mist seemed to be getting thicker and it was slowly enveloping him.

Suddenly the hairs on the back of her neck prickled and she quickly turned around. Standing a short distance from away she saw someone wearing a long black, hooded cloak. The hood of the cloak was pulled so far forward she could not see their face, or tell it they were male or female.

"Who are you and what do you know about my father's plans for Fonso?"

"I knew that would get you here."

The voice was female and for an awful moment Natalia thought it was Vanessa; but she did not recognise this voice.

"If you had no intention of helping Fonso, what was your reason for luring me here?"

"To finish what others were too stupid to do?"

"What are you talking about, why don't you show me your face?"

"You spoilt everything. These past years wasted, everything would have been mine, then you came along and everything changed!"

Suddenly the woman's hands come out from beneath her cloak and Natalia could see she was holding a gun. Everything happened so fast, she didn't have time to move; suddenly she felt pain and felt herself falling to the ground.

Her whole body ached and she was unable to move, as she lay there wondering if she was dying, she could hear a terrible noise.

Suddenly there was the sound of pounding horse's hooves, then voices.

"Natalia; my God, she's been shot!"

She looked up into the eyes of Fonso and the relief at seeing him brought tears to her face. She wanted to leave this place and never come back; she didn't care where they went as long as they were far from here.

Suddenly there was another face, one she did not recognise.

"It's all right miss I know there is a lot of blood, but it is only a flesh wound, it must have deflected off you, but the horse was the one who took the full force of the bullet."

Natalia struggled to get up and saw the blood pouring down Jasper's neck and realised what the terrible noise had been: he was screaming in pain. She pushed the others out of her way and half crawled over to him, kneeling beside him, wanting to take away his pain.

"Oh Jasper I'm so sorry, you knew didn't you? You

saved my life. Please somebody do something; can't you see he is in pain?"

"You might want to look away miss; it is the kindest thing to do."

As she turned around, she was horrified to see he had a pistol in his hand.

"No! I won't let you; if I had been the one who took the bullet would you put a gun to my head, because it is the kindest thing to do? Don't you understand he saved my life? He pushed me out of the way."

Natalia was keeping close to Jasper. It was now her turn to protect him. She looked at all the others and realised there was a policeman and wondered how he happened to be here so fast. Then she noticed a figure lying on the ground. The hood had been flung back revealing her face and there was a dark horseshoe-shaped mark to the side of her head; it was Miriam and Natalia was certain she was dead.

"Miss I can't promise you anything, but I will do the best I can," said the head groom.

Natalia noticed he had a bag in his hand and watched as he gave Jasper something for the pain.

"It is a mild sedative; just enough to ease the pain so we can get him back to the stables. I will then give him something stronger and tend to his injuries where he will be more comfortable."

Natalia nodded in acknowledgement and reassured Jasper that he would be fine.

A cart soon arrived and Miriam was wrapped in a blanket and taken away.

"Miss I must ask you a few questions. Do you think you could answer them now?" asked the policeman.

"I'll try."

"What made you come out here at such an early hour and on your own?"

Natalia looked across at Fonso, before pulling the letter from her pocket.

She watched as the policeman read the letter and wondered how this was going to affect her father, although at this point, she didn't really care.

"Why are you at Holmesby Manor and how did you know where I would be?"

"We uncovered the identity of your kidnapper, he was Miriam's brother. We were concerned she was also involved in the kidnapping and came to question her. It was soon discovered neither of you were in the house. Your maid realised your riding things were missing and your friend here led us to where he was sure you would be."

Natalia looked across at Fonso and smiled her thanks at him; despite him assisting in her rescue, she knew it did not change things; he was no longer safe here. The fact Miriam knew her father wanted to be rid of him was enough in itself. She had to find a way of speaking to him alone, she had to convince him to leave, go back to the safety of Besnik and Luludja.

\*\*\*

It was two days later and Natalia still had not been able to speak to Fonso. She was pacing her room pondering over the very thing, when she heard a knock at her door. She expected it to be Mary bringing up her usual tray of food, as she no longer ate in the large dining room – she had barely left her room. She was greatly surprised when it was her father and wondered what on earth would cause him to go against protocol once again.

"Natalia after your incident with Miriam, it made me realise more than ever your life is in danger whilst living here with me. I think the only safe solution would be for us to fast track your marriage, you would be much safer in the earl's hands."

"Father if my life is in danger, I will be no safer living with the earl and as I have told you on countless occasions: I do not wish to marry him. I only agreed in the first place so you would free the gypsies, but I now realise you had no intention of keeping your end of the bargain. I am also informing you of my intention to leave and no, I will not be going back to the gypsies; I feel they have suffered enough from my family and do not wish to cause them further hardship. I don't know where I will go or what I will do, but one thing I do know: I can no longer stay here."

"If you think you can just walk out that door and not look back, you are surely mistaken, regardless whether you agree or not, you will marry the earl."

"You can drag me kicking and screaming, but there is one thing you have forgotten: you cannot force me to say 'I do' and over the past weeks I have come to know Lawrence; I am sure he would not be party to one who is forced to say 'yes'."

Her father glared at her, he went so red in the face she thought he would surely explode.

"Don't think you have heard the last of this, I always get my way and you will marry Lawrence and it will happen very soon!"

He then stormed out of the room leaving Natalia shaken and frightened, worried as to what he would do.

She paced the room trying to think of a way out of here. *Where would she go? I must speak to Fonso.*

A short time later Mary walked in with her tray of food and the smell of it made her feel ill.

"Mary take it away, I could not possibly eat a thing."

"At least try to manage some tea, I will pour you a cup."

"Thank you Mary, but I don't think I could even manage that."

"Please, it will help you relax. It is a special blend; it is supposed to give one a restful sleep."

"Something I haven't had in a long time. Well if you insist, but just a small cup."

Mary poured the drink and told Natalia to sit in her favourite window seat, try to relax and she will fold down her bed.

Natalia sipped at the hot brew, it was definitely different from any tea she had before. After a while she could actually feel herself beginning to relax. Suddenly she felt extremely tired and her cup slipped from her grasp and fell to the floor. As she bent down to pick it up, she felt dizzy and fell to the floor. She looked up at Mary, but she was having trouble trying to focus and when she tried to speak it came out in a slur. *What's wrong with me?*

Suddenly her father walked into the room and with him was a man she had never seen before. He came over to her and opened the bag he was carrying, he shone a light in her eyes, then put a stethoscope to her chest and she realised he must be a doctor. *Why was he here, she was not sick?*

"I think we should admit her straight away, the stress has been too much for her; she needs specialist care, I will organise her admittance as soon as possible."

It suddenly dawned on Natalia she had been drugged, as her father and the supposed doctor left the room she looked accusingly across at Mary and saw guilt written all over her face.

"I thought you were my friend," she said with a slur.

"I'm so sorry; he said it's for your own good," said Mary, crying.

Natalia struggled to stay alert. The room kept tilting and she knew it was only a matter of time before the drug took full effect. She struggled to lift the moonstone pendant over her head, knowing her father and the doctor would be back at any minute.

"Mary.... you...my...friend.... give......Fonso........ return..... Lul..ud..ja."

It was such an effort for Natalia to speak; she had no idea if Mary understood what she was trying to say. Tears came to her eyes as she struggled to lift the pendant over her head; finally she succeeded, but fell back on the floor and it flung from her hand. The drug was taking hold and she could no longer move or talk. She stared at the colours of the moonstone as it flickered in the candlelight; slowly the colours faded as she slipped into the darkness.

## CHAPTER FIFTEEN

The woman was dressed in a crisp white uniform, not a red hair out of place underneath her well-starched nurse's hat. She was possibly in her late forties and what some would call robust, but in a feminine way. Her name is Fran and she is a nurse at the Bethlem Hospital for the mentally insane.

Often wayward girls are bought to Bethlem Hospital; usually by their fathers and always from wealthy families; in hope that once some time was spent amongst the lunatics, they would be ready to behave and conduct themselves in a manner befitting a lady. If not, their only alternative was to remain in Bethlem Hospital.

Some girls were ready to behave in a matter of hours, but the more stubborn ones would require stronger measures, often left alone in a room with the most crazed patients. Of course, no real harm ever came to these girls, as a guard in the room always watched them. If there was any sign of the girl being hurt, the lunatic would be immediately restrained and the girl was removed and returned to her room.

Surprisingly her shoes made no sound as she walked up the long hallway, it was imperative she remain quiet, for where she was going at this early hour was forbidden.

She slowed as the door came into sight, taking a quick look over her shoulder before inserting the key in the lock. Within seconds she was inside and the door securely locked behind her. She scanned the room looking for its occupant, who as always was sitting in the chair facing the window, looking at the beautiful garden outside.

"Surely a week has not passed already?" asked the voice from the chair.

"Another young girl has been admitted."

"When did she arrive?"

"She has been here almost a week now, she is very beautiful."

"And you thought she would interest me?"

"She was brought here by an old friend of yours."

"Who would that be?"

"The Marques of Mansfield."

The nurse noticed the knuckles go white as they clenched the chair.

"You know he is no friend of mine!"

"I'm sorry. Do you remember Edwina?"

"Yes."

"It is the same with this one."

There was a long silence and the nurse wondered if she had been heard.

"Why are you telling me this?"

"I believe she is of great interest to you, she is the right age."

The nurse walked forward and faced the occupant of the chair, blocking any view of the garden outside. She pulled something out of her pocket and held it out."

"You must bring her to me at once."

"That could be difficult; she is closely guarded."

"Do whatever it takes, I will reward you."

"I will see what I can do."

The nurse bowed her head and quickly left the room.

Quickly locking the door, she walked briskly back to the office and returned the key back to its rightful place before it could be missed.

Natalia was terrified. She was in a room with another girl who was half-crazy; she was not sure if that was the reason she was here, or if her father had left her here and the place had eventually sent her mad. She couldn't believe her father had resorted to such measures, just to ensure she married the earl. She was too scared to sleep at night, as when darkness descended the screams would echo down the halls and each night she would be restrained with heavy leather straps around her wrists and ankles, which were then securely chained to the sides of the bed. The only reassurance she got from this was the girl in the bed beside her was restrained also. She stared up at the ceiling, watching the shadows form as the light began to fade, increasing her fear as her imagination took hold.

"You know sometimes at night they come for you; they do things to you. When you come back, if you come back at all, you are never the same," said the girl beside her.

"Who comes for you?"

"No one knows, as those who have been taken and return are too frightened to tell."

"You're just making this up to scare me."

"No I'm not. You've heard the wailing and screaming at night have you not?"

"I have."

"It is said they are the ones who've been taken. I never sleep at night; I have heard they only take those who sleep."

Natalia was sure the girl was just trying to scare her further, but then she had heard strange noises and the screaming, it was so frightening. She decided she would stay awake and only sleep in the day and watched the shadows grow longer, until they slowly disappeared and there was nothing but darkness, as all lights had been extinguished and night had fully descended.

\*\*\*

Natalia's heart was beating rapidly and she could hardly breathe, she was overcome with panic as a hand was placed over her mouth. She tried to pull it away, but her hands were restrained and there was a heavy weight on her. Really frightened she struggled and tried to bite at the hand, but it was quickly removed and a cloth was forced into her mouth. She felt one ankle freed and tried to kick out, but a large strong hand held it firmly on the bed whilst the other ankle was freed and they both were secured together with a wide leather strap. Her wrists were then freed one at a time and clipped to the heavy belt around her waist. Thankfully the heavy weight lifted from her, but to her horror she felt herself being lifted from the bed and placed on a hard, cold metal surface and further straps secured her there.

"I told you not to sleep; they don't take those who are awake," came a loud whisper.

Natalia tried to struggle, but could not move and realised the cold surface was some sort of trolley, as she could feel herself being wheeled from the room. Her heart was pounding so hard she could hear nothing else and tried desperately to scream, but the coarse cloth was forced further into her mouth causing her to choke.

As she was wheeled down the long hallway, tears slowly rolled down her face; images of brightly coloured wagons and a life much simpler came flashing to her mind. Then her tears flowed more freely as she thought of Besnik. This time there would be no rescue, no knight in shining armour – she was truly alone.

She could feel the trolley slowing, before hearing the sound of a key turning in a lock, then the trolley commenced moving forward and she heard the sound of the door closing behind. *Where have they taken me, what are they going to do to me?* Natalia screwed her eyes tightly shut, she was sobbing so hard she started choking on the gag.

"Can't you see the girl is choking? I didn't have her brought here only to die in my room."

The voice caused Natalia's eyes to instantly open, but a light had been turned on and it shone in her face. She could feel the gag slowly being removed and prepared herself to scream, but suddenly a face loomed over her blocking out the bright light; instantly silencing her scream. As she looked into the eyes above her she wondered if she was already dead.

"I am sorry you had to be bought here in such a manner, but there was no other way."

Natalia's restraints were quickly removed, but she lay there unmoving, *is this real, have I been drugged?*

"I can see my face is a great shock to you, but I must admit you were the last person I expected to see here. I waited for this day for so long, I had almost giving up on ever seeing you again. Hello my beautiful Natalia, my name is Esmeralda and I am your mother."

"I don't understand; father told me you were dead, I visited your grave."

"That is what he wishes everyone to believe. It was under his instructions I was placed here. Fran is the only one apart from the doctor of course, who knows my true identity. Everyone believes I am the most crazed madman of Bethlem Hospital. It serves its purpose I suppose, because I am virtually left alone here."

"Why would father do such a thing, how long have you been here?"

"Not long after you were taken."

"That was years ago. What was his reason?" asked Natalia incredulously.

"He believed I was behind your disappearance."

"Surely he did not blame you for kidnapping your own child?"

"Once we were married, he forbade me to see my parents. He found out I was secretly seeing them. Then when you were taken, he believed it was my doing; he believed I had plans to leave him and safely removed you first. He thought after a time locked up here I would confess to your whereabouts, but of course I had no idea."

"Why did he forbid you from seeing your own parents?"

"He was ashamed of my mother."

"Why?"

"You must tell her," said Fran.

Esmeralda looked from Fran to Natalia, then lifted a

silver chain from around her neck and showed it to Natalia.

"You had this in your possession when you arrived here; where did you get it?"

"I found it in a secret compartment of your jewellery box, along with a photo. Fonso said it is a sign of the Romany."

"Fonso is correct; I am Romany, what is known as a gypsy."

"I don't understand; how can you be Romany, your skin is so fair?"

"My father, your grandfather, was a Gorgio and my parents were much in love. There was no curse between the two; it is a foolish belief. What happened between your father and me was his own doing."

"Obviously father did not know of your true heritage, else he would not have pursued you in the first place."

"He knew; he wanted what he couldn't have. He had no intention of making me his bride; he forced himself upon me."

"You mean he raped you; I am a bas–"

"Don't say such a thing; you were born in wedlock. When your father realised I was carrying his child he made sure we were wed."

"Why would he do that, if he despises Romanies so much? And what about your parents; surely they did not agree to such a marriage?"

"He was desperate for an heir. As you know there is a great age gap between us and as for my parents, I did not tell them what happened; I tried to keep it a secret until I could hide it no longer. Because I was with child no one would marry me and your father knew this. He came to see them. He professed his undying love, which of course was a lie. They believed him and thought it was the right thing to do. Once their minds were made up I had no choice."

Natalia looked at her mother; the sadness in her eyes and the hardship she had gone through. She was still coming to grips with the knowledge she was alive and there was no mistaking she was her mother; it was like looking at herself in years to come.

"Tell me child, why did your father have you brought here?"

"I would not marry the man of his choosing, Lawrence; the Earl of Sherwood."

"Is he the father of your child?"

Natalia looked at her in shock; she had her suspicions, but was not sure.

"There's no need to be frightened, Fran is a nurse; after all she has seen the signs. Did he force himself on you?"

"No, he is not the father."

"The father of your child, do you love him?"

"Yes."

"Does your father know of this man, have you told him the two of you wish to marry?"

"Father does not even know of him, he would never approve."

"You are standing your ground about not marrying the earl; why not do the same and marry the one you love?"

"He is Romany and I am a Gorgio."

Esmeralda looked at her daughter in shock.

"For years they have been banished to the deep woods; how did you come to meet him, let alone fall in love with him?"

"It is a long story, but basically a young boy called Fonso found me badly injured on the outskirts of the forest and risked his life to take me back to Luludja. She has great healing powers; this is where I met Besnik, the one I love."

"Does he know you are carrying his child?"

"No, he has very strong Romany beliefs and a marriage between himself and a Gorgio could not be. What happened between us was not planned, but I will never regret it."

"How do you now feel, to find out you have Romany blood running through your veins?"

"Both shocked and sad I suppose."

"We must find a way to get word to him, but more importantly we must not let your father or the hospital staff know of your condition. The life of your child and possibly yourself are in danger otherwise."

Natalia put a protective hand over her stomach and looked at them in disbelief.

"Your mother is right; it has been done many times before."

"We have to find a way to get you out of here, as soon as possible."

"Mother why is it so important to my father for me to marry Lawrence?"

"Power and greed; a marriage between the two of you would make him more powerful than he already is. He may be older, but he is devious. However to carry out his plan he requires a blood tie with the earl and only you can grant him that."

Natalia sat there in shock. Everything her father had told her had been a lie: the loving marriage and the marble statue he had built, it was only a reminder to himself of his power and what he was capable of.

Suddenly there was knocking at the door.

"We must go; we have stayed longer than we should," said Fran.

"Do not be concerned about the knocking. I believe it is your father's doing, as it is done regularly each night. I'm sure he is disappointed I have not ended my life by now, but yes you are right; we cannot risk you being away from your room too long."

Mother and daughter hugged each other tightly before Natalia climbed back on the trolley. Fran re-fastened the restraints lest anyone see them.

"When can I see you again?" asked Natalia.

"I don't know my child, but know this: I love you and I want you to take good care of my grandchild."

"I love you too, but you speak as though we will never see each other again." Natalia sobbed.

Esmeralda blew her daughter a kiss before turning her back, not wishing her daughter to see the tears in her eyes.

Once they had both left the room, Esmeralda broke down and cried, she cried for all the lost years and for the real possibility she would never live to see her grandchild.

Fran wheeled Natalia back to her room and strapped her back in her bed, neither saying a word.

*\*\*\**

As soon as Fran left the room, the girl in the other bed called out to Natalia, wanting to know if she had gone mad and could she describe the demons she had seen.

Natalia ignored her, she was in a state of shock, from the realisation her mother was alive and the type of man her father really was. Suddenly she felt a flutter and wished she could put her hand to her stomach, a slow tear slid down her cheek, as it was now a reality of a life growing inside her – a creation of her and Besnik. *How could they possibly get word to him and what would his reaction be if they succeeded? Would he come for her, or would it only be for the sake of his child, or would he not come at all?*

Fran put her cap in her locker and put her cape around her shoulders before walking outside the building. She had a half-hour break before having to resume work. She walked briskly glancing over her shoulder, ensuring she was not seen or followed; two lives, possibly three depended on it.

She crossed the road and turned up a side street, continuing until she came to another side street on her left. She paused and quickly looked over her shoulder and then turned up the narrow street where she knew she could find a street urchin. Spotting one at the end of the street, leaning up against a light post and smoking.

"You know you are far too young to be doing such a thing, you will regret it one day."

"Who asked ya?"

"Would you like to earn a nice shiny shilling?"

"Do I look daft; course I would, but depends on what I 'ave ta do?"

"Deliver a letter to a place called Holmesby Manor and it must be there within the hour and delivered to a man who goes by the name of Frederick. I will pay you half now and the other half when you return with a written response, but remember it must only go in the hands of Frederick! I will be waiting for your return at Bethlem Hospital."

"I'm not going near any nut house."

"Suite yourself; I am sure I can find one of your friends who will be willing to do it for less."

"Wait! Let's not be hasty. How bout ya throw in another shilling; aft all, Holmesby Manor's real fancy place and won't be easy ta get into."

"Very well, but remember, within the hour, else the agreement is off. Tell him it's from Fran; someone he once knew."

The boy ran off and Fran waited a few moments before making her way back to the hospital.

## CHAPTER SIXTEEN

Frederick was standing at the base of the grand staircase. He had all the staff gathered, as His Lordship had informed him Natalia would be arriving back home at the end of the week. He was ensuring everything was prepared for her expected arrival.

It wasn't enough she was kidnapped for the second time in her life, then Miriam trying to kill her. It had taken its toll; her doctor had ordered complete rest, but far away from Holmesby Manor and all the unpleasantness.

Her father informed him her time away had done her good and she was anxious to return; she missed the earl desperately and wanted to make official their engagement.

Suddenly something caught his eye outside the window, he quickly dismissed the staff and made his way outside. He stood for a moment and looked around, nothing seemed a miss.

*Perhaps he was seeing things?* He started to make his way back inside, when he saw a scruffy young street urchin. *He probably thought the Manor was easy pickings, well I'll show him.* Frederick headed towards the bushes, ready to give chase, but was surprised that instead of running he actually walked towards him.

"Ya Frederick the butler?"

Frederick was surprised. *How did this character know his name?*

"Well are ya or not?"

"Yes, how did you manage to get past the front gates?"

"Never ya mind. I ave a very important letter ta give ya, 'tis a matter of life an deaf."

The boy knew no such thing; it just gave him a sense of importance.

"Well, hand it over boy."

"Not before ya give me my shilling, I was told I'd get a

shilling."

"Before I hand over any money you must tell me who this letter is from."

"A nurse; says she works at Bethlem Hospital; says her name is Fran and ya know her."

Frederick was thrown for a moment, the only woman he knew by that name he had professed his love to, but she disappeared not long after the mistress died, *could it be her?* He quickly dug into his pocket and handed over a bright shiny shilling. The young lad was thrilled; he didn't think the old guy would fall for it and happily handed over the letter. With shaky hands Frederick carefully opened it.

> *Dearest Frederick,*
> *I do not know if you remember me, but I used to be Mistress Esmeralda's chambermaid. I now work as a nurse at Bethlem Hospital and I am asking for your assistance. I am sorry to bother you after all these years, but I have no one else to turn to. I cannot explain the details in this letter, for fear of it falling into the wrong hands. I am hoping, after all these years you have forgiven me, or at least, are prepared to listen. Please let me know by return letter if you will meet with me, as it is a matter of utmost urgency, lives are at stake!*
>
> *Yours forever*
> *Fran*

Frederick started to walk quickly in the direction of the stables. The young street urchin ran after him.

"Mister ya 'ave ta give a response, else she won't pay me."

"How much was she going to pay you and where were you to deliver this letter?"

"She said if I don't come back within the hour she won't pay me another shilling. I was ta deliver it ta the nut house, but if I don't go soon I won't make it."

Frederick stopped for a moment, he was sure he was being conned, but then he knew Fran; she would not ask for his help after all these years if it wasn't important. He fumbled in his pocket and dug out another shilling. He didn't normally carry around so much money, but he had planned to go to town later in the day and make a deposit at the bank.

"I think that should cover services rendered, but if there is any mention of this letter or your meeting with the nurse to anyone, I will go directly to the local police station and report a theft at Holmesby Manor. I will also be able to give a good description of the supposed suspect and I am sure they will know who I am talking about."

"Don't worry 'bout me, mister, ma lips are sealed. T'was a pleasure doin business with ya."

The boy quickly pocketed the coin and was gone in a flash. Frederick ran to the stables and organised a buggy, with not a moment to waste.

\*\*\*

Fran had been keeping an eye on the clock, she'd been hoping the lure of another shilling would ensure the boy delivered the letter, but as time went on she began to worry. Perhaps Frederick had not forgiven her for leaving so suddenly. She had pondered greatly about asking him for assistance, but she had no choice; there was no one else to turn to – she had no friends; her life was her work.

It was now past the hour and she could no longer wait inside, she had to get out of here, as the walls seemed to be closing in. She made her way to the entrance hoping maybe the boy was waiting outside; *perhaps he was too scared to enter the building.*

She stood on the top step and scanned the area for any

sign of him; there were very few people about and no sign of a scruffy street urchin.

Suddenly she noticed a small buggy travelling at a dangerous speed. *Lunatic*! *He was surely going to run someone over and why on earth would anyone be in such a haste to come to this place?*

The driver reined in his horses, causing nearby people and pigeons to scatter in all directions. She made her way down the steps. She would give him a stern warning about such irresponsible behaviour. The man looked up as he alighted from the buggy, all other thoughts gone from her head. *Frederick!*

Frederick quickly tied the reins, before bounding up the stairs, at first not seeing Fran. Suddenly he saw her face, stopping him instantly in his tracks.

"You are still as beautiful as ever," said Frederick.

"Why did you come?"

"You asked me to."

"I was hoping for a letter; never did I expect you to come in person."

"It sounded urgent."

"It is, I think the best way to explain, is for you to see for yourself."

"I don't understand."

"Just follow me, but please don't say anything."

Frederick nodded and followed her inside the building, pausing whilst she went into the office and returned moments later.

They walked in silence up the long hallway; he could not help but notice the sounds of cries and screams emitting from within. Finally they came to a halt in front of a door and he noticed her nervously look over her shoulder, before inserting a key in the lock. He waited with trepidation as she open the door. She almost pushed him inside before quickly re-locking the door behind them.

*Where the hell were they and what was in this room?* He

suddenly took in his surroundings and the room surprised him, it was not what he expected, certainly not in a mental asylum! It was almost homely, there was a handmade quilt across the bed and pretty cushions; there was no doubt this room was occupied by a woman – there were feminine touches everywhere. Suddenly his eyes were drawn to the chair; it was positioned in front of a window. The woman must be small, as he could not see the top of her head, but could see she had very long hair, it was braided and hung over the side of the chair, all the way down to the floor.

"I have brought you a visitor, I am hoping he can help."

"Can we trust him?"

"I will let you be the judge of that."

Esmeralda rose nervously from her chair; the shock on Frederick's face was evident and Esmeralda wondered if he was going to faint.

"Hello Frederick; it has been a long time."

"It can't be; I carried your coffin; I watched the old man crumble with grief."

"It is me; I am real. It wasn't grief; it was only for your benefit, as it was he who put me here."

Frederick knew he was staring; but he could not believe it; *surely the old man would not do such a despicable thing?*

"It's true; I have been here with her all these years," said Fran.

"I don't understand, why?"

"Control: power and greed. He blamed me for Natalia's disappearance; he believes I orchestrated her kidnapping, he also believed I was going to leave him. He thought by locking me up here I would reveal her whereabouts, but trust me I wanted to find her as much as he."

"But she has now returned; surely you can now be free?"

"How would he explain my sudden resurrection after all these years; after he made everyone believe I was dead?"

Frederick began to pace the room, he knew the old man

was difficult, *but to do such a thing and to deceived them all. What about the doctor, he declared her dead?*

"I can see you have many questions, but I'm afraid we have little time. Natalia's life depends on it."

"She is fine; she has been through a terrible ordeal, but is recuperating, she will be returning by the end of the week," replied Frederick.

"Natalia is here," stated Esmeralda.

"What is this craziness?"

"It was her father's doing, he has put her here in the hope she will behave, for she has refused to marry the earl. If he says she will be home by the end of the week we don't have much time."

"My God, I can't believe he has done all this; but then I see you standing before me."

"There is only one way we can get her out of here and that is for me to take her place. I have seen her with my own eyes; she is the image of me. From a distance I can pass for her; we will have only one chance, but it will require your help. Firstly I need you to find a man by the name of Besnik; he is a gypsy and he is the father of her child."

"Dear mother of God; does her father know?"

"Of course not, why do you think it is so imperative we sneak her out of here? It is only a matter of time before he finds out; I am sure I do not have to tell you what he will do when he does!"

"I will help in any way I can. As for the gypsy fellow, we have one of them working at the stables; he was the one who helped Natalia find her father, I will ask him to find this Besnik."

It was decided: Fran would take Natalia on another of her visits; but she will not return to her room; Esmeralda would go in her place. Frederick would do his best to delay His Lordship from visiting the hospital, at least until they could locate Besnik and hopefully have Natalia safely out of this place.

When Fran and Frederick left Esmeralda's room he asked why she left all those years ago; why did she not tell him what his Lordship had done.

"It is my fault she is here."

"How is that so?"

"I am ashamed to admit it, but it was the lure of money and a better life; something I will pay for the rest of my life."

"What could you have possibly done?"

"His Lordship wanted me to spy on Esmeralda and report back to him. He promised to reward me. I had no idea the sort of man he was, I never thought he was capable of such a despicable thing."

"Why on earth would he want you to spy on her, did he suspect her of seeing another man?"

"No, he was concerned she was secretly visiting her family."

"Good heavens; why would that bother him?"

"Esmeralda's mother is Romany, or what is most commonly known as a gypsy. He was ashamed of the blood tie and was afraid of anyone finding out; he feared it would ruin his plans for Natalia's future."

"My God I had no idea, how did he fake her death?"

"With the aid of the doctor he drugged Esmeralda and left an empty bottle beside her bed with a note. I was the one who found her, I thought she was dead, I hated myself for what I had done; I blamed myself for her death. I could no longer work at Holmesby Manor, not under the same roof as that man. As for you, I was too ashamed to tell you what I had done."

"If only you had told me this years ago; I would have helped you, I was in love with you."

"I was afraid to see the look in your eyes, when I told you what I had done. The only place I could find employment was Bethlem Hospital. It was by mere accident I discovered Esmeralda was here; a secret known only between myself and Esmeralda."

"Surely you could have come to me then."

"Esmeralda swore me to secrecy; she was frightened of what her husband would do. She did not want to jeopardise any chance of being reunited with her daughter."

"Fran as much as I have enjoyed seeing you again, I must get going before my presence is missed. I will speak to the young gypsy boy who resides at the manor; he has a close bond with Natalia and I am sure will help us find Besnik. I will keep in touch; I would like to see you again and not just to help Esmeralda and Natalia."

"You're right; I am wasting time, but I would also like to keep in touch."

She walked with him to the entrance steps and watched him leave, then slowly turned and walked back inside. *Maybe now it was her chance to finally right the wrong she had done so many years ago.*

On the ride back Frederick was remembering the day everyone believed Esmeralda had died, then he remembered the sight of Natalia's unconscious state as she was carried out to the waiting carriage. He remembered that terrible feeling of déjà vu and Mary; she could not stop crying. *Had history repeated itself, was Mary involved like Fran all those years ago*? He decided as soon as he got back he would speak to Mary and hopefully be able to find out what happened that day; but more importantly he must speak to Fonso.

As soon as he mentioned Natalia's name to Mary she burst into tears and was shocked when she admitted to putting something in Natalia's tea; something His Lordship had given her and demand she do. He had told her it was under the doctor's orders and was in the best interest of Natalia.

"Do you have any idea what you have done?"

"I'm so sorry. You have no idea how many times I wish I could turn back time; the look on her face, she considered me, a mere servant, her friend. But there is something I must tell you, when the police found the cabin, the one the kidnapper took her to, they also found her clothes. They were a mass of shreds, the horror she must have gone through, but in amongst it was her small tote bag and in it was a document."

"What was this document?"

Mary pulled an envelope from her pocket, she did not know why, but she could not bring herself to destroy it, nor to show it to Natalia's father. Frederick quickly opened it; he now knew why Natalia had been withdrawn as the ball drew near. It read:

> *Dearest Father,*
> *As per our agreement, I agree to marry the Earl of Sherwood in exchange, for the freedom of all Romany (gypsies) and that they are free to roam the land again, as did their ancestors. Upon my said wedding, this document is legal and binding and all persecution against them is to cease.*
>
> *Signed by,*
> *Natalia Holmesby*
>
> *Signed by,*

"It only has her signature on it, he had no intention of freeing them and I think Natalia realised this. I am sure that is why she called off the engagement. I heard her say it wasn't fair to Lawrence. The night the doctor took her away she asked me to give something to Fonso, but I didn't know if I should."

Mary lifted the pendant from around her neck and Frederick recognised it as the one Natalia always wore. He looked at Mary in disgust.

"Well Natalia is not all right and her life could now be in grave danger. Are you prepared to help her and right this terrible thing you have done?"

"Yes."

"You must promise to reveal this to no one."

"I promise."

"Then follow me; we don't have a lot of time."

Fonso looked up from what he was doing and was surprised and slightly worried to see Frederick and Natalia's maid almost running in his direction.

Frederick looked around making sure no one was about, before speaking to Fonso in hushed tones.

"It is imperative you leave at once and find your fellow gypsy who goes by the name of Besnik. Natalia's life depends upon it, you shall take the small buggy; it will be the quickest and safest form of transport and Mary shall accompany you."

Mary gasped in shock. *He had said nothing about her going to the gypsies*!

Fonso immediately thought it was a trap.

Frederick could see the doubt in the boy's eyes and gave Mary a nudge, prompting her to quickly remove the pendant from around her neck.

"She asked me to give this to you, she said you would understand."

Fonso took the pendant. He knew it was the one Luludja had given Natalia and realised she would not part with it without good reason.

Frederick then handed him the letter and wondered if the boy could read, as he quickly scanned the letter.

"Natalia wrote this, it is written from the heart; no other Gorgio would write such a thing."

"If you have any trouble convincing Besnik, show him this letter and tell him I have seen her mother – she is not dead; her father has in fact kept her a prisoner all of these years."

Mary gasped in shock and Fonso looked at Frederick in surprise.

"Where is she and how can we help her?"

"She is in Bethlem Hospital, it is a hospital for the mentally insane; the same place her father has kept her mother for almost eighteen years. Mary, we have no time to waste, quickly pack a few things and Fonso I shall write a short letter explaining the situation whilst you gather your things. You both must leave immediately; to avoid any suspicion you will go under the guise of Mary's servant."

Frederick explained to the head groom that Fonso would be taking the small buggy, as Mary had a very sick relative and had no time to waste; he need not be concerned about the boy leaving, as they had His Lordship's blessing and both would most likely be away for several days.

The groom thought this odd, but he knew Frederick was his Lordship's most trusted servant, so he need not question it further.

Within the hour both Mary and Fonso were on their way. Mary felt frightened about the journey they had embarked upon, but also felt a thread of excitement; she remembered how Natalia's face would light up when she spoke of the gypsies, the strange people of the deep forest. Fonso was deep in his own thoughts, this all only confirmed his beliefs that Natalia belonged with his people and not with her own kind. After everything that had happened since her arrival here, he suddenly felt a strong yearning for the safety of the deep woods and the sound of Luludja's calming voice. *If only he could have foreseen the danger for Natalia on her search to find her true family!*

## CHAPTER SEVENTEEN

Fonso and Mary were both exhausted; they had barely stopped to rest for fear of wasting precious time. Both hoped Frederick would be able stall the Marques, so that they could safely smuggle Natalia out.

On the journey Mary asked Fonso many questions about the gypsies and he happily answered them, but he also warned her how they felt towards the Gorgio and would not take kindly to him bringing another into their camp.

By the time they arrived both were bracing themselves for a hostile reception. As Fonso pulled the buggy to a halt, Mary's eyes darted in every direction, taking in the strange, colourful wagons, but also for anyone who may wish her harm.

It did not take long for a crowd to gather and Mary could not help but notice the tall muscular man walking towards them. It was obvious he was angry, but her heart quickened a beat with a mixture fear and admiration. Natalia had not said much to Mary about Besnik, only that he had incredible blue eyes. The nearer the tall, ruggedly handsome man came, Mary realised it was Besnik; for he definitely had the bluest eyes she had ever seen. She now understood the look she had seen on Natalia's face when she spoke of him.

"Fonso, what are you doing here with this Gorgio buggy; surely not another damsel in distress?"

"This is Mary, Natalia's chambermaid, I don't have a lot of time to explain; let's go inside Luludja's wagon."

Besnik gave Mary a cold hard stare, causing her body to prickle with fear. She noticed the muscle in the side of his jaw twitch and wondered if he was deciding her fate.

"Besnik please, we are wasting time, we may already be too late."

"What are you talking about?"

"I can't discuss it out here; we must go inside Luludja's wagon."

Once they were all squeezed inside Luludja's wagon, Besnik demanded to know what this was all about.

"Natalia's father has locked her up in the nuthouse to discipline her; the same thing he did to her mother and we thought she had been dead all these years," blurted Mary.

"Start from the beginning, what has happened to Natalia and her mother?" asked Luludja.

"Natalia's father tricked everyone into believing her mother had taken her own life when Natalia was a baby, but he had her locked up in the nuthouse, because he thought she was behind Natalia's disappearance. Then after Natalia was kidnapped from the ball, she wouldn't stop crying and locked herself in her room. Her father made me drug her tea, after which she was taken away to the same, awful place," said Mary.

"Why would a father do such a thing to his own child?" asked Luludja.

"He was very angry because she refused to marry the Earl of Sherwood. He had tried everything to change her mind, but she still refused. Bethlem Hospital is an awful place; he said he would leave her there until she agreed to the marriage, but I know she won't change her mind," said Mary despondently.

Besnik had been standing with his arms across his chest, unmoved by any of the conversation.

"This is terrible, but what makes you so sure she won't change her mind?" asked Luludja.

"She does not love him; she only agreed to marry him in the first place so you could be free, but she discovered she had been tricked!" exclaimed Mary.

"What are you talking about?" asked Besnik.

Mary handed him the document Natalia had written to her father. He quickly scanned it then handed it across to Luludja, who upon reading it began to cry.

"I never meant for her to give up her life for ours."

"Luludja, did you have something to do with this document?" Asked Besnik

"It was the condition on Fonso leading her to her family."

Everyone gasped at her response and it greatly saddened Fonso to think Luludja would do such a thing.

Luludja put her hands to her face in shame. *Once again I have put her life in danger!*

"Besnik, Frederick has written you a letter explaining everything and what he wishes us to do," said Mary, as she handed him the letter.

All eyes watched Besnik as he read the letter, noting the changing expressions on his face. Suddenly he turned and walked out onto the small porch and gripped the small railing and bent over as if in pain.

No one spoke; all wondered what the letter contained, as it had visibly upset Besnik.

"Besnik, what is it, what does the letter say?" asked Luludja.

He straightened then took a deep breath, before turning and coming back inside.

"Natalia is carrying my child," he said hoarsely.

All three stared at Besnik, shock evident on their faces.

"If her father finds out he will resort to whatever measures to ensure she does not have this child. Fortunately only her mother and a nurse are aware of her condition. Frederick has a plan, it could work, but I cannot bring her back here; it will be the first place her father will look."

Luludja got up from her seat and walked behind the curtain to her small room. They could hear her moving things about before reappearing carrying a long slender, timber box about twelve inches long.

"Your mother entrusted me with this on her deathbed, I have no idea what it contains, except that it holds something very powerful and I would know when the time has come for me to give it to you."

Besnik reverently took the box and slowly opened the lid. Inside was a scroll that had been bound by a piece of red ribbon, and when he lifted it out of the box, all eyes saw the box also contained a small red velvet bag. He place the scroll on the table before opening the velvet bag, inside was a ring, a man's ring which was made of solid gold with a square flat top, which had some sort of crest on it. Then he untied the ribbon and carefully rolled out the scroll, there was a letter inside:

> *Dearest Besnik,*
> *Many times I thought of telling you, but I did not want to hurt you or your father. Then as the years went by my secret slowly ate away at me, as you have a right to know. There is a man called the Duke of Aberdeen; he lives in Scotland. He is a man of great wealth and importance. He also knows of the box and what it contains. This man is your true father, a secret only he and I know. What we did was wrong and he has respected my wishes never to look for you; but he hopes one day you will seek him. His only request was I give you his ring, along with the enclosed document. I am sorry my son if I have hurt you.*
>
> *Signed,*
> *Shofranka*

The second page was his official birth certificate, stating he was indeed the son of the Duke of Aberdeen. He felt a mixture of anger and shock that his mother had been unfaithful to his father; the man he loved and had believed all these years was his father. He was glad his father went to his grave with no knowledge of this, for Besnik knew it would have destroyed him.

"Besnik, what does it say?"

He handed the two documents to Luludja before walking outside the wagon.

As Luludja read the letter and birth certificate, she wondered how Shofranka had managed to keep this a secret. *All these years with these documents, we could have been free long ago!*

"Besnik I know this is a great shock, but we must not forget Natalia, the reason we are all gathered here now," said Luludja

"How does this help the situation, I wish you had never given me that box?"

"Your father is obviously a man of integrity, as he agreed to abide by your mother's wishes and not cause heartache for her family, but more importantly he is a Duke, a man with much power, he will be able to protect you all!"

Besnik stood there unmoved and all wondered what thoughts were going through his mind.

"We will leave tomorrow at first light."

Without saying another word, Besnik turned on his heel and walked outside and headed towards the stream.

\*\*\*

Tears came to Fran's eyes as she cut Esmeralda's long hair in preparation for her impersonation of Natalia. It not only saddened her to be cutting away her beautiful locks, but what Esmeralda proposed to do for her daughter would put her life in great danger. *Could mother and daughter successfully switch places and could she safely get Esmeralda back to her room before Natalia's disappearance is discovered?*

Fortunately Frederick had managed to keep the Marques away, but Natalia had become ill and Fran was in a quandary as to what to do. If she sought the doctor's assistance, it would not be long before he discovered her condition, but if she did not receive medical help soon, she could be putting not only the life of the unborn child, but also Natalia's at risk. Fran did not voice her concerns to Esmeralda, she would be against alerting the doctor, but to inform her of Natalia's condition would only worry her further.

Esmeralda told Fran she wanted to see Besnik as soon as he arrived; she wanted to see the man her daughter had given her heart to, the man who is the father of her grandchild. She wanted to know what his feelings were towards her daughter and that he had her and his child's best interest at heart. Fran tried to dissuade her from this, as it was not only a great risk bringing someone to her room, but the fact he was a gypsy, just setting foot in the hospital was putting his life in danger.

Frederick's letter to Besnik had also contained an address, a place where they could find safe lodgings and once they arrived there, Mary would send a runner to deliver a letter to Frederick and inform them of their arrival.

By the time they arrived at the safe house they were exhausted. As tired as she was, Mary knew there was no time to waste; she must get word to Frederick. She scribbled a short note and paid a young boy handsomely to ensure the letter was delivered as soon as possible, before collapsing thankfully into bed. All three knew, once Frederick received Mary's note, things would move quickly.

Fran had also sent off a letter to Frederick, informing him of Esmeralda's wishes and he received both letters simultaneously. He was pleased Besnik, Fonso and Mary had made the trip without incident, but was dismayed at Esmeralda's request, he too was tired, but made the journey to Bethlem Hospital, he must see Fran and see if there was any way he could change Esmeralda's mind.

Esmeralda stood her ground, she said it was the least she

could do for her daughter and the fact she needed to reassure herself her daughter would be in safe hands. It was decided Fran would visit Besnik at the safe house the following morning to explain Esmeralda's request.

The moment Fran laid eyes on Besnik, she had grave doubts about not only him visiting Esmeralda, but Frederick's plan for him to pose as a laundry hand to smuggle Natalia out. Despite his skin tone, the sheer size of him indicated he was definitely not one who would blend into a crowd and she doubted she would find a laundry uniform big enough to fit him.

Once she got over her initial shock, she explained the reason she was here and was greatly surprised when he agreed to Esmeralda's request.

\*\*\*

It was late at night, a time when only minimal staff is required, as all patients were locked securely in their rooms and restrained to their beds. Fran silently wheeled Natalia to her mother's room, she would only have a few moments to say her goodbyes to her mother, much to the dismay of both, but time was something they didn't have a lot of.

The moment Esmeralda saw her daughter, she knew she was not well; anger and hate welled up inside of her, she hated him for the fact he had done this to his own flesh and blood, but also once again she would be denied a life with her daughter. She hugged Natalia so tight, she didn't want to let her go, she still remembered the last time she had tucked her in her crib, all those years ago. Trying her best to contain her tears, she assisted Fran in getting Natalia into the laundry trolley and then covered her with some sheets. The moment the door closed behind them and Esmeralda was once again alone in the room, she broke down and cried; for she feared she would never see her daughter again.

Besnik pulled the cart up to the service entrance as Frederick had instructed, he was pleased most of the lights had been extinguished and the place appeared to be deserted.

Fran had instructed the linen service to come an hour later than usual that night, hoping it would give them the time needed to safely smuggle Natalia out.

Besnik and Fonso were dressed as laundry staff and commenced throwing bags of dirty linen on the back of the cart, they had to ensure they looked the part, in case any of the hospital staff ventured out here, but also if they were seen travelling in the street, they didn't want to draw any undue attention to themselves.

Suddenly Besnik heard the side door open, hoping it would be Fran and not one of the hospital staff. Keeping his hat pulled low, he glanced from under the brim and was relieved to see her pushing a trolley. She quickly wheeled it over to the top of the ramp and motioned for Besnik to come over.

"Quickly, we don't have much time. I'm afraid her health has worsened; God be with you and may you all make it safely to your destination!"

Besnik nodded in acknowledgement and carefully lifted Natalia out of the trolley, ensuring she remained covered by the sheets, not knowing if they were being watched. He placed her close to the seat where he and Fonso would be sitting, then quickly taking his position in the driver's seat. Besnik gathered the reins before releasing the break and after a quick nod to Fran, the cart moved slowly outside and into the darkness. Luck was on their side; it was a dark moonless night and not a star insight. They made their way down the street to the safe house, were Frederick and Mary would be waiting with the fastest buggy Holmesby Manor had to offer.

***

The journey had been long and arduous and all were in constant fear of being caught, wondering if Natalia's disappearance had been discovered.

Besnik was relying heavily on Fonso to lead the way; they were venturing to a land where none of them had been before.

Despite Frederick ensuring they had enough food supplies to hopefully last their journey, Mary was unable to coax Natalia to eat, causing her health to deteriorate rapidly. Mary was overcome with a feeling of guilt, not only for the terrible part she had played in Natalia's incarceration, but also because of it, she might well lose her child. Mary made a promise to Natalia, if she survived this journey, she would forever be her loyal servant.

The sun was just cresting the horizon as the carriage came to the rise of a hill. Fonso put his hand on Besnik's arm, signalling him to stop. When the carriage came to a standstill, Fonso pointed to the horizon to the right of Besnik.

"Are you sure that is it?" Besnik asked.

"As positive as I'll ever be."

From their vantage point, they got a faint glimpse of the ocean; something neither of them had seen before. However it was what was in the forefront that had their attention; above a very steep and rocky headland was perched what could only be described as a castle. There appeared to be only one entrance, as the area was virtually surrounded by sheer cliffs that dropped over one hundred feet to a rocky ocean shore below. It was virtually an island with only a narrow strip of land joining it to the mainland and this was a steep path leading up to the massive gatehouse.

"Why have we stopped?" asked Mary as she leant out the window.

"We have found Besnik's home."

"My God, it's a castle. I have never been in a castle before." Mary gasped.

"I'm sure that includes everyone present, I just hope my father is receptive to a group of vagabonds arriving on his doorstep," replied Besnik.

Besnik gave a quick flick to the reins and proceeded forward towards the gatehouse, hoping they wouldn't be shot on the spot. The going was slow as the path was steeper than first thought and the tired horses were struggling with the load.

"Fonso take over the reins, we need to lighten the load; Mary and I shall walk."

Mary was none too happy about walking, but then as she looked at the jagged rocks below, she realised it was preferable to the horses slipping over the edge, taking the carriage with them.

Besnik used his strength behind the carriage, assisting the horses as they struggled up the steep slope. Finally they reached the gatehouse and all breathed a sigh of relief. Besnik looked around for the gatekeeper, but there appeared to be no one about. He noticed a large bell and realised it was there for the purpose of announcing their presence. He pulled hard on the long rope and the sound seemed to resound off the walls and cliffs below and its echo could be heard for a long time afterwards.

Soon they heard the sound of horse's hooves on the cobbled drive, alerting them to someone approaching the gate.

"What are you peddling?"

"We are not peddlers. it is imperative I speak with the Duke of Aberdeen."

"We don't just let anyone in. What is your call in aid of?"

"Tell him his son wishes to see him, my name is Besnik."

The man looked at Besnik sceptically, taking in the darker skin and the clothes he was wearing. Almost as if reading his thoughts, Besnik lifted the pendant from around his neck.

"Show him this and tell him I have proof, but I can only

give it to him."

The man took the pendant and rode off and Besnik paced back and forth as he waited, hoping his father would help them, *he is our last hope.*

Once again, they heard the sound of horse's hooves on the cobbled drive, causing Besnik's heart to quicken its pace. The rider did not get off his horse and all three held their breath.

"What was your mother's name?"

"My mother was known as Shofranka."

The man looked down at him for a moment, before dismounting his horse and to the relief of all three he unlocked the gate.

Once through the gate's entrance and on the cobble drive, Besnik could see the path was long but no longer steep. He motioned for Fonso to stop and helped Mary inside the carriage, then climbed up beside Fonso and regained hold of the reins.

As soon as they reached the steps that led to the massive entrance doors, Besnik quickly jumped down and opened the carriage door. After helping Mary alight, he carefully gathered Natalia in his arms, he noticed her face was flushed and her green eyes appeared dull and unseeing.

"She is very ill and needs medical help immediately," stated Besnik.

"You should have told me before; we don't want no disease here," responded the gatekeeper.

"She is not diseased; she has been treated badly and she is with child." Besnik's anger was rising.

Suddenly the large doors were opened and all heads turned, there stood a tall man in his late sixties, possibly seventy; he had a shock of white hair, but it was his eyes which drew one's attention; they were the most incredible blue and Fonso knew instantly, this man was Besnik's father.

Both men stared at each other for a moment, neither

saying a word.

"Sir, my mistress is sick," said Mary bravely.

The duke looked at the unconscious girl in Besnik's arms.

"Pardon my rudeness, quickly, bring her inside."

No sooner had they stepped inside the door, than a woman gasped and started to cry as she ran towards Besnik.

"This can't be, I don't understand," she said as she stroked Natalia's face.

"Drina, do you know this girl?" asked the duke.

"She is my sister, but I thought she was dead."

"Sister?" everyone asked in unison.

"Yes, her name is Esmeralda, but she looks so young," exclaimed Drina.

"Her name is Natalia; she is the daughter of Esmeralda. She needs to see a doctor immediately, she is with child," replied Besnik.

Drina gasped as she looked at Natalia, suddenly sparking into action, ordering the maids to prepare a room and a doctor to be sent for at once.

Besnik followed Drina up the stairs and lay Natalia down on the bed. He explained Mary was her chambermaid and was to remain so. He then went back downstairs and handed the box his mother had left in Luludja's care to his father, who then directed Besnik to the study; he had waited a long time for this day, when he would meet his son.

With Mary by Natalia's side and Besnik in the study with his father, Fonso was not sure what to do, so he made his way outside in search of the stables.

\*\*\*

Both men had been closeted in the library until the early hours of the morning. Their only interruption was a tray of food and an update on Natalia's condition from the doctor, he informed Besnik there were no concerns at the present for the unborn child; his concerns were more for the mother and would check on her again tomorrow. He left strict instructions with Drina and Mary and they promised they would carry them out.

Once the doctor had left, Besnik explained to the duke the events that had led him to discover his true parentage. He also explained to him of the hatred Natalia's father had towards all Romanies and their banishment to the deep forest. He hoped his father would not only offer a safe haven for himself, Natalia, Fonso and Mary, but also stop the evil hand of Lord Holmesby, so they could release not only Esmeralda, but all Romany; so they could be free to roam the land again as did their ancestors.

Besnik's father was shocked and horrified, not only at the life his son had been forced to live, but also that a father could subject such cruelty to his own flesh and blood. He made a promise to his son that night: he would do all in his power to protect not only those who arrived on his doorstep that day, but all the Romany people.

## CHAPTER EIGHTEEN

Natalia was almost into her eighth month and despite her being of a petite build, her baby was going to be big and it was difficult for her to move about.

She stood in her room and looked out the window, down at the vast estate below, she thought back to the days when she would ride Jasper, so fast the wind would tug at her hat and the early morning sun on her face.

Suddenly the baby gave her a kick, snapping her back to the present. Then her thoughts went to her mother, she wanted answers and realised the only way that would happen, was for her to tackle the long winding staircase.

By the time she reached the bottom she was exhausted and wondered how she was going to survive another month like this. She leant heavily on the mahogany handrail, not game to sit on the step, for fear she would never be able to get back up. The house was quiet and she was please no one seemed to be about, for she knew there would be a great fuss made if she was discovered downstairs, something she would rather avoid.

She slowly made her way to the library; expecting to find him here, the place he spent most of his time, unless he was outside overseeing the vast estate.

The library door was slightly ajar and she caught a glimpse of him, immediately her pulse rate quickened and the feeling of butterflies had returned to her stomach, depressing her all the more. *I don't know if I can do this.* Suddenly the baby gave a strong kick, causing her to lean against the doorframe. As if sensing her presence he suddenly turned around, the instant she looked into those blue eyes, she felt tears prick the back of her eyes and she could not speak.

"It's not often one sees you downstairs these days."

"I find the stairs difficult," she said, trying to keep the

emotion out of her voice.

"To what do I owe this pleasure?"

She detected an underlying sarcasm, but it gave her the courage to say what needed to be said.

"I want to know why you have not sent for my mother? Surely you must realise I need her now more than ever."

"I have told you before, it is a delicate situation; we must tread carefully."

"I am sick of hearing your excuses, I don't understand what the problem is and don't give me that nonsense about my father. Lachlan is a much more powerful man; he has proven as much by giving the freedom back to the Romanies, your people; why not my mother?"

"Natalia now is not the time to be discussing this, remember what the doctor said: you're not to stress or worry. Sit down and I'll have some tea sent in."

"I don't want any tea, I don't want to sit down. I know you're keeping something from me, but I will not be put off any longer," she yelled.

"Natalia please, think of the child."

"That is all you care about isn't it; your future heir? You're just like my father."

She watched Besnik's eyes narrow as he strode over, he grabbed her arms firmly and stared down at her, she knew she had angered him and she felt a faint flicker of fear.

"Don't ever liken me to your father and it is not just the child I care about."

His grip tightened on her arms, but she refused to let him see her tears; she had come here for answers and she would not leave until he answered her truthfully.

"You are just like him; you want to keep her locked up forever. You don't care about me; all you care about is this child I am carrying. You don't want me to see my mother, I know you spoke to her before we left; what did she say that frightened you?"

"Don't push me Natalia," he warned.

"Or what, you will lock me up too?"

"I'm warning you."

"I hate you, I wish I never met you. You never loved me; you're all the same."

Besnik immediately let go of her and Natalia could no longer hold back the tears. They were streaming down her face. She knew she was losing control, but she could not stop.

"Natalia I can't bring her back," he said softly.

"Why?"

He turned his back to her, almost as if he did not want to look at her, *he's hiding something from me!* Suddenly her tears stopped and her anger rose.

"Tell me why can't you bring her here?"

"Natalia please, you are overwrought; this is not good for the child."

"Tell me why, I know you are hiding something; tell me now!" she screamed.

"I can't bring her back."

"You mean you won't," she said as she pummelled his chest.

"I can't because she is dead!"

Natalia's arms fell by her sides and all the blood drained from her face. *No, this could not be, she had only just found her!*

"I don't believe you; your lying," she said as the tears poured down her cheeks.

"I'm sorry; I didn't want to tell you this way, but I was worried about you. The doctor said we were not to upset you and we had to consider the baby," he tried to put his arms around her.

"Don't touch me; don't ever touch me again. I hate you!"

Besnik's arms instantly fell by his sides and he walked over towards the window, keeping his back to her. She thought she saw hurt in his eyes, but she didn't care. *How could he have kept this from her, why did he not bring her with them?*

"What happened to her?"

"Not long after we smuggled you out, Frederick was unable to delay your father any longer. It didn't take him long to realise it was your mother and not you in the bed. He demanded to know where you were, which of course your mother refused, so he resorted to stronger measures."

"What did he do?" She sobbed.

He turned and the despair was evident on her face, he walked over towards her, but her earlier harsh words stopped him from getting too close.

"Natalia please, it will only distress you further," he said softly.

"Tell me; I want to know," she cried.

He knew he could no longer keep it from her; he had to tell her the truth.

"He ordered the doctor to administer shock treatment, a barbaric treatment to make a patient behave, but she still refused. Your mother had been locked away for so many years without proper food, nor the chance to experience the fresh air of the outdoors, she was not well, something she kept to herself; the treatment was too much for her heart."

"No!" she screamed.

Besnik made to move forward and comfort her, but the look in her eyes were filled with such hate. He watched helplessly as she pummelled the chair beside her, trying to release her anger and her grief, when suddenly she doubled over and let out a terrible scream. He ran forward and caught her before she fell to the floor, as he lifted her in his arms he realised her dress was wet and soaked through. A cold fear came over him, causing him to run for the stairs, calling for Mary or Drina, or anyone close by.

As Besnik made his way up the staircase, Drina appeared, seeing Natalia in Besnik's arms sparked her into immediate action.

"We must send for the doctor, I fear it is the baby," said Besnik, worriedly.

Mary appeared as Besnik laid Natalia on the bed, Drina instructed her to inform the doctor that the baby was on its way.

Besnik looked down at Natalia, her face was paler than usual and despite the cool evening, her face was glistening in perspiration and her face was contorted in pain. Suddenly she doubled up and put her hands to her stomach, the contraction so intense she screamed out in pain. Instinctively he put out his hand and tried to stroke back her damp hair.

"I told you never to touch me, I never want to see you again," she screamed.

He instantly pulled back his hand and moved away from the bed.

Drina saw the look of helplessness on his face.

"Don't take to heart what she says; the pain becomes so great we say things we do not mean. She won't even remember her harsh words once the pain is past."

"Oh I think she knows exactly what she is saying and I have no doubt she means every word of it. Don't worry about me; my concern is for the baby."

"Don't concern yourself with that; he is big and I doubt she'd have carried him much longer, her being such a wee thing and all."

"You think it's a boy, I'm going to have a son?"

"I'm just guessing now don't worry yourself any further, go down to the library and have a drink like all expectant fathers do."

Besnik took one last look at Natalia, her hands gripping at the bedclothes as her body was overtaken by another wave of pain. He stood and watched as Drina cooled her head with a damp cloth and uttered soothing words of encouragement, he turned and made his way downstairs, but not before he heard her words of pain.

"They killed her, they killed my mother, your sister; we shall never see her again. If it hadn't been for the baby we could have waited. This baby is the reason she is dead."

Her words sent chills to his heart. *Surely she could not put blame on one so innocent, one yet to enter this cruel world.* He made his way down the stairs to the library and quickly poured himself a drink. He walked over to the large window and looked down at the angry seas below; this room had been built with the purpose of providing a vantage point, to view any possible intruders who would risk scaling the treacherous cliffs below.

"Don't fret my son she is in good hands now. Soon the halls will echo with the cries of a young babe."

Besnik turned and watched as his father poured himself a generous measure of scotch, then made his way towards the window to stand beside him. It had been a shock when he had met his true father for the first time; seeing those same blue eyes stare back at him dismissed any doubts about him being his father. He had often wondered as a child why his eyes were not brown like all other Romanies and wondered if the man he believed was his father had thought the same thing.

"She hates me and she hates the baby, she blames him for her mother's death."

"So you have decided you are having a son? You might be in for one hell of a surprise, as for her hating you and the baby, it's normal; they blame you both for the pain."

"And you have some experience in these matters?"

"Well no, but I have heard stories of the like," his father said with a smile.

Besnik looked at his father before throwing back the contents of his glass, causing to liquid too burn the back of his throat. He then made his way to the decanter and poured himself another, causing father to look at son. The Duke was unsure about the relationship between his son and Natalia, but he was pleased Besnik had done the right thing by her, making her his wife. The two had remained virtual strangers, but now as he looked at his son, he wondered if it was possible he had feelings for her that ran deeper.

*** 

Natalia's screams echoed throughout the castle and could be heard all the way down to the library, causing Besnik to rush to the door.

"Son, 'tis better you wait here to be called, it can't be long now."

Drina mopped Natalia's brow, cooing words of encouragement.

"One good push and it will all be over," Drina encouraged.

Finally the baby appeared and was letting everyone know he had arrived.

"Well there's nothing wrong with this one's lungs. Congratulations Natalia, you are the proud mother of a beautiful baby boy," said the doctor.

Mary immediately rushed out the door and raced down the stairs to let Besnik know he had a son.

Tears came to Drina's eyes as she lovingly cleaned her grandnephew, for she felt saddened Esmeralda did not live to see this day. She bundled him in a warm blanket and took him over to his mother.

"Natalia he is beautiful and he wants his mother."

Natalia just lay back against the bed exhausted and stared blankly at the ceiling.

Drina looked at her with concern, before instructing one of the maids to prop up her pillows and make her more comfortable.

"Leave me alone, everyone just leave me alone and take the baby with you; I want nothing to do with him," she said before bursting into tears.

Drina was about to comment, but the doctor shook his head and ushered them all out of the room, including Drina and the child. He made sure there were no complications from the birth then he gave her a mild sedative, which would not harm a mother's milk, then he quietly closed the door behind him.

"Doctor the child needs his mother," said Drina.

"Yes I understand this, but sometimes it takes a while for a mother to bond with her child. Right now she needs rest, I will organise a wet nurse until she is ready to accept her son. I trust I can leave her and the child in your good hands."

Just then Besnik came bounding up the stairs, unable to contain the look of joy on his face. However when he saw the doctor and Drina standing outside Natalia's closed door and his son in her arms, his joy turned to concern.

"Is something wrong, why is he not with his mother?"

"She needs to rest; she is not ready to see him yet," said the doctor.

"How can a mother not be ready to see her own child for the first time?"

"Please keep your voice down; you are not helping the situation," said the doctor sternly.

As if to fortify his comments the infant began to cry, causing tears to come to Drina's face, *Esmeralda you should have been here!* She rocked him in her arms and cooed words of comfort and Besnik looked at the child for the first time. He gently put out his hand and touched his soft downy black hair and his skin, paler than his but darker than his mother's. He did not know his eye colour, as he had his eyes tightly closed whilst he cried out, letting all know he was here. Besnik's face instantly softened as he realised *he is my son – my own flesh and blood.*

"May I hold him?"

Drina pulled him closer to her chest. *Men didn't know how to hold a baby; they were awkward and clumsy when it came to one so small.*

The doctor thought it would be a good idea and Drina

reluctantly handed over the child, making sure he supported his head.

As soon as the child was in his arms, he stopped crying and opened his eyes and stared into the eyes of his father, who was overcome with emotion.

"He is so tiny and yet so perfect. How could a mother not want you?" he asked as he looked into his son's tiny face.

"These things sometimes happen, I hear her mother died recently; perhaps she has not yet overcome her grief," suggested the doctor.

Besnik suddenly paled as Natalia's words came back to him. He had not wanted to tell her about her mother the way he had; but she had persisted for an answer.

As he looked down into his son's tiny face, he noted his eyes were not quite green, nor blue, but a mixture of his own eyes and Natalia's.

\*\*\*

It had been over a week and Natalia was still unwilling to see her son and she was refusing to eat, a cause for great concern.

Drina, Besnik and the doctor were in the library discussing the situation.

"Besnik you have not been to see your wife since the birth of your son; this could be a contributing factor to her refusal to accept him."

"I am just obeying her wishes; she said she never wished to see me again."

"You would be amazed at what a woman can say while in the pain of giving birth. Many feel ashamed afterwards, while some never remember saying such things. You must understand giving birth to a child is a pain you and I could never imagine and they need someone to blame at the time; don't take it to heart," said the doctor.

"I am sure she meant every word she said."

"Besnik don't give up on her, please think of the child," begged Drina.

He thought of his young son, the thought of him growing up and never knowing a mother's love. They hadn't even named him yet, as it should be a decision between himself and Natalia, not one he made on his own.

"I will try, but I think I am the last person who should be doing this."

He made his way up the stairs, first going into the nursery as he had done so many times before. He never thought one so little could monopolise one's time or thoughts so much. He gently lifted him out of his crib and held him close, then made his way towards her room. He quietly opened the door, bracing himself for her harsh words, hoping it would not frighten their son. When he entered the room, he could see she was propped up in bed and had her head turned towards the window.

"Natalia, I have someone who dearly wants to see you," he said softly.

She did not move and he wondered if she even had heard him; *perhaps she was asleep.*

He walked slowly around the side of the bed and was shocked at what he saw. If it was at all possible, she looked much paler and her cheeks were sunken and her beautiful green eyes looked dull and lifeless; it was as if she had given up on life and was waiting to die.

"Natalia, we have a beautiful son, one who needs his mother."

She still did not move. Holding his son close, he grabbed a chair and pulled it towards her bed, blocking her view out the window, forcing her to look at him and the sleeping infant in his arms.

"Natalia please don't give up on him; don't give up on life."

He saw her eyes shift to the precious bundle he held in his arms, encouraged by this he leant forward and carefully placed the sleeping child near her breast. Instantly the infant began to stir and started to nuzzle at her breast through her nightgown, his tiny hand grabbed a hold of the ribbon and pulled it towards his mouth. Natalia looked down at him and Besnik saw a slow tear slide down her cheek.

"He knows you're his mother, see how he responded the moment I placed him near you. Hold him Natalia, he needs you; I need you. If you won't do it for me, do it for him." His voice was raw with emotion.

She lifted her eyes and looked at Besnik, tears now running freely down her cheeks. She then looked down at her son, who was now becoming distressed as he pawed and nuzzled through the fabric of her nightgown.

"He's hungry and gets angry if he has to wait too long to be fed," he said with tears in his eyes and a smile on his face.

She looked at him and into those blue eyes, causing her heart to quicken and that sensation of butterflies in her stomach that she felt every time she looked at him. Suddenly there was a loud wail, causing her to look down at the child her arms. Instinctively, not realising what she was doing, she loosened the ribbon on her gown and let him suckle at her breast.

It was as if a fog had been lifted; *this little person is part of me!* Then she remembered the last words her mother had said; 'look after my grandchild for me.' his little hand stretched out over her full breast as he drank greedily. A wave of emotion washed over her and she could no longer contain her feelings she had bottled up so long inside. Her body trembled as a deep sob erupted and then she cried so hard, it frightened her son and he began to cry also.

Besnik was not sure what to do; *should I take him away?*

Natalia realised she had frightened her son and gently stroked his little face, as she tried to contain her tears.

"I'm sorry little one; I haven't been a very good mother have I?"

Instantly the child stopped and resumed suckling at her breast and Natalia looked up at Besnik. *He must think I'm crazy, I bet he is worried about leaving his son alone with me.*

"Besnik, have you chosen a name for our son?"

"I thought we could choose one together."

"If it is all right with you, I would like to call him Emmanuel. It means 'God is with us' it was my grandfather's name, my mother's father."

Besnik immediately got up from the chair and walked to the end of the bed; then started pacing the room.

"Of course, I am sure your mother would have liked that. About your mother—"

"Besnik…"

"You were my sole concern. Yes, you were carrying my child, but my concern was for you. I needed to get you as far away from your father as possible; I wasn't about to lose you again. By the time I had you safely here, your mother was already gone."

"I don't understand."

"It was not an easy journey; we had to travel by the darkness of night. You were not well and I had yet to meet my father. Until then, I had no power over your father…"

"You said you weren't about to lose me again; what did you mean?"

He stopped his pacing and stood at the end of the bed. He could see his son was now sleeping, but his little hand had a firm grip on her finger as if afraid to let her go.

"That night we spent together; you were in a very vulnerable state and to be honest, I should not have acted the way I did. Then when you professed your love for me, I felt a real swine; I was not sure what to say, as I knew you were in an emotional state. I did not want to say something we would both regret in the morning, but by then you were gone. I realised my non-comment had only hurt you more and I wanted to apologise. I managed to find your father's home, but when Fonso informed me of your engagement; it was like a kick in the stomach; I felt angry as I realised your words were just words and was glad I had left things unsaid."

"It's not what you think, I was not marrying Lawrence for love; I had no other choice. What I said to you that night came from the heart."

"I read your letter to your father; Mary found it."

"After that night we spent together I realised I could not marry another man; I could never be with another man; there was only one man I could love, but he did not love me in return."

Besnik walked over and sat back down in the chair, taking one of her hands in his.

"This man you professed your love to, do you still love him?"

The feel of his strong hand over hers and the way his thumb stroked the side of her hand caused a frenzy of sensations.

She looked up into those incredible blue eyes; her heart as always, quickened its pace and she closed her eyes for a moment. Her mind went back to that night they spent together; the passion she felt, the feel of his hands on her skin, his lips igniting the fire that had been smouldering beneath, the way his strong body felt beneath her hands – only he could make her feel whole. She had been kidding herself to think she could live life without him, when in reality she could not. The mere mention of his name or the sight of him made her heart ache and always would. She looked him directly in his eyes and gave him her answer.

"Yes, I love him with my heart and soul."

He stared back at her and she saw the muscle at the side of his jaw clench, as she had seen so many times before. He released her hand and got up from the chair and walked over towards the window. *Had she made a fool of herself yet again?* Her throat suddenly felt tight and she felt tears prick the back of her eyes.

"Right from the day Fonso brought you to the Romany camp you managed to get under my skin. When I placed you on Luludja's bed and looked into those green eyes, it was as if you had cast a spell. I tried hard to rid you from my thoughts, but you had woven your spell and the fact you were a Gorgio and I Romany made things all the worse; what sort of life could we have together? We would be forever cursed, but still you were never far from my thoughts. When I kissed you that day, near Florica's grave, the feel of you in my arms, the smell of you drove me wild. For the first time in my life I felt truly alive."

Natalia could not believe what she was hearing as she looked at his broad strong back. *What was he saying, could it be true?* As if he read her thoughts, he turned and walked over to the bed and gently took their sleeping son from her arms and carefully laid him on the bed, before pulling her up to his chest and kissing her passionately on the lips. Too soon he drew his lips away from hers, but he did not let her go.

"Natalia, I love you with my whole being; having you so close yet so far away these past months was the worst torture I could imagine. I know we both have Romany and Gorgio blood running through our veins, but Natalia, I was prepared to risk any possible curse to spend the rest of my life with you, for a life without you would not be living. Natalia my love, I promise to love and cherish you until eternity, will you marry me?"

"We are already married and what's this about us both having Romany and Gorgio blood?"

"Wait here a moment," he said as he placed her in the chair.

She sat there wondering where he had gone; when a short time later he came back in the room carrying a small wooden box in his hand.

"I saw your mother before we smuggled you from that

terrible place. I got a shock the first time I saw her, the likeness between you was incredible, giving me an insight as to how you will look in your later years. She told me about your father and about her family; but she wanted to know my intentions. I told her I planned to marry you, but not just for the sake of the child, I told her it was for love. She gave me her blessing and asked me to give this to you, but it saddened her, as it is something a mother passes on to her daughter on the eve of her wedding, as you will one day to yours. I think your mother realised despite our best efforts, she would never leave that place. The reason I did not give this to you earlier, I knew you would ask questions and I was afraid how you would cope with the truth."

Besnik opened the box, inside was a beautiful bracelet, a combination of beads, and intricate silver charms. She could see it was very old, as the beads and charms were worn smooth in places from many years of wear, but still very beautiful never the less. Natalia gently lifted it out of the box and Besnik fastened the clasp around her wrist.

"It is beautiful, but how do you know my mother was telling you the truth? She could have just been telling you I was part Romany so you would marry me."

"I have seen a similar bracelet. My mother had one, which her mother gave to her. All Romany women who are wed wear a similar bracelet; it is a sign of being Romany, something to be proud of; as for me being Gorgio, Laughlin is my biological father, something my mother kept secret, even from the man who I thought was my father. Natalia you still haven't answered my question."

"As I said, we are already married. Don't you remember we got married so our son would not be born out of wedlock?"

"Yes, but I never had the chance to ask you properly, nor get an answer."

"I would love to marry you and spend the rest of my life with you and of course, don't forget our beautiful son."

"Natalia you have just made me the happiest man in the world, as for our son, hopefully we can give him some brothers and sisters. Speaking of which, when the doctor says you are well enough, I think it is time you move into the master bedroom, it is far more private and a place we will not be disturbed."

Natalia instantly blushed as he made his meaning apparent by the look in his eyes; she was sure she was the happiest woman in the world, for she could also see the love in his eyes, a love he felt for her.

Printed in Great Britain
by Amazon.co.uk, Ltd.,
Marston Gate.